The Body
in the
Piazza

THE BODY
IN THE
PIAZZA

A FAITH FAIRCHILD MYSTERY

KATHERINE
HALL PAGE

WILLIAM MORROW

An Imprint of HarperCollins*Publishers*

This book is a work of fiction. The characters, incidents, and dialogue are drawn from the author's imagination and are not to be construed as real. Any resemblance to actual events or persons, living or dead, is entirely coincidental.

ISBN 978-0-06-206550-6

For My Good Friend and Fine Writer Valerie Wolzien
It's Always About the Journey

When you travel your first discovery is that you do not exist.
—ELIZABETH HARDWICK, *Sleepless Nights*

ACKNOWLEDGMENTS

Many thanks to my HC publicist Danielle Bartlett, my friend Emilio Bizzi, Dr. Robert DeMartino for medical expertise, photographer Jean Fogelberg, my agent Faith Hamlin, guide Claire Hennessy in Florence, my editor Katherine Nintzel, HC director of library marketing Virginia Stanley, and the staff of the Hotel Residenza Farnese Roma in Rome (especially Paolo).

Authors often thank family members, and although that doesn't seem a sufficient enough word for the gratitude I feel for all you do for me—and for your love—here it is: a world of thanks to my husband, Alan, and my son, Nicholas.

I have taken some liberties with actual locations and a few descriptions, but not many.

THE BODY

IN THE

PIAZZA

CHAPTER 1

Faith Fairchild was drunk. Soused, sloshed, schnockered, pickled, potted, and looped—without a single sip of alcohol having crossed her lips. She was drunk on Rome. Intoxicating, inebriating Rome.

It had started before the plane had touched down when she glimpsed the sea—"Mare Nostrum," "Our Sea," the Romans had called it. Soon the coast gave way to towns, fields, and the green serpent that was the Tiber. On the bus from Fiumicino into the city, the views were not as spectacular, but there were occasional patches of brilliant roadside wildflowers and long rows of twisted pines—Respighi's *Pines of Rome*—flashed by. Leaving the highway at the city limits, the streets narrowed abruptly. The flowers were in planters now outside stucco-sheathed apartments and shops painted just as she had imagined them—yellow ochre, burnt sienna, raw umber, deep rose—Italian Crayolas. Dense traffic had caused the bus to slow to a crawl, an imposing vessel upon a mighty ocean of motor scooters and tiny cars, darting perilously like schools of minnows into the oncoming traffic lane, honking as if the road had been usurped rather than the other way around. She'd laughed to herself at the host of metaphors Rome was already inspiring.

When the bus left the airport, it had been filled with the excited clamor of arrivals speaking so many different languages it was impossible to distinguish one from the next. As riders got off and others took their places, Italian dominated. They were probably talking about the weather or mundane problems at work or home, but their gestures, faces, and the musical quality of their voices suggested that they were debating Verdi versus Puccini or heady matters of state. Faith wished she had had time to study the language and vowed to sign up for at least an online course when she returned.

The bus stopped abruptly, immobilized by the traffic. "Could it always be like this?" Faith said to her husband.

Tom Fairchild shrugged, intent on maintaining the tiny perimeter of space they'd claimed on the crowded bus.

"*Scusi,*" a man next to Faith said. "This morning it is a, how do you call it, 'strike'? Yes, strike by the *trasporto* workers. It will be over in a few hours. It's very usual."

"What are they asking for?"

"*Tutti.* Enjoy your stay." He got off and was soon making faster progress on the sidewalk than he had been on the bus. "*Tutti*"—Faith knew the word—"Everything."

She didn't mind the delay. It gave her more time to look out the windows. By the time they reached their stop and she stepped onto the Corso Vittorio Emanuele's sidewalk, her head was already filled with the sight of places she'd only seen in photographs, paintings, or on the screen. She'd grabbed Tom's arm repeatedly at the views—St. Peter's, Castel Sant'Angelo, the Ponte Principe—and now as she wheeled her small suitcase—for once she'd packed lightly—across the street and into the Campo de' Fiori toward their hotel, she grabbed his arm again. If heaven were in any way a reflection of life on earth, the Campo de' Fiori market *had* to be the model. Stall after stall was filled with the kinds of produce she'd only seen in the pages of glossy food magazines. Artfully arranged crates of ruby-red and pearl-white radicchio, shiny dark eggplants, silken orange zucchini blossoms, and shimmering silver-scaled fish, none of which had been sprayed with fixative or whatever else stylists used to achieve perfection for those photo shoots. One stall was filled with stacks of white porcelain, another with colorful pyramids of spices in cello-wrap. All she needed was a large basket—and a kitchen. She stood transfixed before a display of more kinds of mushrooms than she had ever seen in her life and knew that she'd have to come back to Rome, rent an apartment, and cook. For now—and why had it taken her all these years to get to the Imperial City?—she would have to be satisfied with just dreaming.

She glanced up and her eye was drawn to a rather forbidding-looking bronze statue of a hooded monk that towered incongruously over the bright white canvas umbrellas sheltering wares, and she made a note to check the guidebook. Who was the enigmatic figure? Rabelais—didn't he spend time in Italy?—would have been more appropriate. But nothing seemed to be curbing the bustling crowd's appetite, and Faith realized that the sight of all this luscious food had awakened her own. She was starving.

They'd boarded the plane in Boston at dusk last night. Faith had brought her own repast, a ciabatta roll stuffed with fresh mozzarella, prosciutto, sliced tomato, and basil that gave a nod toward her destination, while Tom had said he'd opt for whatever the galley served up. That had been "steak tips with seasonal vegetables." She'd commented pointedly that the vegetables must represent some fifth or even sixth season as yet unknown to man and he'd responded by asking her to order a meal for herself. Like the old joke, the food might be lousy, but the portions were too small—especially in this case, when the airlines were cutting back on everything from pillows to peanuts. Tom had consumed his meal and hers, too, commenting that he liked the challenge of eating from those little trays with doll-size cutlery.

Faith was an unashamedly admitted food snob. It went with the territory. She'd started her successful catering business, Have Faith, in the Big Apple just before meeting Tom and restarted it in the more bucolic orchards of New England when their second child, Amy, began nursery school.

Since she'd eschewed the breakfast offered in flight—what looked like some kind of ancient Little Debbie snack cake and brown-colored water passing for coffee (she'd sniffed Tom's cup)—Faith hadn't had any food for hours, never a good thing in her book, and the only question now, here in foodie paradise, was where to start?

"Happy, darling?" Tom asked. The trip was an anniversary one and had been his very own idea. "A significant anniversary deserves a significant marking," he'd said.

She wrapped her arms around his neck and kissed him. People didn't do that in the Fairchilds' neighborhood back home; they *did* in Rome.

"Very—and very hungry."

"The hotel's not far, so why don't we check in and then eat? The rooms won't be ready this early, but we can leave the bags."

"Okay, but let me get one of these little tarts first," Faith said. They were passing a bakery, the Forno Campo De' Fiori smack on the square, and she had her eye on what looked like some kind of *crostate* oozing with apricots that was seductively displayed with other pastries, pizza, and panini in the window.

Tom decided he needed one, too, *and* several pignoli-studded almond cookies. Munching contentedly, they were soon making their way across the market to the street leading to the hotel. As Faith passed the monk's statue, the morning sun cast his shadow in their path and, feeling superstitious, she pulled Tom to the side to avoid walking through it. Kind of a "step on a crack, break your mother's back" thing she told herself. She also told herself "better safe than sorry." *Nothing* was going to spoil this trip.

She adored her two children: Ben, despite his occasional irritating teen attitude—had she and her younger sister, Hope, similarly known absolutely everything in the world at that age?—and Amy, feet still planted firmly in childhood with a passion for Harry Potter. Yes, Faith could honestly say that most of the time she not only loved her children but liked being with them. That said, she was joyfully anticipating the almost two weeks stretching out before her sans the crises that made up her everyday life: a science project due tomorrow and not started; a mean girl spreading rumors that Amy had B.O.; and every Sunday morning the mad dash to get the Reverend Thomas Fairchild in a clean collar and matching black socks—well sometimes one was navy blue. When Faith had mentioned the possibility of the trip to her closest friend and next-door neighbor, Pix Miller, Pix had immediately offered herself and husband, Sam, as in loco parentis not just in spirit but in fact. Empty nesters, they would simply move next door for the duration. "It will be fun," she'd said. "And good practice for grandparenthood." Pix was a bit older than Faith and like Virgil guiding Dante had steered her through the perilous shoals of everything from toilet training to how to get the teacher you wanted at Aleford Elementary.

After the Millers' offer, the rest of the plans fell into place with surprising ease. Faith's assistant, Niki Constantine, was more than capable of running things at Have Faith for the duration with the help of Trisha Phelan, one of the firm's part-time workers. Niki was a new mom and had been bringing the baby to work with her, which would continue until, she told her boss, "The little darling learns to walk and becomes a nuisance." Since she spent every waking minute of the tiny girl's life cuddling her adoringly, Faith doubted Niki would regard Sofia as a "nuisance" even when the baby became ambulatory. Of course things could change once she hit her teens.

And so Tom and Faith would eat, drink, and be merry. Just the two of them, the way they had begun all those years ago.

Meeting at a wedding reception Have Faith was catering at the Riverside Church on New York's Upper West Side, what Faith did not realize until the wee small hours of that fateful night was that the handsome friend of the groom had come to town from Massachusetts to perform the ceremony, changing out of his robes immediately afterward. Earlier in the evening, Tom Fairchild had literally swept her off her feet: one dance as the party was winding down, one song—Cole Porter's "Easy to Love"—and one ride across Central Park in one of those horse-drawn carriages she'd previously thought strictly for tourists, never realizing how impossibly, absurdly romantic they were. When Tom had revealed his occupation, surprised that she hadn't known, it was too late. She was hooked.

Daughters and granddaughters of men of the cloth, Faith and Hope, a year younger, had made a pact to avoid that particular fabric, knowing the kind of fishbowl existence it meant. Years earlier their mother, Jane Lennox, a Manhattan native, had put her well-shod foot down, insisting that her fiancé, the Reverend Lawrence Sibley, could tend to a congregation in her hometown as well as any other place. Sin was not dependent on locale. Well, perhaps in some cases, but she had been firm, and he accepted the call to a parish on the city's Upper East Side. Jane, a real estate lawyer, found them a bargain duplex when their daughters were born. Not exactly a moss-covered drafty old manse with inadequate hot water, but the Sibley girls had still had to grow up under a congregation's omnipresent eye—"Are those girls old enough for that kind of makeup?" and "Did you hear about the way the Sibley girls danced at the Young People's last get-together?" Hope's occupation—she'd gone straight from *Sesame Street* to Wall Street with her own subscription to the *Journal* before she turned ten—met with general approval, Faith's years in the wilderness trying to figure out what and who she wanted to be less so. Even when she did finally find her true calling, the parish was puzzled. "A cook?"

Not until raves started appearing in the *Times* and elsewhere did they wake up and smell the coffee—coffee it was exceedingly hard to get booked.

Tom was consulting the map. Rome was new to him, too. They'd been to Northern Italy during their honeymoon, but no farther south than Siena.

"We came down Vicolo del Gallo, so this is definitely the Piazza Farnese. The hotel should be on that street over to the side there." He pointed.

"More like an alley," Faith said, hoping it would be quiet. The piazza was almost empty, especially compared to the neighboring market square. She knew from the hotel's online information that the imposing building across from them was the Palazzo Farnese, built during the Renaissance. For many years it had been home to the French embassy. A French flag and the flag of the European Union hung above the wide main entrance. Two ornate fountains that looked like huge bathtubs occupied opposite ends of the large cobbled square.

Another thing to check out in the guide, Faith said to herself. There had to be a story behind them. She'd had every intention of reading up on Roman history and the major sights but, in the end, skimmed the introductions in several books and told herself that this way she'd be coming to everything fresh. She'd memorized a few key phrases that would take her far: "*Quanto costa?*" and "*Vorrei mangiare.*" "How much?" and "I want to eat something." She wouldn't need Berlitz for deciphering a menu. Faith's food linguistic skills spanned all nations.

Her plan was to wander, eat, and wander some more. Emilio Bizzi, an old friend originally from Italy who lived near Aleford, where Tom's church, First Parish, was, had given them his Late Renaissance, Early Baroque suggestions, a tour the Fairchilds were already calling "The Caravaggio, Bernini, Borromini Trail." It would be fun to follow it all over the city, giving them a focus for the three days they had for this part of the trip. She wasn't going to miss the Colosseum, though. Or the Spanish Steps. Or the Trevi Fountain. Or . . . they'd just have to come back.

"Come on, there's the hotel," Faith urged Tom, picking up her speed. "We can eat our lunch by the Bernini fountain in the Piazza Navona across from Borromini's church and then find the nearest Caravaggio. Three birds in one fell swoop."

A breeze off the river was blowing her thick honey-colored hair across her face. She pushed her sunglasses up on top of her head to keep her locks in place and get a better sense of where she was. From the street, the hotel looked like the ancient monastery it once had been. The Fairchilds paused a moment to take it all in. The outer front door, which had been pulled back, was painted deep blue; its thickness suggested a fortress more than a place dedicated to worship. Large stone urns overflowing with scarlet geraniums flanked the inner door, which led into the lobby. Definitely not Motel 6, Faith thought, or any other U.S. chain. If this lovely space had been stamped out by a cookie cutter, she wanted one for her own *batterie de cuisine*—someone had exquisite taste. As she moved toward the desk across the gray-and-white marble tiles, she thought about the silent feet of the monks that must have trod here as well and realized that following all sorts of footsteps was going to be one of their greatest pleasures this trip—from the Etruscans to the Romans to Renaissance princes and Baroque beauties with a glance ahead at all those Daisy Millers on the Grand Tour of Europe. Perhaps ending up with Fellini and *La Dolce Vita*?

"*Buon giorno,* may I help you?" a pleasant-looking man asked from behind the desk. "Are you checking in?"

What about us shouts American? Faith wondered to herself. It used to be you could tell someone's nationality from his or her shoes. Then she realized that the name of the U.S. airline was easy to see on their luggage tags and English was more than a good guess.

"*Buon giorno,*" Tom said. Faith was proud of his accent, especially since he knew less Italian than she did. "We're the Fairchilds."

The man virtually leaped around the counter, hand outstretched to grab Tom's. "Francesca's friends! I am Paolo! Anything I can do, you must just ask. Francesca and I are from the same village," he added as he shook Faith's hand heartily as well. Those magic words: "From the same village," "Same hometown," "Went to school together." Shared space, the international Open Sesame. Faith had known that Francesca, one of the main reasons they had selected Italy as their anniversary destination, knew someone at the hotel. It was why they had booked it, but it was a stroke of luck to meet Paolo the minute they walked in.

Francesca Rossi had been eighteen when she came to New York City with a carefully guarded secret and plan. She was on a student visa and started working for Have Faith when Faith's assistant Josie Wells went to open her own restaurant, now a legend, in Richmond, Virginia. Francesca grew up cooking with her mother and grandmother in Tuscany, and Faith had been happy to have the young woman on her staff that tumultuous spring just before Faith's marriage to Tom. It hadn't been long before she realized that Francesca was keeping more than her *nona*'s ragu recipe from her. In the weeks that followed, employer and employee bonded on the quest to right an ancient wrong, its roots in post–World War II Italy. Francesca went back home, and the Fairchilds had a joyous visit with her and her family on their honeymoon soon after. The newlyweds had been feted by what seemed like the entire population of the town, high in the mountains outside Florence.

A few years later Francesca herself settled down, marrying Gianni Rossi, a very distant cousin who managed the family vineyard and olive groves. Children and plain old life kept Faith and Francesca from seeing each other in person—the Rossis never made the oft-promised visit to the States, and the Fairchilds didn't get back to Italy—but the two women had stayed in close touch.

Besides wanting to see Francesca and her family, the Fairchilds were in Italy as gourmet guinea pigs. Francesca had been giving small group and individual cooking lessons for years, relying on word of mouth to promote herself. Now she and her husband had set themselves up as a full-fledged culinary school offering weeklong classes that included accommodations, trips to local markets, and other excursions. Francesca had called Faith, begging her to come for the first session to help work out any kinks that might arise.

When she mentioned the call to Tom, Faith had been extremely surprised when he suggested they make Francesca's venture the destination for an anniversary trip. Tom's culinary expertise extended to grilled cheese sandwiches, opening a can of Campbell's cream of tomato soup, and his tour de force: pouring boiling water through a small strainer filled with his favorite Irish Breakfast tea leaves. He was also very good at ordering pizza from Aleford's Country Pizza, extra sauce, extra cheese, no anchovies. Faith had explained he might encounter an anchovy or possibly something else overly pungent or unfamiliar—she was thinking *lardo,* that savory cured pork fat, which looked like what it was, but Tom had dismissed her admittedly halfhearted misgivings— she really wanted to go—and said he'd try anything. Plus, he'd always wanted to learn to make pasta from scratch. Who knew? The school was in the middle of a vineyard, which might have had something to do with his enthusiasm, but Faith accepted Tom's newfound interest for whatever it was and mentally started packing.

"Normally the rooms are not ready yet, but I will check. I think yours might be," Paolo said, going back behind the desk. He picked up the phone and soon turned to them smiling even more broadly, if that was possible.

"I think you will like this one, but do not hesitate to tell me if you want another or need anything. I will show you the elevator," he said, handing them a large key attached to a heavy length of brass elaborately embossed with the name of the hotel.

As he led the way through a pleasant sitting area and a small bar, he said, "I know you are here for this new project of Francesca and Gianni's, the cooking school. Some of the other people taking the course are staying here, too. A few arrived like you today, some have been here all week. *Tutti è molto simpatico.*"

Faith was happy to hear this, although Paolo had already struck her as someone who always looked at the glass as half full and would declare most people *molto simpatico*. She wanted to keep these precious days in Rome to themselves, however, and did not intend to try to track down and assess their fellow students. Time enough when they would be rubbing elbows with them in the Rossis' *cucina*.

Paolo ushered the Fairchilds into the tiny elevator and they went up to the third floor, locating their room at the end of a curved hallway. Room 309 was spacious with a high ceiling, soft, pale-green damask-patterned wallpaper, and heavy darker green and gold silk curtains, which Faith immediately pulled all the way back from the tall windows, flooding the space with the late morning light.

"Look, Tom, palm trees!" she cried.

He came over by her side. "Mediterranean, not Floridian, but tropical nonetheless." He kissed her lightly as he said, "I love that it takes only a couple of palm trees to make you happy. And to think my sister told me after she met you at the shower that you were going to be 'very high maintenance.'"

He kissed her harder, pulling her away from the window. Even as she felt her body responding, Faith spared a fleeting thought for her sister-in-law, who had tried so hard to marry her brother off to someone of *her* choosing. Tom had never mentioned the "high maintenance" comment before, but it came as no surprise and was the least of Betsey's almost lethal endeavor.

"Nice-looking bed. Good size," Tom was murmuring.

Faith recalled the hotel's description of their double rooms. "A *letto matrimoniale*."

Tom was already pulling down the spread.

"An apt, very apt, term, don't you think, Mrs. Fairchild?"

"So long as we don't fall asleep. Everyone says the way to get over jet lag is to stay up as late as possible and get on the local time."

"Oh, I have no intention of falling asleep," Tom said. "And unless I miss my guess, you don't either."

And then there weren't any more words.

Afterward Tom *did* fall asleep. He suddenly went from wide-awake to deep slumber, and Faith didn't have the heart to disturb him. She lay on her side, looking at him. He hadn't changed much since their chance meeting at the catering job she'd blessed ever since. The laugh lines around his mouth and at the corners of his eyes were more defined, as were the ones on his forehead—the ones that didn't come from laughing. There was a bit more salt in his rusty brown hair, but he was as lean as ever, despite being what her aunt Chat called upon meeting him, "a big, hungry boy." During the early days of their marriage, Faith had been astounded at how fast milk and other staples of Tom's diet ran out. Now she had two of these boys; Ben had inherited both his Dad's metabolism and food preferences.

She slipped from between the sheets and got dressed. One of the things Faith had also noted from the hotel's Web site was its rooftop terrace. She left a note about her whereabouts on her pillow, grabbed the key, guidebook, the small travel journal her sister had given her, and a bottle of water before tiptoeing out the door. A silent exit wasn't necessary, as her husband routinely slept through major thunderstorms and only awoke if one of the children or Faith sneezed, but she felt it was more dramatic—and

Rome was drama personified, or whatever the term was for places. As she climbed the stairs across from the elevator, assuming they would lead to the terrace, she thought of all those Hollywood extravaganzas—*Ben Hur, Spartacus,* and *Cleopatra* (where there was as much drama on-screen as off). They might be cheesy, but they were fun to watch.

The rooftop terrace was not a terrace but a roof, an extremely large one surrounded by a low wall and iron railings. It was the top of not only the former monastery but also of the buildings immediately adjacent, creating a flat open space that extended almost back to the Piazza Farnese. Faith leaned over the railing and peered down to the narrow street. She could see some children kicking a ball around one of the fountains and the corner of the newsstand next to a *caffè*. Two priests were strolling slowly toward the piazza; their long, dark, well-tailored robes seemed a cut above the similar garb she'd noted on American priests. Cassocks by Armani?

The rooftop area that belonged to the hotel had been outfitted with several small tables and chairs. They would have been at home in a garden—white-painted ornamental cast iron and, like the hotel keys, not going anywhere.

Planters overflowed with several kinds of geraniums, ivy, and bright ruffled petunias. She smelled jasmine and located a wall of it screening a small canvas swing for two. The perfect spot to toast their arrival once Tom woke up, Faith thought. They might be able to pick up a bottle of something at the small grocery store they'd passed near the Campo de' Fiori.

She went over to the opposite side of the roof and looked down at her palm trees. Someone had placed large terra-cotta pots of small lemon and orange trees in a row in front of the wall as an additional barrier. The nearby elevator shaft had been disguised by a trompe l'oeil espaliered orchard with small birds. The fresco was faded and peeling, which, for Faith, added to its charm. She walked to the far end of the roof.

It was impossible to sit still when there was so much to see—domes and steeples piercing the Della Robbia blue sky; a glimpse of the Tiber; the large formal garden that belonged to the French embassy; balconies, some strung with wash, all with pots of flowers; and open windows revealing someone reading at a desk, a small kitchen with just a hand stirring a pot visible, and a cat asleep in the middle of a sun-dappled bed. Seagulls circling overhead made her think of their cottage on the coast of Maine, but these cries were different. Laughing gulls with Italian accents? There were no additional barriers here aside from the railings, broken in spots, and she drew back hastily.

Returning to the table where she had left her things, she drank some water. It was a warm day, not hot. Perfect weather. Perfect setting. She heard the door from the stairs open and turned, expecting to see Tom, but it was another man, who immediately said "*Buon giorno*" and lifted the Panama hat he was wearing. He was carrying two books and after Faith returned the greeting, he walked toward the jasmine-sheltered swing. Passing her table, he paused and picked up her guidebook.

"British or American?" he asked.

"American. And yes, I've never been to Rome before."

He laughed. "Then please allow me to give you an essential piece of advice, admittedly cribbed from E. M. Forster's *A Room with a View,* and urge you to emancipate yourself from your *Baedeker* or whatever you have purchased as its modern-day equivalent."

"That would not be difficult, as I have not yet had time to read any of it, but surely I will need it to know what things are," Faith said, feeling as if she had stepped into a Forster or James novel and only just preventing herself from adding, "kind sir," to her remark. For that she would have needed a hat herself, or parasol. His British accent, more reminiscent of Sir Alec Guinness than Sir Mick, intensified the notion.

"You already have everything you need in order to ascertain the true nature of things." Her new friend, for she instantly hoped he would become one, pointed to his eyes, ears, mouth, and head.

"May I?" He indicated the empty seat across from her.

"Please," she said, wishing she had more than a bottle of water. The scene called for vino and small plates of antipasti. As he sat down, she asked, "Is a map permitted?"

He raised his hands in mock horror. "Worse than a guidebook! The point of travel is to get lost. But perhaps you are one of those travelers who needs to be able to tell one's friends that one 'did' the Borghese, the Sistine Chapel, and so on."

"No, we're not like that. We do have a bit of a plan—a friend gave a suggestion. We call it the Caravaggio, Bernini, Borromini Trail. We thought we'd wander from one artist to the other."

"I thought you seemed like a sensible woman. I can always tell. A focal point is different from a checklist, as you surely know."

He leaned back in the chair and stretched his long legs out. He was wearing light tan trousers and a well-pressed white linen shirt. His feet, however, were incongruously clad in dusty brown suede desert boots.

He followed her glance. "I walk a great deal—and it's also an affectation. Like the hat. My name, by the way, is Frederick Ives and I am called 'Freddy.' I also have a ridiculous middle name, which I will reveal upon closer acquaintance, one I am positive will ensue. Now tell me who you are, literally. Not simply your name—a good place to start—but tell me all. You said 'we,' so you are not a solo traveler and I am quite, quite sure you are not with some sort of ghastly American tour group. Since you are wearing a wedding band I assume a husband is somewhere about, more's the pity. Although you could be a divorcée wearing a ring to stave off unwanted attention, inevitable with such beautiful eyes, or sadly a widow, but I don't often have that kind of luck."

In Rome for only a few hours and here she was, already dally-

ing in a pleasant, harmless flirtation! Faith had pictured exchang-
ing a meaningful glance with one or more handsome *signors,* but
with native speakers the kind of wordplay she was engaged in at the
moment would have been far beyond her linguistic skills. To have
such luck a few hours off the plane! And Frederick—"Freddy"—
Ives was not unattractive. Not at all. An older man. She guessed he
was in his late forties. She studied him more carefully.

Freddy's hat was covering his hair and what she could see was
fair, hard to determine whether any of the threads were silver, or
missing. His initial, courtly gesture had not provided more than a
second's glance at what lay beneath. His boots had obviously taken
him into sunny climes, as his face and arms were deeply tanned,
making his blue eyes quite startling. Why was it that some men
grew even more attractive with age, while women were fight-
ing a good fight, eventually surrendering to the inevitable—
comfortable shoes and Not Your Daughter's Jeans?

Faith took a breath and fervently wished she could change the
water into wine to suit the mood, but that was not her department. How to tell all? Where to start? She followed his suggestion.
"My name is Faith Fairchild—"

"I'm so glad," he interrupted. "It's perfect for a heroine. I was
trembling with fear that it might be 'Mabel' or 'Maude.' No, I take
that back. I like 'Maude,' just not for you. Go on."

Somewhat nonplussed, Faith plunged back into the conversation, giving Freddy the CliffsNotes version of her life so far, which
seemed to delight him, and he further interrupted only twice to
comment on how extremely unlikely it was that she should be a
cook—"One thinks of Mrs. Beeton"—and also a minister's wife—
"too Trollope."

Faith was enjoying herself very much. All these literary allu-
sions. As an English major she'd pictured herself married to someone who would read what she read and they'd sit sipping sherry in
front of the fire, discussing books while little Elizabeth (*Pride and*

Prejudice) and little Nicholas (*The Great Gatsby* and *Nickleby*) slept in their wee trundles overhead. Thank goodness she had met Tom instead, and while they shared some of the same tastes in reading, they had totally avoided tweeness.

Still it had its attractions. Just as she was about to ask Freddy for his own *vita,* the door from the hotel opened and this time it *was* Tom, followed by a member of the hotel staff bearing a tray with a bottle of Prosecco in an ice bucket and several little bowls with olives, nuts, and some sort of Italian Chex Mix equivalent. Faith jumped up and hugged her husband in delight.

"Ah, the bridegroom cometh," Freddy said, standing also.

"Tom, this is Frederick Ives. Freddy, this is my husband, Tom Fairchild."

"I think we need another glass if you would, Antonio," Tom said, putting his hand out to greet his wife's new companion, who immediately shook it heartily, saying, "I would not dream of intruding. You are obviously a man of exquisite sensibilities, and priorities. I envy you this moment in your maiden *Roman Holiday.* First times are rare in life."

Tom laughed. "That's exactly how I feel. *La dolce vita.*" The men exchanged looks, and it was Faith's turn to laugh. School-boys, both of them.

Freddy picked up the books he hadn't opened. One was a small notebook; the other was a copy of Graham Greene's *The End of the Affair.*

"I would be honored if you would be my guests for dinner tonight at an *hostaria* not far from here. I selfishly want to watch your enchanting wife's face as she tastes their *carciofi alla giudia* and your nice one, too, Reverend Tom, when you drink the golden Frascati from my friend, the owner's, private source in the Alban Hills." He paused and then added in a surprisingly intense voice, "I don't know when I will be in Rome again, and I won't be here long this time."

The Fairchilds accepted his invitation. Nine o'clock at Hostaria Giggetto on the Via del Portico d'Ottavia. Their host would meet them there.

Antonio was opening the door for Freddy when Faith realized she had an unanswered question.

"But what do you do? You never said."

"Oh, I write guidebooks. Ciao."

Chapter 2

Excerpt from Faith Fairchild's travel journal:

Know I will have neither the time nor the inclination to keep this systematically, so I'll just write down some things to remember—especially food and people like Freddy Ives, although I doubt I'll be running into anyone else like him on this trip or, in fact, ever. As soon as I started to write in here, I immediately heard Freddy's voice quoting Oscar Wilde's Gwendolen and why she kept a diary, "One should always have something sensational to read in the train." I doubt very much that I will have anything sensational to write about. Being off the leash is sensational enough.

Freddy definitely brings out the reader in me, maybe because he looks a little bit like Peter O'Toole in "Mr. Chips" and I'm making a separate list in the back of this journal of books I need to read or reread when I get home, that place across the pond, which seems very far away right now. Pause to gaze out window. This journal is turning more into stream of consciousness than anything else.

Called to tell Pix we'd arrived safe and sound. She put the children on and I doubt they miss us, which is only fair, as I don't miss them—at least not yet. Ben wants us to bring him back a Vespa (as if) and Amy is 6 boxes away from selling the most Girl Scout cookies in her troop and would we buy some more? Am picturing self as old lady surrounded not by stacks of newspapers like the Collyer brothers, but stacks of Tagalongs and Thin Mints. Tom did not get on, as he unfortunately found out what the roaming charges are before we left home, so no calls to chat with anyone. Had to tell Hope not to phone unless dire emergency and bad haircut does not count.

We had a picnic lunch in the Piazza Navona, which we found by chance thereby reinforcing the Freddy Method of sightseeing. On the way we came across a street lined with wonderful antiques shops, the goods all beyond our reach with the terrible exchange rate. Cannot do the math in my head, so am counting the euros as dollars but not mentioning this system to Tom. At a panetterria nearby we bought three yummy panini: proscuitto crudo with fresh mozzarella, artichoke fritta—eggy and still warm—and one with roasted vegetables drizzled with truffle oil and sat to eat on a stone bench by Bernini's Fountain of the Four Rivers facing Borromini's Church of St. Agnes in Agone (want to remember at least some of what we've seen). A guide was describing the piazza in English to a small group of sturdy-looking travelers. Judging from the prevalence of Birkenstocks with socks, as well as fanny packs worn on tummies and men wearing those polo shirts with penguin logos (what brand is this anyway?), I pegged them as Americans. Maybe shoes and dress are still clues. Elder Hostel or some other similarly educational program? The guide was giving them their money's worth and I decided it wasn't cheating to eavesdrop. The fountain's four rivers are the Nile, symbolizing Africa; the Danube, Europe; the Ganges, Asia; and the Rio de la Plata for the Americas. The Plata's muscular arm was said to have been raised to protect the giant from the collapse of Borromini's facade, and the Nile was similarly posed, covering his eyes in disgust. A bitter Baroque rivalry, literally carved in stone! Unfortunately the guide added that the fountain was completed before

Borromini even started the church, so no dis intended. I was hoping she'd be leading them to a Caravaggio next, but they were headed for the Pantheon. At least we knew the direction to go, but we ended up sitting and people watching instead.

Then we needed coffee and then we decided to go back to the room again, and then . . . Now I'm waiting for Tom to finish his shower, so I can get ready to meet Freddy for dinner. Am feeling festive, so will wear only posh frock I brought—a jersey Eileen Fisher pale gray number with a cropped sweater in the same color that I adore. It's so light it feels like a cobweb, with tiny crystal beads like dewdrops. Something Titania would wear. Feel as if I am being possessed by Victorian lady novelist, or teenage girl. Oh Freddy, what are you doing to me? This journal is going to be one of those things I burn before my children pack me off to a home. Too embarrassing.

We are going to the restaurant by way of the Pantheon. Or that's the plan anyway. I have the feeling this is going to be one of those things like my never having been to the top of the Empire State Building despite every intention. Tom's done finally—and another note to self: have never met a woman who couldn't get dressed to go out faster than a man. More later. Feel as if we have been here for a week at least. Could it be only last night we were at Logan?

"You're not tired?" Tom asked. "You didn't sleep at all today. I did and I'm still feeling a little bushed."

They were walking along the Tiber. The night was warm and lights from the bridges and buildings on both sides of the river reflected up into the sky, still dusky blue.

"I may not sleep until we get back on the plane if the rest of the trip is like this," Faith said. "I don't want to waste a moment. I remember feeling this way when I was a teenager. I could stay up all night and my eyelids never drooped the next day. Remember that bumper sticker Samantha Miller had on her car when she was in college—'I'll sleep when I'm dead'?"

"I do, and I also remember thinking it was pretty extreme. I prefer Millay and the image of burning a candle at both ends to give off a lovely light. But, wife o' mine, this is your trip. Sleep or don't sleep, whatever your heart desires."

"I'm looking at it," Faith said, and they stopped to kiss. She hoped this would get to be a habit while they were in Italy. They certainly weren't going to be able to do it on Aleford's Main Street. Millicent Revere McKinley, the embodiment of the defunct Bostonian Watch and Ward Society, would come flying from her little clapboard cape strategically located by the town green and throw a bucket of water on them.

"Here's our turn, the Via Arenula," Tom said. "The third left will take us to the Via del Portico." While they had taken Freddy's advice and ignored printed material earlier, Tom was charting their route to the restaurant from their stop at the Pantheon, map in hand.

The street was lined with shops, most of them closed. They were in the historic ghetto of Rome, and it was after sundown, signaling the start of the Sabbath. Yet some nonkosher restaurants were open, Faith noted, and enticing smells were coming from the crowded tables set up outdoors. She was hungry; lunch had been a long time ago.

Hostaria Giggetto was at the very end of the street. Freddy was sitting at one of the tables and strolled out to meet them. Kissing Faith on each cheek and clapping an arm around Tom's shoulder, he was wearing a black collarless shirt underneath what Faith's father always called an "ice cream suit," vanilla white linen. For a moment it occurred to her that if Tom had been wearing his work clothes, they would have made interesting bookends.

"Come and sit down. I hope it's all right to sit outdoors?"

"It's perfect," Faith said.

Tom was nodding his head in agreement and perhaps awe, gesturing toward three dramatically lit Corinthian columns and the partial facade of a ruin so close to their table they could almost touch the stones.

"Incredible," he said.

"The columns are all that remains of the temple of Apollo," Freddy said. "Augustus named this portico in honor of his sister, Octavia."

"Probably to make up for her scummy husband," Faith said firmly. "I mean, it's the ancient version of putting your husband through medical school or business school and then getting dumped. In her case, it was supplying him with an army and whatever they called K rations. Okay, he left her for Cleopatra, pretty tough competition, but he could have said no, I'm a married man."

Freddy was laughing. "And don't forget Octavia raised their son along with a passel of other assorted offspring. She was a bit like Victoria in being the progenitor of all sorts of future heads of state. Kings, kaisers, tsars, not so different from emperors, although I don't think Caligula and Nero would have made it into her 'Granny Remembers' book, had she still been around. And now we need some food and a great deal of wine over which you can tell me all—perhaps not all—you've been doing since we parted."

The waiter approached and Freddy said, "Please ask Claudio to select some wines for us and he may as well choose the whole meal so long as one entrée is today's fish. Just start us off with plenty of *fiori di zucchina, carciofi alla giudia,* and *filetti di baccalà. Grazie.*"

"*Prego, signore.*"

"Who is Claudio? The chef?" Faith asked.

"No, he's the grandson of Luigi Ceccarelli, known to one and all as 'Giggetto,' who started the restaurant—hence the name—in the 1920s after he served in the war. It had been an ancient inn, one of those Caesar-was-here-type places or perhaps it was Remus even further back wanting a little *fritto misto,* despite his early penchant for vulpine milk, after dispatching his brother. Later I'll take you inside and Claudio's father, Franco, who took over from his father, Luigi, will take us to see the wine cellar, which has enough Roman masonry to satisfy what I am very much afraid may be an unhealthy touristic leaning on your part. Oh, and I asked for Claudio because he does all the buying. Gets up at an ungodly hour to go to the markets."

Healthy or unhealthy, Faith thought that by the time dinner was over they wouldn't need a guidebook. All they had to do was keep Freddy talking, a happy prospect. Apparently Tom had the same thought.

"So Augustus built this in honor of his sister."

Freddy shook his finger at him. "Naughty, naughty. Soon you'll have me telling you that it was the foyer for the Theater of Marcellus next door. Spare a thought for the poor lad, a favorite of his uncle's but dead at nineteen. This entrance also led to a vast array of temples, libraries—the Circus Flaminius in short. Ah, saved. Here are the courgette blossoms."

It was soon apparent that the man who eschewed anchovies on his pizza was a huge fan of them mixed with ricotta and stuffed into the golden flowers, even more golden after being lightly battered and fried. Faith filed the preference away, thinking she could now try Tom on one of her favorites: *spaghetti alla foriana,* that heavenly combination of anchovies, raisins, plenty of garlic, walnuts, and pignoli (see recipe, page 233). The waiter placed another appetizer on the table. It was the *baccalà.* Small chunks of cod that looked like the fish part of fish and chips, seemingly commonplace. But these morsels! Anything but commonplace. Perfectly done, and it was hard to believe they hadn't come right from the ocean, bypassing boats and markets. Freddy advised a tiny squeeze of lemon that brought the flavor out even more. Judging from the starters, it was going to be a memorable meal.

She sighed and sipped some wine. Octavia's portico was facing her, and for a moment she gave a thought to the kind of monument she might erect for Tom's difficult sister, Betsey. Her own sister was easy. She already worked in a temple of sorts—one not to a deity, but mammon. Quite apart from that, Faith would choose something elegant yet warm for Hope—maybe a Carrara marble plinth. She smiled to herself at the direction her thoughts were taking.

Freddy was smiling, too, as he watched them eat with such obvious relish. "Before the artichokes arrive, which will require our utmost concentration—it is my favorite dish in Rome—tell me, what did you look at today?"

Faith abandoned her sculptural speculations. "People mostly, mobile, and immobile as in the Piazza Navona Berninis. We had a picnic lunch there."

"I like that piazza, although it's a bit large. Our Piazza Farnese is more intimate. And of course those poor Berninis in the Navona. You Yanks snapped off their fingers as souvenirs when you were bivouacked there during the Liberation. Odd thing to put on a mantel."

"As odd as your Lord Elgin's Greek trophies? As I recall there was a bit of statuary pillage there, too," Tom said.

"Ah, you have me there, I'm afraid, Reverend. But we digress. Any Caravaggios today? My favorites are just off the Piazza Navona in Chiesa San Luigi dei Francesci. The Saint Matthew cycle. Stop in if you missed them. I suppose I go back whenever I'm here because I am poised to identify with him as an old man, as he is depicted in the last of the three paintings. Wrinkles abound and Matthew's taking dictation from an angel—unfortunately mine own writing has quite obviously never had the benefit of divine intervention, but I hope to share those noble marks of age, lines earned by living. And then of course there are his marvelously filthy feet."

"Filthy feet?" Tom said, scraping the last flakes of cod from his plate.

Freddy lifted his foot from under the table. It was clad in the same well-worn desert boot as earlier, unless he had numerous pairs of similar vintage. "Yes, quite a brouhaha about it. Not the thing, don't you know, to portray a saint with plebian dust on his soles."

His imitation of a "tebbily" upper-crust Brit was all too accurate and Faith found herself wondering what his mysterious middle name was. Something from *Debrett's,* like Cholmondeley, pronounced for reasons no doubt dating back to William the Conqueror as "Chumley"?

Before she could ask, the waiter placed one of the *carciofi alla giudias* in front of her. The sight of the crisp, steaming artichoke, its choke removed and the petals fanned out like a sunflower, drove all thoughts from her mind save one: eating it. She was familiar with the dish—a kind of artichoke onion blossom—but had never tasted it and vowed it would be the first thing she tried to replicate back home. Although it might lose something in the translation, or rather transportation. It seemed meant to be eaten just where she was, under the Roman sky.

Her husband had what could only be described as a dopey grin on his face, the kind engendered by either good food, good sex, or both.

"Do you think Francesca could teach us how to make this?" he asked.

"Old friends of ours, Francesca Rossi and her husband, Gianni, live in Tuscany and have just started a cooking school. We're going there for its first week, their maiden voyage," Faith explained to Freddy. She'd told him they were in Italy to celebrate their anniversary but hadn't mentioned the school.

Freddy looked surprised. "It's a common name, all three, but I rented a small place from a Rossi family near Montepulciano while I was writing a book on the hill towns many years ago. Of course it's the people you know. Maria and Mario had a daughter, Francesca, who was married to a man named Gianni, with whom I enjoyed many happy glasses of Vino Nobile. They had three small children who must be quite big now. Francesca spoke often of her time working with a chef in New York City. The Rossis are the ones who steered me to our hotel also. I believe wholeheartedly in fate, not coincidence."

Faith believed the same thing. Coincidence was showing up at a party with the same dress as another guest; fate was what happened afterward. And Freddy was definitely fate.

He continued, "Like your delicious wife, you cook? I applaud you, Thomas. I have studiously avoided any involvement with the preparation of food lest it detract from my appreciation of it. Or that is what I tell myself."

Tom was nodding thanks to the waiter who was replenishing his wine. "Well, I try. Keep my hand in, so to speak."

You old fraud, Faith thought to herself, storing her husband's comment away for future teasing. And apparently the wine is making you start to sound like Bertie Wooster. Tom was a big Wodehouse fan.

She was savoring one of the crisp, golden-brown *carciofi* leaves. The secret had to be starting off with such a flavorful, perfectly ripe artichoke and using only the freshest oil.

"*Carciofi alla giudia* may be the most famous dish to come from the Roman ghetto—'ghetto' is an Italian word," Freddy said. "In fact, most of what we call Roman cuisine is really *la cucina ebraico-romanesca,* the food that was developed out of necessity in the ghetto. Between roughly 1555 and sometime in the 1800s, Jews were confined to a seven-acre area surrounding where we are sitting now. There were five thousand of them, far, far fewer today, and the area has shrunk in size. These apartments are now the most prized in Rome, but for hundreds of years, in addition to not being able to leave the area during the day, or even go out into the ghetto itself at night, Jews were herded to mass in a church you may have passed on your way here, Sant'Angelo in Pescheria. They also had to wear yellow hats. Color sound familiar?"

"I've read about this," Tom said. "When the Romans invaded Judea, they brought their captives to Rome as slaves. There were periods though, weren't there, when Jews were allowed the freedom to worship, own property, and live where they chose? A rabbi friend told me the Roman Jewish community is the oldest in Europe."

Freddy nodded. "It was the isolation that gave rise to the dishes we have before us, but you're right that prior to the 1500s there were periods when it wasn't so bad—especially if you were a physician. A lot of the popes were smart enough to call, say, Dr. Shapiro instead of the local barber with his jar of leeches." He looked away from the Fairchilds and gestured dramatically toward the entrance of the restaurant. "Ah, the arrival of *Il Primo*! And Claudio has given us *Rigatoni all'Amatriciana,* I see."

The waiter set steaming bowls of the pasta in front of them and returned with a wedge of pecorino Romano, which he grated on top and left. Faith was familiar with the dish, deceptively simple— *guanciale,* a kind of Italian bacon; onions; garlic; olive oil; and *peperoncino,* the Italian spicy crushed red pepper whose zing took the pasta to another level. She was going to have to pace herself. There was still a second course and *Il Dolce,* dessert, to come. And possibly a *contorno,* side dish. No food would go to waste, though. Fortunately her husband was a bottomless pit, and from the way Freddy was attacking his plate, he seemed the same.

Silence reigned comfortably for a bit as they ate. The growing dark and soft light from the votive candles on the table had created a sense of intimacy, as if they had known each other for a long time.

Freddy picked up the thread of their conversation again. "It was those years of forced separation that gave rise to things like these delectable artichokes. The ghetto wasn't exactly a place where one could plant veggies, and the Tiber had a nasty habit of overflowing, its waters creating a rather noxious cocktail. Jewish housewives relied on spices to both preserve food and add flavor. Plus they fried what they could in olive oil. We are also sitting on the site of an ancient fish market, hence fish as a staple in their diet, a happy accident giving us, among other tasty bites here, a fish soup that I hope will be one of tonight's offerings."

He looked somber for a moment, a cloud across what had been a relaxed and happy face. He pointed toward the portico. "After dinner, I'll show you the plaque over there. It's the kind of thing I seem to be able to memorize: 'On October sixteenth, 1943, here began the merciless rout of the Jews. The few who escaped murder and many others, in solidarity, pray for love and peace from mankind and pardon and hope from God.'

"Over a thousand had assembled that day bringing the amount of gold—one hundred and ten pounds—they were told would save them from deportation. In my mind's eye, I see them still gathering, weighing, trusting. Only fifteen returned, all adults. None of the two hundred children made it. The irony—such an inadequate word almost always—is that Il Duce didn't have a problem with Jews. The old some-of-my-best-friends-are thing, but in his case, it was a fact. A number of the original founders of the *fasci di combattimento* were Jewish. But Mein Führer wasn't having any of it."

The narrow cobbled street was filled with echoes and visions. Faith had to close her eyes for a moment. When she opened them, their plates had been removed.

Freddy filled their glasses and raised his, spilling a few drops on the table and his notebook. "*Memento mori*. Now we must switch to *cin-cin* as a toast and talk of other things."

By the time the next course arrived, they had covered the recent elections in the States, the solution to Italy's economic woes—"The entire country is covered in masses of white canvas umbrellas much of the year like a giant Christo wrapping, surely these manufacturers, these tentmakers, can step up to the plate," Freddy suggested. They moved on to the notion—and the obscenity—of colonizing the moon. "Would serve them right if it *is* made of green cheese and not the good kind, but some horrible dyed concoction," Faith offered.

As the main course was arriving, Claudio himself brought a side dish of emerald green *asparagi,* simply prepared with olive oil and lemon. After the meal, he promised, he and his family would give the Fairchilds a tour of the restaurant.

Il Secondo turned out to consist of three wonderful dishes: the fish soup Freddy had mentioned; plus *filetto di cernia,* grouper, the fish in a fragrant white wine and mushroom sauce; plus spring lamb—*abbacchio*—*alla scottaditto,* which Freddy obligingly translated as "finger blistering," an act Tom cheerfully undertook, grabbing one of the crispy, seared chops from his plate and passing it to the others. Faith was happy to see that Freddy was not one of those "If you wanted it, why didn't you order it" types and was obviously willing to share, calling for additional bowls for the large serving of soup that had been placed in front of him. Many an unhappy marriage could have been prevented if the bride or groom had been firm on this essential act or walked away when refused. This thought led Faith to another. She'd noticed right away on the terrace that Freddy wasn't wearing a wedding band. Some men didn't wear rings, though. She felt herself relax even further into the mood of the evening; it was time to move from the political to the personal.

"Did you grow up near London?" It was an opener and usually people proceeded from childhood to their entire life stories.

"Clever minx, but I'm on to you. I have no desire to kill the cat in this case, though. No, I did not grow up near London. My family is from the north of England, not far from York. Part of the Roman wall went through our backyard. Such engineers. Such big thinkers. Like all little boys of my type I was sent away to school, where I was educated by sadistic masters and learned quite a bit in the process despite the beatings or perhaps because of them. I will never know, will I? And then to university and now here." He grinned. Faith knew he knew it wasn't what she'd wanted at all.

"Always been a writer, then?" Tom came to the rescue.

"No," Freddy answered, and unlike most people, who go on to fill an ensuing silence after a while, he appeared content to sit and watch them quietly for the rest of the night.

"Do you get back to England to see your family often?" Faith wasn't quitting, and going on the assumption that he must travel a great deal for his work, she thought the question was not out of place.

"No," Freddy said again and then laughed, a laugh that was almost like a bark, startling the young couple at the next table, who, having finished their antipasti, had been engaged in locking lips.

"I wander 'lonely as a cloud.' I cannot disappoint you any more, Faith my sweet. Ask me anything. Well, almost anything. My parents are both dead. I am an orphan with no siblings. I tried being married once, but couldn't get the hang of it and, much to the relief of my wife, stopped trying. She now lives in Shropshire with her much nicer husband and four children, none of them mine, and she sends me a Christmas card each year. And now, pudding? Or if I may suggest instead, an espresso for me—you two must go to sleep and get on local time—*un liquore* for you, perhaps a limoncello if they have some of the della Costiera, as I'm sure they must. Then we can walk back by way of the Pantheon, which you need to see at night. There is an acceptable *gelateria* nearby for afterward. Mo's, the best in Rome, is too far—near Vatican City. But you will be in Florence and can go to Carapina as many times as possible. I'm quite fond of Italian ice cream. All those flavors, much like your original Howard Johnson's without the orange roofs."

"So you've spent some time in the States?"

"Don't you think I've shared enough information with you for one night, dear lady? We must leave something to talk about the next time we meet, as I'm sure our paths will cross again, although not immediately. I leave Rome early tomorrow morning."

Faith, too, was sure their paths would cross again and pictured the three of them walking off at the end of the evening into the fog à la Claude Rains and Humphrey Bogart, except it was a clear night and Rome, not Casablanca.

He ordered their *liquori* and his espresso. Faith sipped her li- moncello appreciatively—she wanted to remember the brand— and then Freddy shooed them off for a tour of the restaurant while he proceeded to write in the notebook that he'd closed and placed next to him on the table when they'd arrived.

What Faith had thought from the outside would be a small interior turned out to be a maze of delightful rooms ranging from banquet proportions to an intimate patio with a few tables tucked away at the rear. The wine cellars were impressive for the number of bottles and the brick walls that dated back to the original fish market. Claudio and his father were enthusiastic guides, pressing a bottle of a favorite Frascati on them. The Fairchilds had no dif- ficulty promising to return as soon as possible.

When they came back outside, Freddy was engaged in writing. He snapped his notebook shut as soon as he saw them and said, "The Pantheon, I rather think now."

"Just the brief look we had before coming to the restaurant was a revelation," Tom said. "It's the kind of place that a photograph can't capture. It sounds quite inane, but it's so *big* and the oculus is truly like an eye to the heavens. I'd very much like to see it at night."

"Not inane at all, exactly right. When you come back to Rome, which you will even if you don't go to the Trevi Fountain and toss a coin, try to go to the Pantheon when it's raining. I have a small store of special memories and one is of being under that eye during a sun shower. I was quite young and felt like some sort of male transfiguration of Danaë. The golden mist hung in the air and even the puddles on the floor looked molten. Ah youth, truly wasted on the young, as Shaw, that curmudgeony vegetarian, aptly said."

He stood up, tucking his notebook in his jacket pocket. "*Andiamo!* Before you both turn into pumpkins. I shouldn't be keeping you up so late, but I'm a very selfish man. Ask my ex-wife. I can say that now, since you know all."

Faith was quite sure they did not even come close to knowing all about Freddy.

"Could you ask the waiter for the check?" Tom said.

"Done. Remember I said it was *my* party. Now I very much want some *nocciola* gelato. I suggest we indulge in that delightful Italian ritual known as *La Passeggiata,* a leisurely evening stroll."

How long had they been eating? Hours, Faith knew, but the time was stretching out even further, and despite the meal she had just consumed, she realized there was still space for gelato, even a *doppio,* two scoops and yes, one would definitely be *nocciola*—hazelnut.

They strolled out into the night. The street was starting to get crowded, and Faith was reminded that Italians ate late. Freddy led them to the commemorative plaque, and they stood quietly in front of it for some minutes before he linked an arm through each of theirs, moving them back the way they'd come. He pointed out a small stone arch leading to an alley to the right of the restaurant that he told them would take them on the kind of pleasant wandering he espoused—"where way leads on to way." Faith thought again of all the footsteps they were following in Rome.

"But," Freddy added, "not tomorrow. Having forbidden you the more conventional tools of travel, I've made arrangements for you to go to the Borghese, where you will gaze upon Berninis, Caravaggios, and all manner of gorgeous things. Paolo has the information. It was too late for me to get you to the Sistine Chapel with a small group, and I forbid you to go any other way. In any case, you will love the Borghese. Mostly I go to be thrilled by the sublime Pauline herself, so erotic, that lusciously smooth marble."

Faith had seen pictures of the statue of Pauline Borghese, Napoleon's sister. She was reclining seductively, half nude on her Empire marble chaise longue. Tickets to the Galleria Borghese had to be purchased at least several days in advance, and she wondered how Freddy had managed it.

"You strike me as good walkers, but not fanatics—no jolly hockey girl thick ankles on you, Faith my love. So you might have a leisurely breakfast—the hotel lays on quite a nice spread—and walk to the museum and gardens. You'll bump into a number of famous sights unless you're careful. Afterward you can have lunch at 'Gusto—very chic, but very good, it's near the Ara Pacis—then make your way to the Forum. I know you want to see the Colosseum, my little Daisy, and thankfully that kind of Roman fever— malaria—is not the kind of danger it once was. Not to say there aren't others . . ."

Before he could elaborate, if he was, they were at the Pantheon, dramatic, impressive in the long floodlight beams, all Freddy had promised. They stood for a while in the center of the square by the fountain, gazing at the front before walking completely around the exterior, the massive dome looming over them, omnipresent. Afterward, he led the way to the *gelateria,* which had a long line of customers whose happy chatter in several languages sounded like flocks of various kinds of birds, among them the passionate couple at the table next to them in the restaurant.

As they reached the Corso Vittoria Emanuele, Faith thought she would always remember this moment, like those "store of memories" Freddy had mentioned. She had a store of them as well. She assumed most people did. Flashes of intense, perfect happiness that existed in one's mind as if they were being relived that instant. This flash was the three of them standing perfectly still, waiting for the pedestrian sign to change while the traffic whizzed by in front of them. Their gelatos were gone, but the flavor lingered, and above, the Roman night hung suspended, a canopy of light and dark.

When they got to the Campo de' Fiori, she remembered to ask Freddy about the large bronze statue, even more forbidding at night.

"Ah, Bruno. Reduced now to a convenient meeting place. We say, 'Meet me at Bruno' and everyone knows where to go. You must be familiar with the Dominican supposed heretic Giordano Bruno, Tom."

Tom nodded. "Was this where they burned him, then?"

"I'm afraid so. Rather a popular spot for public executions, those highly popular precursors to the horrid reality shows on the telly, or melees at soccer games, that captivate audiences now. The market didn't move here until the mid-nineteenth century. Before then it was in the Piazza Navona. Bruno was put to death in 1600. Poor man. He'd spent most of his adult life outside Italy, where his ideas about an infinite universe and other things such as the solar system met with more favor than here. Anyway, he thought the madness of the Inquisition had subsided and came back. Homesick, I imagine. Italians usually are when they leave for any length of time. His bad luck that the embers were still smoldering. Rather literally."

"Who put the statue up? Surely not the church," Faith said.

Freddy shook his head. "It was erected at the time of Italy's unification, late 1800s, by the Freemasons, primarily. It's still a symbol for all stripes of independent thinkers, or those who imagine they are. They have a kind of fair every year, but you'd have more fun at the Befana Toy Fair in the Navona, especially at its end during Epiphany in January. La Befana would never bring coal to you good children," Freddy said. "And even if she did, it's made of chocolate nowadays."

They walked into the Piazza Farnese, which was completely empty, in contrast to the somewhat rowdy crowd that had spilled out from the many restaurants and bars lining the Campo de' Fiori market. The change was so abrupt that Faith found it unsettling. Not so much as the shadow of one of Rome's numerous cats flitted across the cobblestones.

"These must have been baths originally, yes?" Tom asked. "Only a modern contemporary artist would design fountains with tubs like these."

"Indubitably. And not just any fountains, but ones from Cara-calla. Aaah, the thought. I would not have liked to live in that time—pestilence and no single-malt Scotch—but I would like to have indulged in the baths. Just look at those tubs." Freddy flung out his arm toward the one near the street to the hotel. "Solid granite, excellent for holding the heat and lovely nubiles pouring ewers of scented water for me to splash about in. In point of fact, they were not baths, but fountains from the start, extremely deco-rative conversation pieces in the Baths' vast gardens, but I imagine them otherwise, functional objets d'art. I'm glad they didn't end up as landfill. The Farneses moved quite a number of bits out of the Baths luckily. So much of Rome has been someplace else at one time or another. And speaking of time, I must bid you good night and farewell. I will be leaving early in the morning. Do ask Paolo to show you my room, by the way. I always have the same one. Such an old fuddy-duddy, but it is the hotel's largest and has what was once a tiny chapel at one end, perfect for me to contem-plate more venal things. There are lovely frescos on the ceiling above it and also the bed." He put out his hand toward Tom's, shaking it firmly.

"You're not going back now?" Faith said. She wasn't ready for the night to end. She'd pictured them sitting on the rooftop terrace together for a while.

"I must, my pet." He kissed her on both cheeks. He smelled ever so faintly of lime. "But we will keep in touch. Maybe I will come to that Aleford place of yours and eat some Indian pudding. I see you are shuddering. I forgot, not a native New Englander. And here am I such a lover of all things Transcendental. We'll have lobster instead. Surely you will allow that. My card." He drew one from inside his jacket pocket.

Faith took it. The address was a post office box in London and there was no phone number. "Frederick L. Ives," she read aloud. It sounded like "Frederick Lives" and she smiled. "Surely you know us well enough now to divulge your middle name."

Freddy bowed. "I must confess it to be 'Lancelot.' Mater was an ardent Tennyson fan. She did not consider the effect of the consonant before the vowel."

And he was gone.

Faith was hungry. It was long past breakfast time in Aleford. Much to her husband's surprise, she was up and dressed well before 7 A.M., the time the hotel started serving their *colazione*. The fact that Tom was not just a morning person, but an extremely *early* morning person, had been one of the few major differences between them. That and the entire Fairchild family's penchant for games of all sorts—active outdoor ones and the indoor type involving boards, game pieces, and cards. Faith knew at an early age that someone else was going to have to play Candy Land with any kids she would have. What she didn't know was that someone else was going to have to play its grown-up equivalent with her spouse. Scrabble, Boggle, Othello, even Clue—she resisted them all.

"Something smells heavenly and I need coffee," Faith said as they walked into the pleasant breakfast room. The buffet that extended the length of the room on one wall boded well.

"I don't think I've made myself clear," said a voice to their right. It belonged to a woman, and although she spoke with an English accent, it sounded like the kind Freddy had been imitating, not using. "I can see that you have an egg thingy out, so that means you must have eggs in the kitchen. Why then is it apparently impossible for one to order two of them poached?"

Dressed in a starched white jacket, the young man who had brought the Prosecco up to the terrace the night before bent down toward her and answered. His voice was too soft for Faith to catch much apart from many uses of the word "*signora*."

The *signora* flushed and stood up, speaking even more loudly to the man next to her. "I will be making sure that none of our friends come here, Roderick, and filing an immediate complaint to the management, although I sorely doubt that will do anything in *this* sort of place."

Faith almost started to giggle. The woman made it sound like a bordello. "I suppose I'll have to make do with some of their dry toast," she said. "The fruit looks spoiled."

She was tall and had an extremely long oval face some might unkindly associate with winners of the Derby. Her chin and nose completed the picture. All that was missing was a feed bag. Faith assumed Roderick was the woman's husband, but they looked enough alike to be mistaken for fraternal twins. They were cut from the same cloth—and the cloth was tweed. His took the form of a jacket, and hers a skirt, both bagging—the elbows and the seat, in her case. Good tweed lasted forever, and judging from the rings on her fingers and her earrings, at some point money had not been spared on any of their attire. But tweed! In Rome in the spring! Faith made her way to a small table for two in the corner where she could continue her observations as other guests arrived.

At the moment it was just the four of them, unless the English lady had a Corgi tucked under her chair.

"Yum," Tom said, clutching his plate. "Did you see what's on the buffet? Cake and cookies for breakfast! What a sensible idea."

There were two kinds of cake. One looked like a lemon sponge and the other was layered with custard and topped with chocolate. In between, cookies were arrayed in tempting rows on a large tray. The egg "thingy" referred to a kind of frittata with small, whole sausages—kind of Italian mini-franks, Faith thought—baked into the puffy omelet. Then there were plates of cured meats and cheeses, including fresh mozzarella. Plus slices of luscious-looking tomatoes, mounds of fresh fruit that was not in the least spoiled, yogurts, muesli, a huge jar of Nutella—Tom's preferred spread— several kinds of juice, crackers, breads, and warm *cornetti,* the Italian equivalent of a croissant. Jams of all kinds, more pastries. A large bowl of creamy ricotta stood next to jars of three kinds of honey for drizzling. In short, it was the breakfast that Faith had dreamed about with a hotel so near a market like the one at the Camp de' Fiori. It was not, however, in the least like a typical Italian breakfast, most often eaten standing up or on the run and consisting of a sweet roll dunked in cappuccino or a *caffè latte.*

Now, what should she have?

But coffee first.

By the time the Fairchilds finished, each table was occupied. The picky Englishwoman was still tucking in with a large slice of cake and, despite her voiced objection, enough fruit for a family of four on her plate. The only other traveler who had attracted Faith's attention was a young woman sitting alone who looked as if she'd be more at home in a hostel. Her visible piercings were on her earlobes and nose. She was dressed all in black, and her spiked hair was cut short. Beneath the violet and chartreuse streaks, it looked blond. But hard to tell. She'd gone straight for the coffee and quickly drunk three cups before turning to the buffet.

*   *   *

"Happy?" Tom asked. They had stopped for a moment in the Pi-azza Farnese, which was as empty as it had been the night before.

It was very late Saturday, or rather early Sunday. They had lingered over dinner well past midnight. Faith felt as if she were looking through some sort of View-Master, those funny contrap-tions she'd had as a kid with reels of Disney's *Snow White* plus things like the pyramids and shots of the Amazon that had been in a drawer at her grandparents' house. She'd been astonished to dis-cover they were still made when Ben had received a SpongeBob one some years ago.

But it was the perfect image, she thought. Click, and it was the walk to the Borghese, window-shopping on the Via Condotti, elegance she could never afford even with a stronger dollar, then click and they were stopping to climb the Spanish Steps. Click, the small Keats-Shelley Memorial House museum that clung to one side. They stood in the tiny room where Keats had died so young and looked out the window as he had, gazing at the boat-shaped fountain in the Piazza di Spagna he was said to admire for its lion heads at the prow and stern. Since the train to Tuscany didn't leave until after lunch the next day, they had decided to go to the English cemetery in the morning to see both Keats's and Shelley's graves—Keats with the sole identification: "Here lies one whose name was writ in water."

Another click brought the Borghese, the gardens and the mu-seum itself. The Berninis seemed to breathe, even tremble, Proser-pine forever seeking to free herself from Pluto. In the next picture they were sharing a mound of mouthwatering *fritto misto* at 'Gusto followed by an equally outstanding crunchy, thin-crusted pizza covered with cherry tomatoes, black olives, tomatoes, arugula, and two kinds of cheese—Parmesan and fresh mozzarella. Faith had had to wander in the adjacent *emporio* with its array of cookware and cookbooks. Tom had suggested a cab back to the hotel, what with the wine at lunch and what with . . .

And then back to the views. Ancient Rome at last. The cab driver, Stefano, had proved to be an accidental tour guide, providing a running commentary on everything they passed, interjecting his own description of his native Roma: "We are a historic lasagna!" Really quite an ideal way of thinking about the layers and layers that made up the Eternal City, the people, the food. Faith resolved to write a postcard to Freddy with the metaphor. And then, click, there was the Colosseum ("When it falls, so will Rome," Stefano had quoted the old saying, adding that it was publicized now to discourage people from chipping away at it). Click: wildflowers growing in the Forum next to pieces of the grandeur that once was there, scattered about like a child's discarded building blocks. A final shot: dinner at a place that looked and smelled good from the outside, proving even better. And now the question.

"Happy?" Tom said again, muffling his wife's obvious reply with a long kiss.

A kiss that was abruptly interrupted by the sound of people running. Faith broke away from Tom to look. There were two people, and one appeared to be chasing the other. They were racing across the piazza toward the fountain just in front of the Fairchilds. Tom grabbed his wife back and folded her in his arms, pulling her out of their path. The second figure gained on, then tackled the first. Faith watched, aghast as the two were locked together in a violent embrace, thrashing about on the hard cobblestones. Suddenly there was a single shout, an exclamation almost of surprise. Tom and Faith stood frozen, staring. What had come before had occurred with stunning speed and now time briefly stopped. One person got up; the other didn't. Faith buried her face back against her husband's chest, afraid to look.

And then speed again, the noise of racing footsteps, but only one pair. She lifted her head and caught sight of the fleeing figure. It was a man. Young. A face like the faces they had been seeing astride scooters, sitting in *caffès*, on the sidewalks all day. Nothing out of the ordinary. Except what had just happened, she was sure, wasn't ordinary at all.

The person on the ground was trying to sit up. The face was in the shadows, but as they went to help, they could see it was also a man, dressed from head to toe in black.

Not quite to toe. His shoes were brown. Well-worn desert boots. Faith knew those shoes. Knew the man.

It was Freddy—and he was clutching at the handle of a knife that had been thrust into his body just below his heart.

Fate, not coincidence?

CHAPTER 3

Freddy's eyes were closed. He was clutching at his chest, fumbling for the knife. The blood from the wound was beginning to seep onto his dark shirt.

"Freddy, no! Don't try to pull it out!" Faith screamed. His hand dropped to his side and his eyelids fluttered open. "We're getting help! Just hold on!" Dimly aware that Tom had his phone out, she moved nearer and gently cradled Freddy's head in her lap, Tom knelt down beside Faith. "I've called one-one-two," he said. "The operator spoke English, thank God. I told her a man had been attacked and was seriously injured. She said help would come immediately."

The Italian equivalent of 911 is 112, and it was one of the things both Fairchilds had learned before the trip. Tom was spreading his jacket over Freddy—surely in shock—and Faith quickly added the cardigan she was wearing.

"Faith, Tom," Freddy whispered.

"Don't try to talk," Tom said. He took Freddy's hand.

Freddy shook his head. "Too late. Stupid. Should have known." He was groping inside his jacket with his other hand.

"My pen." The words were barely audible. With obvious effort, he repeated them. "My pen."

Tom reached into one of the inside pockets and pulled out a fountain pen. "Look for his notebook, Tom," Faith said. "He must want us to write down what he's saying."

A name? Did he know who had attacked him? she wondered.

The previously empty piazza was rapidly filling up with people, but it felt as if the three of them were completely alone on a stage.

"His notebook's not here," Tom said. "His wallet and anything else he was carrying are gone, too. Just the pen."

Freddy brought his hand up and pushed at the pen. "You have to stop them. They're going to ki . . ." He slumped back, exhausted by the effort. "Pen," he said once more, and then all was silent save the welcome sound of the police—the raucous two-note wails Faith had noted until this moment with mild annoyance. Now they sounded like the horn of Gabriel.

Guards from the French embassy were streaming out from the entrance on the piazza, joining the *polizia* who were jumping from vehicles ranging from motorcycles to Lancias. The French force had what looked like small machine guns at the ready; the Italians were holding pistols. It was terrifying. Faith assumed that Tom's call must have been followed by so many others that the police decided to send a battalion. The ambulance arrived, and one of the Italian police shouted into a bullhorn. The onlookers melted back against the perimeter. Faith and Tom didn't move.

"*Non parlo l'italiano,*" Tom said loudly. "*Sono un americano.*"

The EMTs rushed to Freddy and the Fairchilds moved out of the way. One of the policemen walked over to them after speaking to two others from the force that was rapidly encircling the area. He did not look friendly. He *did* look in charge "Your names?"

"Mr. and Mrs. Thomas Fairchild. We are in Rome on vacation. The injured man is Frederick Ives, British. A friend of ours," Tom said.

They were loading Freddy into the back of the ambulance. Faith cried, "Where are you taking him? We need to go, too!"

The policeman didn't pay the slightest attention to her request and the vehicle sped off. Suddenly she felt the full weight of being in a foreign country. "We have to be with our friend! Please!"

He ignored her again. "Your address here in Rome?"

Tom gave him the information and answered the questions that followed as well. Home address in the United States, arrival and departure dates. Occupations. The inspector appeared to be filling out a form. Faith had heard about Italian bureaucracy—one friend described the lengths she had had to go through simply to buy postage stamps—but this was intolerable. Next it would be mother's maiden name. But it wasn't.

"Which of you was holding the knife?"

A nightmare. A complete nightmare!

Tom asked, his tone puzzled, "Do you mean did we touch the knife?"

"*Did* you touch the knife?"

Was the first question a trick? Could the man possibly think they had attacked Freddy? Faith wondered. That they were some-how a team of deadly U.S. crooks who were expanding their turf to Rome?

"No, neither of us touched the knife. We did not want to do any further injury to Mr. Ives."

"Then who did?"

Tom sighed and described the attack, finishing with the state-ment: "His wallet is gone as well as any other papers like his pass-port that he may have been carrying."

Their interrogator raised one eyebrow. "You seem to know the contents of Mr. Frederick Ives's pockets well, Mr. Fairchild. While sadly Rome suffers from pickpockets, purse snatchers, and other forms of petty crime, violent crime of this sort associated with a robbery is uncommon here."

His somewhat smug expression conveyed his opinion that brutal muggings were to be found on every street corner in the United States. He shrugged. "But there are always hotheads who might carry a knife like this as a persuader and then get carried away. Tell me, did your friend use drugs often?"

"I'm sure he didn't use them at all!" Faith exclaimed. "And we need to go to him *pronto*!" She wasn't sure that was the correct word. It was how Italians answered the phone, but she hoped her tone would convey her urgency.

"*Sì*." The inspector walked away from them and pulled out his mobile. He listened, said something, and motioned to the same two men he'd spoken to earlier, one of whom promptly tossed the cigarette he had been smoking onto the cobblestones. After a brief conversation, the inspector returned alone to the Fairchilds.

"I am sorry. Your friend is dead."

Tom tightened the arm he had around Faith's shoulder.

"Are you sure?" she said.

He nodded. The fact of death had softened his expression.

Out of the corner of her eye, Faith could see the police unwinding crime scene tape, kicking the still smoldering cigarette butt out of the area.

And then she started to sob.

It was a Rome not many tourists get to know—the Serious Crime Squad headquarters. The Fairchilds were offered coffee. Tom took it; Faith knew it would choke her. Hours passed, most of them spent waiting to tell their story, and whatever they knew of Freddy's, to what seemed like an endless stream of officials. Tom was quizzed more closely than Faith. He had seen enough of the assailant's face to provide a good likeness using an Identi-Kit. To Faith the only unusual features were thick dark eyebrows that stretched across his forehead in a straight line, as if drawn with a marker. But she was able to add that his black sneakers were Converse—she'd noted the blue All Star logo when he ran off—and that he'd also been wearing black Diesel jeans with a short black Ferragamo leather jacket. Unlike the United States, where this sort of information had met with extreme doubt in Faith's past police investigations—who noticed things like this?—the police in Rome seemed to expect that a woman of taste would have instantly recognized such labels.

Finally, they were told they were free to go but not before yet another individual told them how rare this sort of robbery gone wrong was in Italy. And especially in that part of Rome. "Now if it had been around the train station at that time . . ." several people had told them, shaking a verbal finger, as if Freddy had somehow become an affront to the city by being murdered in a good part of town.

A police car drove them back to the hotel, dropped them at the entrance, and sped off, almost grazing the sides of the narrow street. They rang the bell next to the ancient door, locked for the night, although little was left of its hours now. When there was no answer, Faith lifted the heavy iron knocker, feeling Shakespearean and wishing with all her heart she could, in effect, "Wake Duncan with thy knocking!"

Paolo answered, pulling back the door and securing it to the wall. His eyes were red. He'd obviously heard the news.

"*Signore* Ives. I cannot believe it. None of us can. Come in, come in." He took Faith's hand and pulled her into the lobby. "Go to your room and I will bring you some *camomilla*. Could you eat anything? A little *pane*? Or better, some *brodo*?"

She shook her head. He started to tear up, as he had apparently done before. "He has been coming here for many years. A friend to us all. I'll bring the *camomilla*. You need to have something and then sleep if you can. You must stay here until you feel you can travel. I will call Francesca."

But what Faith wanted most was to leave Rome. It would pass. It would have to. Freddy would be upset to know he'd put them off his beloved Città Eterna for long. As she thought of his reaction, she told herself she had to stop thinking of him as if he was alive and not just off temporarily on a journey.

"The train isn't until the afternoon. If we could stay in our room until then . . . ," Faith said.

"But of course." Paolo looked a bit hurt. As if she needed to ask was written all over his face. Gravely solicitous, he walked them to the elevator.

"Mr. Ives told us he was checking out," she said. The thought that had been plaguing her all night returned full force. Freddy said he was leaving early. Why had he stayed—and where?

"He did, even though he had the room for another week. He had paid in advance, so I told him it would be here if he changed his mind."

The fatigue and shock of the night dropped from Faith so abruptly that for a moment she was startled. Her mind began to race.

"So there isn't anyone there now? Freddy wanted us to see it and said we were to ask you to let us in. That it was the finest room in the hotel, with some interesting features."

Paolo nodded. If he thought her sudden request odd, he gave no indication. Her husband, however, was looking at her with an expression she knew all too well. "Stay out of it, Faith" could have been written in a comic strip balloon coming from his mouth.

"I will bring the key with the tea." Paolo bowed slightly as the elevator doors opened.

"Faith . . . ," Tom began as soon as they were in their room.

"You said his pockets were empty and so did the police. I just want to find his notebook. Maybe he left it in his room. I noticed at the restaurant that it had one of those alphabetical address sections in the back. The only address we have is a post office box in London, and something tells me the same is true on the hotel register, especially as he has been coming here so long. He probably doesn't even have to sign in at all. There may be some next of kin and it's only decent we find them. They can't ship a body to a post office box."

"The British embassy was sending someone and will take care of all that. You heard the inspector. I know how you feel. It's rare to meet someone and become such instant close friends, especially at our age, but we only knew Freddy briefly, and our part in both his life and death is over."

There was a knock on the door and Paolo entered with a tray. He set it down and told them he had instructed the staff not to disturb them. He handed Faith the key to Freddy's room as well and left.

Faith sipped the hot tea. Chamomile blossoms were the Italian answer to Sominex, or for that matter Prozac as well. A cure for sleeplessness, anxiety, and all sorts of other ills. Paolo had added honey, and soon the sweet liquid was making her both drowsy and calmer. Tom was already lying down. She joined him, resolving to only close her eyes for a moment before going to search Freddy's room.

An hour later she was awakened by a shaft of sunlight streaming across her face through the windows they had neglected to cover. For a moment, she luxuriated in the warmth of the bed, Tom's steady breathing, and the thought of the beautiful city surrounding them. And then she remembered.

Freddy was gone. Forever. And she owed it to him to find out what had happened. Robbery gone wrong—the detective's conclusion? She didn't think so. Thieves in Rome preyed on tourists in daylight, snatching purses, drawing your attention to a pigeon dropping or other mess on your back, then grabbing your wallet or backpack. Or the gangs of children employed to surround and cut off a target, creating a disturbance while one of them, or an adult, stole your camera, phone, and suitcase. The area around the train station *was* dangerous, and not just at night.

No, this wasn't like that. Both men dressed in black, dressed so as not to be seen. Had it started with Freddy tailing his killer or someone else, discovered and forced to flee? Then there was the young man's expensive clothing. Well, that could be due to the nature of his work—pickings good lately?

Yet, it all still came down to Freddy. Who *was* Frederick Lancelot Ives?

Any hotel guests who had not departed were lingering at breakfast and the hall was empty as Faith quietly slipped from their room. Freddy's room was on the same floor as the Fairchilds,' but at the far end. She hadn't dared to hope that the room had not been cleaned, but the first thing that greeted her was the sight of the unmade bed. Knowing Freddy wasn't coming back immediately, the staff must have skipped making it up, pressured by other housekeeping demands.

Yet aside from the bed, the room appeared not to have been occupied at all. There was nothing in the wastebaskets save a spent tube of Italian toothpaste, Pasta del Capitano. Faith was sure Freddy would have told her he used that brand because of its captivating name and the picture of the Capitano himself, complete with nineteenth-century mustachio. It was a large tube, indicating that Freddy had been in Italy for some time, or it could just have been his preferred paste.

The armoire was empty, as were all the drawers. Nothing under the bed. The minibar looked untouched. The room had to be, no question, the nicest in the hotel. Freddy was right about that. The ceilings above the bed and the small marble altar in the alcove that had once been a private chapel were covered in celestial frescoes, a giant sunburst positioned above the *letto matrimoniale*. The only clue that Freddy had been there was the faint smell of the lime cologne he wore. She knew that the scent would always bring him, and those awful moments, back.

Faith went to the window. It was at the front of the hotel and looked straight across into the French embassy. The embassy shutters were closed, but the street was starting to come to life. She pictured Freddy looking out yesterday morning. He had taken the time to draw the drapes and fold the shutters back, seeing what she was seeing now before he left. Left to go where? She turned away, closed and locked the door, before taking the stairs to the lobby. She didn't want to smile at anyone in the elevator.

For once Paolo was not at the desk. A young woman who seemed to know who Faith was introduced herself. "I am Carolina, what can I do to help you? The breakfast is over, but I can get you and your husband anything you want to eat."

"*Grazie,* but we are fine for now. Here is the key Paolo gave me. Please tell him I thought it was a very beautiful room, very special."

"Our best. *Signore* Ives always had it." Carolina's face fell. Faith broke the somber silence voicing a thought she'd had on the way down.

"Did Freddy, that is *Signore* Ives, leave a suitcase or anything else in your storage closet when he checked out to pick up later in the day? If so, I wonder if I might look to see whether he had packed the book he was going to lend me."

"*Sì.* His case is here. I put it away myself. I must remember to ask Paolo what we are to do with it now." Carolina gave a deep sigh.

Faith followed her to a closet beyond the bar and watched as Carolina unlocked it. There were a number of bags in it. The one Carolina pointed out as Freddy's was a good-size one behind the others. It didn't have a luggage tag or anything else to distinguish it.

"I must go back to the desk. If you will put it back when you are finished, I will lock the door again."

Faith set the case flat on the floor and unzipped the outside pockets, which were empty, before opening the main compartment. She felt like a voyeur as she went through Freddy's things. Invading his personal space. But she had to.

He packed neatly. Extremely neatly. And, like the room, the contents offered nothing. They were impersonal to what she was sure was a considered degree. No one could ascertain anything from it except that what Faith had seen Freddy wear was what he wore all the time—there were duplicates of the two outfits, including an extra pair of his signature shoes. His toiletry kit revealed he preferred an American nonelectric-brand razor and the cologne was made by Penhaligon's, a nod to his British roots? And very expensive ones at that?

She sat back on her heels to think about what this lack of information might mean. Both the room and now his suitcase were devoid of receipts, stamps, a souvenir postcard, letter, crumpled note on the hotel stationery, not even a used *biglietto* for the bus, although she and Tom had been surprised to see that no one ever used these tickets, hopping on and off without stamping one in the machine. Even a nun! Stefano, the taxi driver, had told them the widespread practice was putting him out of business.

Carolina had said there was just the one item. Faith would have expected a computer case or an electronic notebook in the suitcase. Freddy was a writer. Surely he didn't create entire books using only the small notebook he carried.

There were two choices in cases like this—the conscious obliteration of one's tracks. Freddy didn't want his movements traced, either because he was a good guy—or a bad one.

There was a book at the bottom of the case, but it was not his notebook. It was the Graham Greene he'd been about to read when Faith met him on the rooftop terrace. *The End of the Affair.*

She took it with her.

*   *   *

Tom was still asleep. There was no need to wake him. The train didn't leave for hours. Paolo had put a basket of small pastries, biscotti, rolls, butter, and jam on the tray with the tea. She had not thought she would ever be hungry again, but she was. She filled a napkin with some biscotti, buttered a roll, and took a bottle of water from her bag. Then, slipping quietly out of the room, she climbed the stairs to the roof. Tom would know where she had gone.

She assumed the terrace would be deserted and so it seemed. The hotel guests would be making their ways to Vatican City, the Capitoline Museum, or other parts of Italy, having "done" Rome. Faith sat on one of the small chairs next to the jasmine-covered trellis that hid the swing she'd thought she and Tom would have shared. Another time. Yes, they would come back.

She spread her small feast on the table and broke off a piece of biscotti. It was going to be another glorious day, the sky already an intense blue and cloudless. The sun felt good.

"This is a fine time for you to be getting scruples."

The woman's voice was so close that it startled Faith and she dropped the cookie. There *were* people on the roof and they were on the swing, out of sight, but only a scant few feet away. What to do? Cough? Leave?

"Just because you're paying me doesn't mean you own me!" a second woman said angrily.

They were speaking English, but their accents were purely American. Americans who had grown up or spent a great deal of time south of the Mason–Dixon Line.

This wasn't friendly girl talk, so one or both was likely to get up and leave at any moment. There was only one thing to do if Faith wanted to find out who the women were. She gathered up the remains of her snack in the napkin and her water, retraced her steps on tiptoe, then came back, selecting another chair farther away and noisily scraping it against the concrete. From her new spot, she couldn't hear anything, but a face peered around the trellis and seeing Faith gave a little wave.

"*Buon giorno,*" she said.

Faith half expected the greeting to be followed by "y'all."

"*Buon giorno,*" she said, recognizing the woman from breakfast yesterday. She'd come in as the Fairchilds were finishing. She appeared to be in her thirties, and even at the early hour was in full makeup. Her deep auburn hair, lacquered in place, was styled as only big hair can be. An older woman with the same grooming regimen had accompanied her. They had made a beeline for the coffee.

Faith returned to her snack, eating slowly, and stared at the tops of the palms. It wasn't long before both women emerged from their jasmine tent and nodded to her as they passed.

Not a moment too soon. Tom came on their heels, saying, "I thought you'd be here. But it's been long enough. We need to take a walk, love."

His words suggested she'd been there a while, and she was glad the two women hadn't overheard him. Although the exchange Faith had overheard could mean nothing more than the one asking the other to smuggle the Gucci scarves, Fendi bags, and Bulgari bracelets that put her way over the limit allowed by customs in her luggage, she didn't want them to know she'd been eavesdropping.

"And I'm hungry, too," Tom added. "We need to get something to eat before the train." He took her hand, pulled her to her feet and into his arms.

"Yes, let's take a walk," she said, holding him close. "It's our dream trip and I'm not forgetting that. Do you know what I think we should do?"

"Haven't the foggiest."

"I want to go to church and see the St. Matthew Caravaggios, especially the one with the dusty feet. I want to pray and light candles for Freddy. And then I want to go to the Trevi Fountain, throw two coins in, and find some more great panini." Her voice caught at the last words, and she ended with a sob.

Tom stroked her hair. "This sounds perfect. Just what he would have wanted us to do, I'm sure."

Faith shook the napkin out and wiped her eyes. Several pigeons swooped in to peck at the crumbs. She kissed her husband, their embrace lasting long past the pigeons' consumption of the unexpected treat. The roof was completely empty of all forms of life when they finally let go of each other and went down the stairs to pack.

It wasn't until she got to Termini, the train station, and saw all the families crowding the platforms for a day out, the women holding bouquets, that Faith remembered it was Mother's Day here, too, Festa della Mamma. Sitting on the train, waiting for it to leave, she thought back to last year's Mother's Day. Her family had served her breakfast in bed and she had pretended to be very surprised. Both kids were comfortable in the kitchen, having started cooking with her at an early age. Ben had produced a delicious omelet oozing with fontina and thin shavings of smoked turkey, as a change from ham, he'd explained. Amy had made popovers, and Tom, well, Tom gave her flowers. After church they'd driven down to Norwell, Tom's hometown on the South Shore, where they'd had a late lunch with the Fairchild clan, afterward piling into canoes for a paddle on the North River.

Faith's own mother didn't believe in Mother's Day, declaring that every day was mother's, father's, and children's day. That the May date was invented to sell cards, flowers, and perfume. She'd always thanked Faith and Hope for the cards they'd made at school and then the whole occasion had vanished once they were older until Tom appeared, askance at the attitude. His mother got flowers; Faith's would, too. And Faith noticed that Jane very quickly began to enjoy the custom. She was glad she'd remembered to order them for both mothers before she'd left. But here she was, childless in Italy, and she felt quite a pang looking at all the happy families on the train and with such good things to eat, she suspected, tucked in all those baskets and boxes.

It was almost departure time, and as usual one lone traveler was making a dash for the doors. Faith was amused to see Goth Girl from the hotel lunge in at the last moment and then search for her seat, the cool expression on her face replaced for the moment by confusion and finally, relief.

It seemed they were almost immediately in the country, and Faith tried to focus on the passing scenery. A lone line of cypress trees atop a distant hill stood out against the blue afternoon sky. They looked almost human, with their stark limbs lined up for some kind of *danse macabre*. She instantly recalled the image from Ingmar Bergman's film *The Seventh Seal,* and shut her eyes tightly.

"Honey, we're almost there. Wake up." Tom was gently shaking her shoulder.

She opened her eyes. The train was slowing. They were in the outskirts of another city. It couldn't be Florence. Much too soon. Although the Eurostar train cut the time in half, to under an hour and a half. How long had she been sleeping?

"Come on. If we don't get off, we'll end up in Venice."

"Not a bad thought," Faith said. "Another time."

She grabbed her carry-on bag and followed Tom to the storage area where they'd stowed their two cases. She'd put together a wardrobe of white tee shirts and jeans plus two sweaters, black crop pants, the one dress, shoes for walking, sandals, and flats. A raincoat, socks, and underwear completed her packing, except for some scarves and a necklace she'd bought several summers ago in Brooklin, Maine, at Sihaya Hopkins's glassblowers studio—a thin gold wire with a selection of beads in several sizes. Sihaya worked in the tradition of Italian glass, molten layers of dense color, so it seemed appropriate to bring her work as Faith's only jewelry.

"Did you catch what the conductor was announcing?" Tom said.

Faith had been aware of something coming over the loud-speaker, first in Italian, and then in English, but hadn't paid attention. They were at the right stop and she was concentrating on getting off without leaving anything behind. "No, what was it?"

"He was apologizing for the train being seven minutes late. Can you imagine that happening on the MBTA?"

She could not, and it was yet another indication of how civilized things were here.

Francesca had told them to go outside and stand in front of the station and that someone would be there waiting holding a sign that said CUCINA DELLA ROSSI, the name of the school. As they exited the platform, Faith heard the very distinctive ringtone Ben had installed on her phone for the trip: the opening to *2001,* which her son was very surprised to learn had been composed by a man named Richard Strauss in 1896, not John Williams. Ben thought his mother needed something that wouldn't go unanswered, something dramatic. She fished her phone from her bag in a panic and hit "answer" only to hear two voices, one very childlike and the other octaves below, say in unison: "Happy Mother's Day, Mom."

Faith tapped Tom—who was smiling broadly—lightly on the shoulder. She was glad that Yankee thrift hadn't stopped him from arranging this particular roaming charge.

"Oh, you sweeties! What a wonderful surprise!"

"We miss you, Mom," Amy said, but she sounded quite cheerful. "The Millers are taking us to lunch with Danny and Samantha!"

The two Miller children still living in the Boston area were former babysitters and permanent idols for both her children.

Nope, Amy might say she missed her, but life didn't get any better than hush puppies at Redbones in Somerville, the Millers' favored spot near both kids' apartments.

"Have fun and say hi to everyone for us."

"So, did you get me a scooter yet?" Ben said, the laughter in his voice indicating what he thought the chances were.

"Not exactly, but we did get you something."

Two somethings: a bright red Vespa holding up a snow globe containing the Colosseum; tacky, but Ben would love it. Also a Ferrari mouse for his computer. She'd find things for Amy in Florence.

She started to hand the phone to Tom, who shook his head and mouthed, "Send them my love." Yankee thrift had kicked in.

"Love you from Dad and me."

"Love you, too," and they hung up, no doubt eager for the chance to sit in awe as Danny, now Dan, Miller described his adventures in the world of IT and Samantha talked about her job at the Gardner Museum, all the while drinking lemonade from Mason jars at the down-home restaurant.

Outside the train station, they spotted the sign immediately, especially as the man holding it was waving frantically at them and calling their names. He rushed over to them.

"I'm Gianni. We are going to have such a *meraviglioso* time." The word needed no translation and he grabbed their bags, motioning them to a large van parked in what Faith was sure was an illegal spot, but since there were many other vehicles angled in the same way, it apparently didn't matter.

"We are waiting for a few more. Two people are already in the *macchina*. Why don't you get in?" He had stowed their bags in the back and was returning to his spot, speaking rapidly all the while.

Maybe opposites do attract, Faith thought. Gianni's wife, Francesca, was a woman of few words, at least when Faith had known her, and exuded a quiet serenity, unless extremely provoked, which

Faith had also witnessed those many years ago. She'd seen family pictures over time, but they hadn't done justice to this extremely handsome man—tall, slender, but muscular, his warm smile and sparkling blue eyes crowned by a picturesque mop of dark brown Michelangelo curls.

They got into the van and had just introduced themselves to the couple inside—Len and Terry Russo from Livingston, New Jersey, whom Faith recalled seeing in the hotel lobby getting their key from Paolo—when Gianni returned with the rest of the guests in tow, and more introductions were made as he put the rest of the luggage away.

Faith had seen all of them before in Rome—in and out of the hotel.

There were the two southern women, Harriet and Sally Culver, an aunt and niece from Louisiana; the passionate couple from the restaurant and *gelateria,* who turned out to be Sky Hayes and Jack Sawyer, from Beverly Hills; and finally—Goth Girl! Her name was Olivia, apparently no last name or one she wasn't willing to share, nor did she divulge her country of origin, although from the girl's accent, Faith was willing to bet a sizable ranch in the Outback that Olivia was an Aussie.

An interesting crew. *Molto simpatico?*

Gianni appeared to be able to drive while providing a running commentary on what they were passing, speaking over his shoulder with greater frequency than felt comfortable to Faith, but he obviously knew the road.

"We will return tomorrow morning to choose ingredients at the Mercato Centrale, which is next to the Basilica di San Lorenzo, so you will have time if you like to run in and say hello to the Medicis."

It was obvious that Gianni was in high good humor and born to be the host of this sort of venture. Faith had known all too many people whose dreams of owning restaurants and inns went up in smoke when they were faced with the reality of always being pleasant and always "on" for their guests.

As eager as she was to get to the villa, Faith wished Gianni would slow down so she could soak up this first sight of the Arno Valley, surrounded by steep hillsides covered with olive groves and vineyards, creating giant patchwork squares with fields of grain. And everywhere bright red poppies swayed in the breeze. Far off in the distance the kind of miniature hill towns so alluring in the misty backgrounds of Renaissance paintings jutted out from the horizon.

Gianni turned off the main road, built by the Romans, he said, onto a smaller one, and then made a few more turns until they were on a dirt road shaded by a canopy of oaks and lined with those tall pines that seemed to know just where to grow for maximum effect. Just beyond, there were acres of vineyards. She was suddenly very hungry—and dying for a glass of wine.

A few minutes later they were there. Villa Rossi. A much larger place than Faith had imagined. The walls of the house were stone, earth tones that gave way to bright terra-cotta roof tiles; the shutters had been painted a soft green with a hint of silver, like olive trees. Wisteria tumbled from a small iron balcony over the front door, and roses of all shades and sizes filled large planters as well as partially covered the garden walls. These last were *exactly* as she'd imagined. And there were palm trees!

Francesca was running toward her, arms outstretched.

"Faith!" She hugged her tight, whispering in her ear, "I am so sorry. So sorry. Paolo called. We knew *signore* Ives, all of us. But I am also so happy you are here." She let go and stepped away. "I cannot believe it!" She turned to give Tom a hug and greet the other guests.

As they crowded into the hallway, a voice drifted out from one of the rooms to the side.

"Now, we absolutely must tell this woman that I bathe in the morning and you bathe in the evening. This is the sort of place that is always running out of hot water. Roderick! Did you hear what I said? We have to—"

"Yes, dear, I heard," he said, cutting her off.

Even without the use of his name, Faith would have recognized that voice anywhere.

Maybe not *tutti è simpatico.*

CHAPTER 4

Francesca asked everyone to gather in the spacious living room. Once they were all settled, she stood in front of a fireplace large enough to roast an ox, or, Faith thought, more likely Tuscan boar. She wasn't sure how long the house had been in the Rossi family, but she knew the main structure was over two hundred years old. She looked at the tiled floor and the stone lintel at the door into the hall, concave with wear, and once more she thought of all the footsteps she was following.

She was trying to give Francesca her full attention, trying not to let her mind wander back to last night and today's early morning hours, as it had been periodically, adding a surreal quality to the journey and now the arrival here. She kept seeing Freddy's face—animated under that hat on the hotel terrace, savoring the *carciofi* at the restaurant, and contemplative in front of the Pantheon beneath the dark velvet Rome sky. She wanted to remember those faces. The faces when he was alive. But the one that dominated all the others was the last face, his dying face. This was the visage she so desperately wanted to forget.

Faith forced herself to look around the room instead, taking

in the details, so obviously Francesca's own touches. The woman
had always had brilliant taste. There were bouquets of hydrangea,
roses, and trailing ivy throughout—fragrant, but not cloying. A
brightly polished copper container on the table in front of the
couch was heaped with lemons so perfect they looked fake, their
authenticity betrayed by their aroma. It was going to be a week of
tastes and smells, as well as delights for the eye. The late afternoon
sun lit an array of Tuscan pottery lining the shelves of an antique
bookcase. The vivid colors and exuberant patterns—fruits, vegetables, and whimsical animals—distracted Faith for a moment
as she thought how nice it would be to have platters and pitchers
like these at Aleford, especially during those endless dark New
England winter days.

"I think we are all here, yes?" Francesca said.

The photos she had been sending over the years had not lied.
If anything, they didn't do her justice. She appeared only slightly
older than the eighteen-year-old she'd been when she'd worked
for Faith in New York City. Her long, gleaming chestnut hair
was pulled into a loose knot at the nape of her neck and her
skin was smooth, not a trace of a wrinkle, and lightly tanned. If
she'd gained baby weight after any of her three children, it had
disappeared, but she did retain that glow Faith associated with
pregnant women. And it was a glow reproduced on so many of
the paintings of the Madonna she'd been seeing since she'd arrived. Mary must have had an exceptionally easy baby—no colic
for sure.

"*Benvenuti,* welcome, everyone," Francesca said, standing
straighter.

"We are going to have a wonderful week, starting now. After we talk a little here, you will find your rooms upstairs. Your
names are on cards on each door and your luggage is being placed
there now. I hope it is all to your liking, and if you need anything,
please let me, Gianni, or one of the staff know."

Faith did not think it was her imagination; Francesca was undeniably casting a nervous glance at the British couple. Her English was fluent with a lovely lilt, but she'd stumbled over the phrase "to your liking."

"We will begin by introducing ourselves, break for an hour so you can unpack, rest if you like, and then we'll meet in the kitchen to make an antipasto to go with the wine tasting that has been arranged for you before our dinner. Tonight I have prepared most of the meal, since you have all been traveling, but for all the other nights, *you* will be the cooks from start to finish!"

She was beaming, and Faith was happy—relieved to see that most of the faces in the room were reflecting Francesca's enthusiasm. Only Goth Girl—she had to start thinking of her as "Olivia" instead—and the Brits had neutral expressions.

"Faith and Tom, why don't you start? It was Faith who gave me my very first job at her catering company when I was studying in the United States many years ago!"

Faith wished Francesca hadn't revealed Faith's occupation. She didn't want to intimidate the others, and also she could evaluate how things were going much better if she'd been incognito.

She nodded to Tom. Let him speak. He was used to it.

"As you've just heard, I'm Tom and this is my wife, Faith. We're delighted to be here and even though my wife has certain skills, mine are limited to opening a can and dialing, so I'm hoping to change some of that by the end of the course. We live in Aleford, Massachusetts, about twenty minutes outside Boston, and have two kids, one who unfortunately has just entered his teens and a third grader who still happily likes to sleep with her stuffed animals."

This last sentence brought some smiles. Other parents? But what Faith was noting in particular was that given the chance, Tom, the sky pilot, was flying under the radar. She well understood his wish. Invariably, revealing his profession made people want to keep their distances, and watch their mouths, or the opposite.

The couple from New Jersey was sitting on the couch next to the Fairchilds.

"We're Len and Terry Russo from Livingston, New Jersey, not far from Manhattan, you cross a state line for a totally different state of mind—or so they tell me," she said. "We've heard all the Jersey jokes." The gentle fun she was poking at herself reminded Faith of that famous *New Yorker* cover by Saul Steinberg where a map pictured a bustling Manhattan from Ninth Avenue down absorbing most of the vista, Jersey a tiny strip, the rest of the United States even smaller, and the horizon dotted with China, Japan, and Russia in minuscule type. It was a Manhattan mind-set she shared, much to her husband's bewilderment.

"We're here because we love to cook," Terry continued, "and, well, as you can see, we love to eat, too."

Both Russos were carrying a few extra pounds, but not much. Faith was surprised the woman had mentioned it, and her husband did not appear happy with the remark. The man was actually scowling. They looked to be in their late forties, and when it seemed that this was going to be the extent of Terry's remarks, Gianni, who had come into the room, said, "The name 'Rossi' is 'Russo' in Southern Italy, so we're related!"

That did the trick, and Len Russo relaxed visibly. "*Paisan!*" he called out. Gianni's personality, Faith realized, was going to be a major asset for Cucina della Rossi.

A strident voice broke into her thoughts.

"We are Roderick and Constance Nashe from Surrey. I think you will find we are not novices in the kitchen, having had a great deal of experience with fine dining and the execution of many cuisines."

She shot Faith a look that clearly threw down a glove—my knife skills versus yours any day. Faith also noted that Constance did not deem it necessary to mention that Surrey was in England and one of the wealthiest parts of the country. One was just supposed to know these things.

"Oh, this is going to be so much fun!" The speaker actually clapped her hands together. "I mean, my aunt and I want to learn *everything*. We are total beginners, but we just *love* Italian food! Oh, I'm Sally Culver and she's Harriet—"

"Sugar"—Harriet interrupted her niece—"the last time anyone called me 'Harriet' was when Daddy caught me sneaking peach schnapps from his liquor cabinet around the time dinosaurs were still roaming the bayous. Call me 'Hattie,' y'all. And you've probably guessed that we're from Louisiana."

Faith noticed Hattie was wearing a wedding band, but her niece wasn't. Perhaps to make up for it, she had a diamond and sapphire cocktail ring that she'd definitely have to take off before kneading pasta dough.

After the Culvers, the room descended into what was soon an uncomfortable silence. The remaining three people looked at one another and then all of them spoke at once, stopped, and finally Olivia plunged in.

"I'm Olivia. Here to learn." The intimation was that the rest of her fellow students were good-time charlies, dilettantes, culinary lightweights.

More silence.

"Where are you from, dear?" Hattie asked. "I'm getting a hint of *Crocodile Dundee*. So you're Australian?"

"Something like that," Olivia said, and slouched back in her chair. She'd picked one far from the rest of the group by the windows.

"I guess that leaves us. We're Sky and Jack from sunny California," said the woman Faith had noticed at the Hostaria Giggetto and afterward at the *gelateria* that first night in Rome. A very passionate pair, judging from their behavior between courses. Maybe they were on their honeymoon. Their wedding rings were shiny, and Sky's was coupled with a diamond as big as the Ritz. She looked younger than Faith, although it was hard to tell her age.

Good genes or maybe a good plastic surgeon. Whatever the cause, she was a stunning California girl with more than a passing resemblance to Farrah, except with updated hair—blond, yes, but straight, a glossy silken curtain hanging to the top of her almost bare shoulders. She was wearing a tank top with whisker-thin straps. Her eyes, or contact lenses, were emerald green.

"We thought it would be fun to do something different. I mean not just go look at museums."

"Not that we don't like that," Jack said. "Anyway, we're hoping to wow people when we get home with some gourmet meals."

If Sky was Farrah, Jack was Malibu Ken—toned, buff. He exuded health and he was also blond. Adopting the current fashion among men his age, he looked like he needed a shave. It was oddly attractive. Alone or together, Sky and Jack turned heads. Faith had had an Uncle Sky, short for Schuyler. She doubted that was the case here, imagining flower-children parents who fortunately hadn't saddled their daughter with something groovy like Rainbow Starlight.

The couple was sitting close; she was almost in his lap. Faith noticed that Olivia was regarding them with an expression of loathing, which quickly disappeared when she saw that Faith had seen it. Olivia was here to cook. Clearly she was not going to have any patience for those who might have other things in mind.

"Such a wonderful group. From so many places," Francesca said. "It is just what Gianni and I have hoped. Now, before you leave, one last thing. Breakfast—*colazione*—will start in the dining room each day at seven for the early risers and go until eight thirty. It will be buffet-style, but if you want something you do not see, please let us know."

Constance Nashe didn't even let a millisecond go by. "I suppose it isn't going to be possible to get a cooked breakfast." She stated it as a fact. "Poached eggs, proper toast."

"That is no problem at all. You just need to tell me what you would like as soon as you come down, or the night before with the time you want it in the morning, and it will be ready. We have wonderful sausages and tomatoes, so we can do a full English breakfast if you like. Even the beans, although they may be a little different."

Not canned, Faith thought, noting with glee the disappointment on Constance's face at having her demand satisfied. She was obviously a woman who enjoyed making those around her uncomfortable, even when it meant her own needs weren't met.

"You will find a folder in your rooms with information about our house and the grounds. I think you will especially enjoy our pool. We have given you the schedule for each day, but it may change. We want to know what *you* would like to do, so the outings are suggestions, although we planned them with a view toward introducing you to this area in the short time we have—markets, wineries, some historic towns, and of course, Florence itself starting tomorrow morning. We have tickets for those who wish to visit the Duomo and other places. There is a map of the city and also some other maps in the folder."

She took a breath. Faith felt proud of her former employee. Francesca was doing very well.

"We have one other student who will be joining us during the day. You will meet him later this evening. I think you will enjoy Jean-Luc. He has restored an old property a short walk from here and is originally from France. He has invited the class to visit his villa on Tuesday and will talk about the renovation process he went through if you are interested. I can tell you it took much longer than he thought! But it is a beautiful home now. Oh, I almost forgot. You will be cooking from sheets I will give you each day in the kitchen, but at the end, you will have new ones without the food spills in a binder to take home."

She looked at her watch. "One hour—and then meet back here?"

There were murmurs of assent and people started leaving to go to their rooms. Faith and Tom went over to Gianni and Francesca.

"So far, so good. Everybody seems happy to be here," Tom said. "I can't wait. I'm not bad at nookie, but have never tried my hand at gnocchi."

Faith had forbidden him to repeat this joke, which he had tried out on her some weeks before, and she was only happy that at the moment the audience was limited to their two friends.

Gianni laughed uproariously and Francesca looked puzzled. Faith gave her husband a look. A wife-type look.

"Okay, okay." He was laughing, too. "I had to try it once, didn't I?"

"Not really," she started, and was about to elaborate when Francesca pulled her to the side. "Could you come into the kitchen for a moment or do you need to freshen up?"

"No, I'm fine. And I'd love to see the kitchen. Tom, why don't you unpack your things?" This wouldn't take long. Tom had packed even less than she had. "If you're not in the room, I'll find you where?"

"Definitely checking out the pool."

The reverend had obviously decided he was on vacation, Faith thought. And she would work at getting in the same mood. Tom saw much more death than she did—and he had also not had the same amount of contact with Freddy. She looked out the French doors that led to a patio and spotted the pool, an inviting turquoise oblong farther down the hillside. It, the garden, the pleasure of cooking again with Francesca, would all help her to move on. And move is what she did, following Francesca down the hall and through the dining room, noting the sizable wooden table, long and wide, easily seating the entire class and then some. The kitchen was conveniently located off the room.

The Rossis must have gutted whatever was here, Faith thought. She had expected the *cucina* to match the rest of the house, but instead it was a sleek modern restaurant kitchen with slip-resistant rubber foot-friendly flooring, stainless appliances, and enough workstations to accommodate up to sixteen students. Under each table, she glimpsed everything that would be needed—bowls, measuring cups, pots, pans, strainers, etc. Knives and other utensils would be close at hand in the drawers, she was sure. Yet this would never be mistaken for a teaching kitchen in the United States. A window had been pushed out to provide a wide sill with space to grow fresh herbs, the glazes on the pots a splash of color. Braids of garlic and dried peppers hung on either side. Several containers of oils sat next to rows of earthenware jars no doubt filled with all sorts of olives, dried mushrooms, and fruits and vegetables preserved in a variety of ways. Francesca had been the one to teach Faith how to make the best glazed fruit, eggplant caponata, and an Italian version of olive tapenade. There were serving pieces of the same pottery on display in the living room piled on one counter. Faith felt her whole mood change.

"It's gorgeous! I can't wait to start cooking," Faith said. "You and Gianni have done an amazing job, I hope you have some 'before' pictures. How do you say 'dream kitchen' in Italian?"

She was suddenly very much aware that her enthusiasm was having no effect on her friend. In fact, the woman looked close to tears.

"I have a big problem and I'm very worried."

Faith thought she knew and was instantly sympathetic.

"Constance?"

Francesca shook her head. "I can handle her. She is just like my mother's friend Lucia; something always has to be wrong to make them happy. No, none of the students. It's our assistant. Alberto. He has disappeared."

Excerpt from Faith Fairchild's travel journal:

So much for the pool. Tom is sound asleep on top of what looks like an extremely comfortable bed. Cucina della Rossi is going to be a big

*success. They have done everything right. The house is beautiful,
and if the other rooms are anything like this one, they'll be turning
people away. It could be in one of those Tuscan-style coffee table
books—the bed has a sheer muslin canopy, very romantic—and
the walls are the color of goldenrod. They must have scoured the
countryside for the antique furniture, a beautiful armoire and chest
of drawers. There's even a tiny balcony just big enough for a table
and two chairs, perfect for morning espresso or an evening digestif.
Anyway, we're here and I am determined to have a good time. I can
be sad, impossible not to be, but I'm with my beloved (although not
much company at the moment) and that's what's important.*

*I'll write about my fellow students later. Have to wake Tom soon
and get down to the kitchen. We're making antipasti for tonight's
meal. Wonder what it will be. But want to make note of these people
at some point. A mixed bag. At least we all share a love of good
food. I think. But poor Francesca. Not even open twenty-four hours
before a major problem. I wanted to tell her this was going to happen
a lot, but she doesn't need to know that yet. What she needs now
is a solution. Apparently months ago she found the perfect sous chef,
Alberto. Someone from another village (maybe this was a mistake?),
and they have been working side by side to get everything ready.
Last night they all said buona notte and trundled off to bed. The
Rossis and staff are sleeping in what used to be the Italian equivalent
of a granary, which they remodeled for their use and any overflow
guests. When Alberto didn't show up for his morning cappuccino
Gianni went to his room and discovered that he was gone. Also all
his things. The bed hadn't been slept in. This without a word to
them or any other indication that he was planning to jump villa.
They've put the word out to get a replacement and I offered, but
Gianni's sister is filling in for now. Not a good solution, tho. Besides working in the kitchen, Alberto was acting as the handyman,
helping Gianni, and she can't do that. She's about five feet tall and
her arms are like linguine. First Francesca was afraid something hap-*

pened to him, but after she discovered some truffles stored in a place only the three of them knew about were missing, she moved straight to livid. More later. Tom's awake and it's time for some vino.

Before moving into the kitchen, Gianni invited the students for a glass of cold Prosecco served on the terrace, which extended across the rear of the house. Lavender and rosemary the size of small shrubs lined the walls, and a pergola covered with vines provided shade. It smelled, and looked, heavenly. Whether because of the wine or the beautiful setting or both, by the time the group moved indoors, it was a convivial one. Faith noticed that Roderick Nashe had managed to snag several refills, and his face was looking much less like that of a country squire confronting a poacher, his habitual expression heretofore, and more like a country squire hoisting a tankard or two after riding to the hounds. Even Olivia seemed almost cheerful.

They had just started to go indoors when a man appeared from around the corner of the house. He looked Italian and Faith immediately assumed it was the wayward sous chef returning with a plausible excuse for his absence and his sudden need for the truffles—his Vespa had been stolen? A relative needed an operation? Anyway, whatever the reason for the sudden absence turned out to be, Faith was very relieved to see him. Gianni's sister seemed like a lovely person but was clearly not up to the chores.

Except it wasn't Alberto.

"Jean-Luc! Just in time." Gianni went to greet his neighbor. "Come and meet everyone. We are about to start preparing, and more important, getting set to eat, the antipasto."

"Since I have brought the wine for our tasting, I knew you wouldn't start without me."

He was smiling broadly, conveying the impression that there was nowhere else he'd rather be at the moment than with all of them. He was going to be a fine addition to the group, Faith thought.

Seeing him closer, she realized he was older than he had appeared at first. His curly dark hair was streaked with gray, yet he carried himself with youthful athleticism. He was stylishly dressed in a pale yellow linen shirt and trousers the color of cocoa.

"Before I learn your names, please call me 'Luke,' since so many of you are Americans, I understand. When I was working in Colorado a long time ago—a young man's adventure—they gave me the nickname and I think I will be 'Luke' for the week again."

Glancing at her fellow classmates, Faith noted they seemed as taken with the man as she was, even Constance, who had acted positively, and even slightly nauseatingly, girlish when he shook her hand.

About to introduce herself in turn, Faith felt the words stick in her throat in reaction to the smell of lime that hit her full force as he approached. It was the same citrus cologne that Freddy had worn. She swallowed hard. Coincidence. Only coincidence. The brand, Penhaligon's, was no doubt sold in Florence at all the upscale *farmacias*. She tried to sidestep the memory, stammering out that she was Faith Fairchild and lived in the United States near Boston, Massachusetts. Tom took over, asking the man what part of France he was from and how long he'd been living in the neighborhood. She knew it wasn't because her husband had picked up on her confusion. It was what he did. A natural interest in people that went with his turf, even sans collar.

"I am from a small place near Nice, but this is now my adopted country. I have been doing my best to help the Italian economy for many years, though I bought my villa here only four years ago."

Gianni was ushering people back into the house toward the kitchen. "Jean-Luc—oh, I must remember you are an American cowboy for these days—*Luke* speaks perfect Italian even with his French accent, which means he has been able to talk to the men working on his place. I think this is why he has been able to do so much in so little time."

The kitchen drew oohs and aahs. Gianni's sister handed out white chef's aprons and kitchen towels. Faith noticed that, like herself, Olivia, the Nashes, and the Culvers all placed the towel at the front of the apron over the drawstrings for easy access, indicating their familiarity with professional kitchen routines.

"No toques?" Luke asked.

"No hats at all, just keep your hair back if it is long," Francesca said firmly. "Now, we have twelve people, so all week you will be cooking in groups of four. You must tell me how you would like to be divided. I thought couples might split up, as often the groups will be cooking different things and this way you will learn more, but if you would rather stay together please say so."

"We'll split up," Len Russo said quickly, earning a glare from his wife. He added, "So we can learn more stuff, hon."

"Good idea," Faith said. She knew being with Tom would make her crazy. She'd want to snatch the knife or the whisk from his hand and do everything herself.

The Nashes also split up, and Faith noticed Constance sidling over to Luke. Oh dear, there could be tears before bedtime, she predicted. She doubted the handsome Frenchman went in for tweed. The Culvers opted for separate groups with more protestations about wanting to learn *just* everything and *truly* loving Italian food. Jack and Sky stayed together. Faith was not surprised.

When everyone was at a station, Francesca said, "We are going to make *crostini,* a simple and delicious way to start the meal. First of all, let me tell you the difference between *crostini* and *bruschetta,* which we will also make during the course. '*Crostini*' means 'little toasts' and '*bruschetta*' comes from '*bruscare,*' to roast over hot coals. The biggest difference is the kind of bread. For *bruschetta* we use a rustic, country-type bread, similar to sourdough, and we slice a larger and thicker piece than for *crostini,* which uses a different bread as well—a white, baguette-type loaf. One of the nights when we are cooking outdoors, we'll do *bruschetta* over the coals. The simplest way, which we like best, is rubbing the slightly charred bread with garlic and topping it with our own olive oil—maybe a little fresh basil and diced tomato."

"I'm starving already!" Hattie called out.

"Good. We want everyone to bring a good appetite. Now each group is going to make a different topping for tonight's *crostini*, which we will toast in the oven under the broiler. You can also make *crostini* by brushing some olive oil on each side and baking the bread. I like to have sometimes the extra crunchiness the broiler makes."

Each group sliced bread at their tables and Gianni's sister—what was her name? Faith wondered—whisked the baking sheets away to the oven. Francesca explained that she had selected quick toppings, but that she would include others in the recipe packet.

"One of my favorites is a traditional spread we make from cooked chicken livers, sage, rosemary, a little cognac, sometimes a little anchovy, coarsely chopped and mixed together, but it takes an hour. There is also a fashion now in Italy for making Mexican *crostini* with a kind of Italian guacamole. You can put anything you like on top of the bread!"

She looked over at Faith, and Faith knew Francesca was thinking of the first time she'd had the south-of-the-border avocado spread—at a restaurant in New York City when her boss had finally been able to get the young girl to reveal her real reason for coming to the States. So many years had gone by. It had been another century and another life.

Faith was in a group with Olivia, Sally Culver, and Len Russo. They were going to be assembling *crostini* topped with thinly sliced fennel, olive oil, and salami that Gianni told them came from a nearby farm. Once they started, Len was taking so many "just a little tastes" of the meat that Faith was afraid they wouldn't have enough, but it was soon clear that it didn't matter. He was having a good time, as it seemed the rest of the room was, and she had to remind herself she wasn't on a job. Although she added a bit of fennel frond to each *crostini* as a finishing touch.

It soon become obvious that Olivia had worked in a restaurant, and perhaps attended some sort of culinary institute. She was all-business, which Faith had been expecting. What she hadn't been expecting was the way Sally handled a knife. Someone in the bayou had taught the woman well, but when Faith asked how she'd learned, she flushed and said she watched a lot of cooking shows on cable. It seemed to Faith that she slowed down after that, even fumbling twice. On purpose?

When they were done, the *crostini* looked beautiful arranged on the colorful platters. Cameras and phones came out of pockets and photos were snapped. Sally Culver had been documenting the entire process, checking out the other groups, too. Her camera was very professional, a cut above Faith's own, which was perfect for the trip, but when she imagined the quality of the food photos Sally's would achieve, she felt a little jealous.

Besides Faith's group's salami/fennel effort, there were a fig and prosciutto topping; smoked salmon, mascarpone, and capers; fresh tomato and ricotta; as well as some prepared by Francesca—melt-in-your-mouth slices of lardo; and Asiago cheese and smoked ham with a drizzle of fennel honey. Fennel was the new something, Faith noted to herself. Fennel pollen, fennel honey, just plain fennel. Maybe the new smoked paprika? Or was that dating herself?

While the "chefs" were finishing up, Gianni and Luke had prepared the wine tasting in a room off the living room that the Rossis called their library. French doors led outside and, besides a wall of bookcases, there was an entertainment system hidden in a beautifully carved tall chest should anyone have a craving for Italian or satellite TV. Faith pictured herself instead curled up in one of the overstuffed armchairs reading cookbooks, one of her favorite things to do— even if she never cooked any of the recipes. She'd spied some on the shelves along with an assortment of fiction in several languages.

Soon they were sampling the delicious *crostini* and tasting two reds: a 2008 Rosso di Montalcino and a 2009 Chianti Classico, as well as two whites: a 2009 Moscato di Terracina—this was Faith's favorite, the Muscat grape went perfectly with the hearty flavors of the various *crostini,* especially the salmon—and a 2010 Collio Pinot Grigio. As the antipasti disappeared, she slipped back to the kitchen to see if she could help Francesca get dinner on the table and learned that Gianni's sister was named Gianna. Had to have been major childhood confusion there when calling out the back door.

The Rossis on both sides were pitching in to make Cucina della Rossi successful. Francesca's parents had the children for the week at their house, close enough so she or Gianni could run over to see them, but enough out of the way so their parents could concentrate on the cooking school. Gianna was prepared to stay until they could find a replacement for Alberto. The kitchen was filled with fantastic smells, and as they cooked, Francesca and her sister-in-law chatted away. Faith found it very relaxing not to have to follow a conversation and busied herself with the pasta course— *pappardelle,* a broad fettuccine, made that afternoon, tossed in a light porcini mushroom cream sauce, finished off with a little butter. They could hear the others entering the adjacent dining room. It was time to plate, and Francesca asked Faith to shave some pecorino over each portion.

And they heard something else. A knock on the kitchen door.

A very loud knock.

Francesca and Gianna opened the door together quickly. A young man stood without. In less than a moment all three were engaged in rapid conversation.

"Do you speak English?" Francesca said loudly, taking a step back and motioning Faith over.

"*Sì,* yes," he said and added another "yes," firmly.

"Say something to us." Francesca folded her arms across her chest.

He appeared to consider several options and then with a smile, recited, "Mary had a little lamb that was white. Like snow. And everywhere the lamb go. Even the school. I know one about a boy, Jack, and a pie, too."

After she stopped laughing, Francesca told him to wash his hands and serve the pasta Faith had prepared.

"And you only speak English to that lady and the rest of the students. *Capisce?*"

He nodded and said to Faith, "I want to learn better. Tell me when I make a mistake. I am Mario."

Francesca said something to him in Italian that Faith figured was "get going," since he scurried over to the sink.

"Go, eat, Faith. Join the others. You are not here to work," Francesca said.

"I gather Alberto has been replaced?"

"It's a miracle. Or maybe not. I shouldn't be surprised. When you live where I do word travels fast. Mario heard we were looking for someone at the *caffè* on the square. He had stopped to eat on his way back from visiting some family near Chiusi. He lives in Rome and just left a job at a restaurant there. He would be happy to be here for the summer and save some money."

Faith was puzzled. She didn't think the job paid that much. "What do you mean?"

"We will give him room and board besides his wages. He rents an apartment in Rome in an area popular with foreign students coming to take courses now, and his roommates will have no trouble finding someone until he goes back in the fall, even though rents there are very high."

"So, win-win," Faith said and started to leave the kitchen, needing no further encouragement to join the group. She knew that *Il Secondo,* the course after *Il Primo,* the pasta, was rabbit. Francesca had prepared it by placing a mixture of rosemary, sage, salt, pepper, and lardo into slits she'd cut, and then spreading more of the mixture over the meat inside and out. In another pan she was roasting carrots and potatoes very simply with olive oil and the same herbs as a side dish, caramelizing them slightly at the end with a little raw sugar. A variety of cheeses were ripening on a large board, so Faith knew there would be that course before *Il Dolce*. And what would that be? A simple fruit preparation or something richer? Some kind of panna cotta or maybe the lusciously rich *semifreddi* that Francesca had also introduced her to all those years back—hazelnut, pistachio, chocolate, coffee. She left the kitchen amazed that she could still think about food after all the *crostini* she'd eaten.

Mario was indeed an answer to their prayers, and she sat down next to Tom content in the knowledge that with such a big problem solved, there would only be minor ones, if any at all, for the rest of the session.

Excerpt from Faith Fairchild's travel journal:

Every woman's dream. An incredible meal and no dishes to wash. Tom is sitting with Gianni and some of the others having some grappa. For a man who normally nods off before the ten o'clock news, he's become an immediate convert to the Italian way of life. I'm the one who crashed and am writing this in bed. Trying to figure out what I'm feeling, who I am here. Not thinking about Freddy, just about me, Faith. I read somewhere that when you travel you lose yourself. Not sure. More that you try to find yourself I think. Hard to do in Aleford, where I'm always Reverend Fairchild's wife; Ben and Amy's mom; or that food woman, the caterer. Tomorrow we go to Florence. The market and then we're free until the afternoon, when we'll return to cook. Want to see all the things am supposed to, but also plan to wander. Need shoes. Or gloves. Or maybe both.

CHAPTER 5

Could she be morphing into a morning person? Faith wondered as she followed Tom quietly out of the house. No one else appeared to be up, although there were faint noises coming from the kitchen indicating breakfast was being prepared. The Fairchilds had decided to walk into the village and have their *colazione* with the locals. They left a note for the Rossis on the table where someone would be sure to see it saying where they were—Mario had solved the Alberto problem, but the last thing their friends needed was to find another empty room with no Fairchilds, or explanation, in sight.

"I keep pinching myself, *cara mia*. Can't believe we're here and I'm not struggling with my sermon—or the vestry," Tom said.

Faith squeezed his hand. The path that Gianni had pointed out last night was wide enough for two to walk abreast. Rolling fields and vineyards stretched as far as the eye could see on either side, the dark red ochre soil a reminder of the richness of the Tuscan earth.

"Oh, Tom," she exclaimed as they came across a solid field of poppies. "It's like *The Wizard of Oz,* except good poppies and I'm not Dorothy and you're not a lion or made of tin or straw."

"Otherwise, exactly the same, I agree," he said with an indulgent smile. "I don't know whether we can find ruby slippers in Florence, but I'm pretty sure there are plenty of red leather shoes. Although no clicking your heels until we absolutely have to go home."

"Agreed."

She was in no rush either. A girl could get used to this sort of leisure—a stroll like this with her husband, as well as knowing she'd return to a bed and room made up by someone else.

They were beginning to pass farms and other kinds of square dwellings, built of stone and roofed with rounded clay tiles, the style typical of the region for centuries. Soon they saw the massive ancient walls surrounding the hilltop village and the steep road that they assumed would take them to the center.

"Smell the acacia? It's those yellow fluffy flowers on the shrubs over there," Faith said, pointing. "A kind of mimosa."

"I didn't know you were going in for horticulture these days. You're beginning to sound like Pix. Not a bad thing, of course."

Pix Miller and her family had been born clutching Life Bird Lists, magnifying glasses, flora and fauna identification charts, and all manner of other nature lore necessities. Tom's family, too, were always pointing out constellations and talking about things like the next salamander crossings. Faith figured it was a New England thing.

"Tuscan acacia honey, probably some made from these very blossoms, is one of my favorites. We have to be sure to take a few jars back."

"Ah, gastronomy, not botany. I should have known. Now, which *caffè*?" They had arrived at the main piazza, the heart of every Italian city and town, a place almost never empty—crowded day and night with an ever-changing mix of ages whether natives or tourists. It was too early for any tour groups, but the three *caffès* that fronted on it were bustling with customers on their way to work, and those who'd retired from everyday occupations. These last were mostly playing cards on the tables outside, empty cups lined up in a row. Faith pointed to a spot at random and they went in to stand at the counter.

After consuming two *caffè lattes* and a buttery *cornetto,* Faith felt extremely content. Such a nice custom, these very civilized but efficient breakfasts. Why didn't Aleford have places like this? There wasn't even a Starbucks.

They wandered the narrow streets leading off the piazza, pausing to take photos. Faith's camera was tiny enough to fit in her pocket, and she found she was drawn to details rather than broad vistas—iron doorknockers shaped like lion heads, Egyptian faces, medieval imps; and lines of wash blowing in the breeze: blue workmen's pants, sheer lingerie. Window boxes and planters overflowing with lush blooms and always, always arrays of fruit, vegetables, cheeses, displays in bakery and butcher shopwindows. Back at the piazza, they tried the church door, but it was locked, and reluctantly they decided they'd better head back so they wouldn't keep the others waiting for the trip to Florence. For a moment Faith wished they weren't on a schedule and could create their own rhythms the way those around them seemed to be doing. The card players had moved their chairs into the shade and pigeon-breasted older women—*nonnas,* grandmothers?—were crossing the expanse, carrying baskets, on their way to shop. Was there a local outdoor market today? Faith hoped she hadn't missed it; she'd ask Francesca which day it was.

As they walked out of town, they passed the paper obituary notices, some with photos, that Italians post on walls to announce a death and funeral arrangements. It struck Faith as a sensible way to get the word out in a village this size, although she had seen them in Rome, too. An ever-present reminder that in the midst of life we are in death. Some of the notices were over a year old and the weather had obscured the print. Plastered against the old stones, they were very moving.

"So, what do you think of our fellow class members? We haven't really discussed them," Tom asked as they started down the hill.

"I could do without the Nashes. Did you hear her almost bite Len Russo's head off when he called Roderick 'Rod'?"

"I guess this means 'Connie' is out, too."

"Definitely. Anyway, a group like this is always a mixture of serious cooks and people who want a different kind of vacation— maybe to one-up their neighbors. 'Oh yes, we're serving the *osso buco* recipe we learned to make in Italy.'"

"Hey, I'm planning on saying that very sort of thing. Except gnocchi."

"Don't even go there, Tom."

"I like the Russos." He hastened to return to the subject at hand. "Although they don't seem to like each other at the moment."

"I agree. Something's going on there. I get the feeling this is make-or-break time, as in stay together or head for divorce court. Not so with the Californians, that's for sure."

"Nope. Sky is quite the babe. He'd be nuts to leave her."

"Hold on, Reverend!"

"I can look, can't I? And don't tell me you haven't noticed Jack."

"Not my type."

They stopped for a moment while Faith demonstrated what her type was and then continued toward the house. She realized she hadn't told Tom about overhearing Hattie and Sally Culver on the terrace in Rome. The exchange about it being a fine time to get scruples and being paid. It was impossible to tell which woman had been speaking even now after meeting them. She relayed the experience, and Tom thought she was making a mountain out of a molehill.

"Or however you say it in Italian. I'm thinking we should take some conversation classes when we get back. But, Faith, the Culvers are not a mystery. I think you're right and they're probably just trying to get around the customs limits. Not right, but not such a big deal. Nothing too criminal."

He didn't need to spell it out. It wasn't murder.

When she didn't say anything, he stopped and faced her, putting his hands on her shoulders.

"I know you like to believe that there are secrets lurking everywhere, secret secrets and secret crimes. The people here are just your average multinational gathering of folks with stuff. Everyone has stuff, but there's nothing deep or dark at Cucina della Rossi."

He slid his hands down and embraced her, saying softly, "I've come too close to losing you too often. This last business in New York was the worst. It's time to stop." Stepping away, he smiled. "Now let's pick up the pace a little. They may not have cleared away the breakfast things. I could do with another bite or two."

Her husband could always do with another bite or two, Faith thought. She was slender now, but she knew that as she got older she'd be jealous of the Fairchild metabolism, watching Tom indulge as she counted her calories. He was right about stuff, though—everybody had it, unwanted baggage. And maybe he was right about stopping—not that she'd sought out any of her previous close calls. But he wasn't right about secrets. In her experience, a group like this was hiding any number of things. Which reminded her. Goth Girl, a disguise?

"We forgot Olivia," Faith said. "I think she's going to grow on me. And no, not like mold, which is what her dark appearance suggests. The girl has to be a cook, really good amateur or pro. She's the real deal. I can always tell."

"So that's everyone," Tom said. "Our companions in whisks."

When had he developed this penchant for terrible jokes and puns? Faith wondered. Pretty soon he'd be regaling the group with "A priest, a rabbi, and a minister walk into a trattoria" or the like. She'd have to be vigilant and nip this in the bud.

They could see the roof of the Rossis' house, shining brightly as the sun hit it, but they were closer to another roof of an even larger place. Was it the neighbor, Jean-Luc's? Which reminded Faith they'd left him out.

"What about neighbor Luke? He's part of the class," Faith said. "You've spent more time with him than I have. He certainly seems to know his wines—and grappa." She'd been asleep but woke up as Tom slipped under the covers last night. When he'd kissed her, there was a faint trace of the strong afterdinner drink on his lips. Grappa was distilled from pomace—the skins, pulp, seeds, and stems left after the grapes had been pressed. Waste not, want not. Faith had had the feeling the men hadn't put the grappa in their espresso, one of the ways she liked it, but in the small bulb-shaped glasses she'd seen on the sideboard in the dining room with a refill or two.

"Very pleasant guy, and yes, he's like those Frenchmen who can tell you what side of the hill the grapes were growing on and whether there was too much or too little rain that year just by glancing at the label on the bottle. He really does seem more Italian, though. Hard to say why. Maybe because when he speaks it, he sounds so fluent."

Faith had noticed his accent, too—that there wasn't an accent.

"He was telling us," Tom went on, "about the way everyone around here finds remains of Roman mosaics and other objects when they dig down for foundations, make a new road, or plow up a field. A treasure hunt."

"And did he do that? Find something?"

"He's been excavating around an old well at a site on his property and has found some pottery shards and glass he thinks date back to the Romans. He wants to take down some outbuildings that aren't historic, sheepfolds and a pigsty, an oasthouse—you know, for hops—that are too far from the villa to be used for guests or a garage. We were talking a lot about it because Gianni is eager for him to get going. He wants to lease the land to expand his vineyard, but Luke is waiting to do it with a team of archaeologists."

"He really expects to find something?"

"Absolutely. And for some reason, Etruscan, not Roman. Although since we're right in the heart of Etruscan civilization—'Tuscany' comes from the Roman word '*Tusci,*' which is what they called them—it makes sense that he has hopes."

"All I know about the Etruscans is that they were very enlightened when it came to women and produced all that wonderful art, especially those terra-cotta sarcophagi. I don't know whether it's in a museum near here, but I'd love to see the one with the life-size smiling couple reclining in each other's arms. She's feeding him a little tidbit, maybe bread dipped in acacia honey. And the frescoes—everyone's playing an instrument or dancing. Happy people. It will be interesting to hear more about why Luke thinks there's a site in his backyard."

"I think the buildings are much farther away than his backyard. He owns a lot of acreage, but—"

Whatever Tom was about to say was halted by an argument that was occurring on the front terrace by the drive. They were walking right into the middle of it, although at the moment, the argument was one-sided. Constance Nashe was making her points loud and clear; the Rossis were trying in vain to get a word in edgewise. The other students were in the van, watching the scene unfold through the open windows.

"I specifically informed you that Roderick and I had rented a car so we could make our own way. Now, there is no more to be said. We will meet you at the market."

Francesca looked distressed. She started to say something, but Constance actually held up her hand like a traffic cop.

"Come, Roderick."

Gianni stepped in front of them. Faith could tell he was ready to explode. "We are only trying to make things *pleasant*"—he spat out the word—"for you, Mr. and Mrs. Nashe. It is extremely difficult to park in Florence. You need a special permit to drive in the center. You will find nothing within walking distance of the Central Market and will miss the various vendors we have arranged for you to meet with tastings of olive oil, balsamic vinegar, wine, cheese, sausages, fruits, and other things."

Faith had the feeling he was trying to overwhelm them with images, tempting images.

It wasn't working.

Constance moved her fingers from cop to a dismissive wave. "We shall have no trouble parking."

"But we will be meeting to come back to prepare tonight's meal later this afternoon. You do not need your car."

"We may take a little run up to Fiesole. We know Florence."

Faith had to turn away to hide her smile. The way Constance said "know" made the glorious city sound like a must miss, or a déclassé destination akin to Blackpool in Britain or Branson in the United States. Not *our* sort of thing. And in any case, something that had been crossed off their list.

Francesca said something softly, and Gianni stepped back.

"Of course you must do as you like. We will be at Baroni for some of the tastings at ten o'clock. It is easy to find the Baronis. Ask any of the other merchants for Paola and Alessandro."

Constance gave a regal nod and walked off to what Faith now realized was their car, a small white Fiat that had been there yesterday, too, which explained how the Nashes arrived before the others. Faith also realized she hadn't heard Roderick say much of anything since she'd met him except "Yes, I'd like another" when the wine was being poured.

Tom and Faith got into the van and she moved to the rear, taking a seat next to Olivia.

"Bitch," the girl said and then hastily amended her expletive. "Not you, Mrs. Fairchild, her."

It was hard to disagree.

❋   ❋   ❋

While Gianni drove, Francesca provided the running commentary, pointing out Lake Trasimeno in the far distance and other sights. Gianni's observations had been a bit livelier and more colorful, but Faith was glad his eyes were now firmly fixed on the twisting road. She'd heard about Italian drivers and was now living it. Cars, trucks, even buses sped past them on blind curves horns blaring, which she hoped was a way to alert the oncoming traffic but thought was more likely a declaration of another sort.

She leaned back and thought about her fellow students. What were the Nashes doing in a class like this? When she'd first written about their plans, Francesca had described Cucina della Rossi as aiming somewhere between agritourism and luxe. They wanted to offer guests more than comfortable accommodations, which is why they'd invested in the pool and other amenities—each room was en suite—but they weren't in a class with some of the cooking schools located in grand *castellos* and palazzos with everything from Wi-Fi to indoor and outdoor pools, tennis courts, stables, a spa, and yes, by the way, a kitchen where guests could learn to dice an onion or maybe make pesto. Francesca and Gianni wanted to attract people who were not just passionate about food but also interested in where it came from, starting the first day with the large market in Florence and then other outings closer to home visiting small producers and touring wineries. Francesca had reminded Faith in one letter that the Slow Food movement, which emphasized, among other ideas, the use of local, traditional foods, began in Italy before spreading like wildfire internationally. It was Carlo Petrini, taking a stand in the 1980s against a McDonald's at the foot of the Spanish Steps, who started it. She'd told Faith that she and Gianni wanted their school to reflect these values—it was the way they ate, the way their families always had. Faith agreed heartily. Fast food not only tasted horrible but also was horrible for you. Francesca didn't have to deal with a drive-through in her village, nor was there one in Aleford, but the town was surrounded by them. Until she realized she could buy the toy and not the meal, Faith had had a struggle keeping Ben and Amy away from the siren call of that oxymoron, the Happy Meal.

But while they might not be Wimpy aficionados, the Nashes didn't strike her as acolytes of Prince Charles either, although Constance bore more than a passing resemblance to Camilla. Why weren't they at one of the multistarred spots, if only to be able to name-drop once they were back in England—"Dear Lorenzo—a Medici, you know" and so forth? Maybe it was cost. Hard to tell with those tweeds. Then again, Surrey was a wealthy locale.

She could hear the Culvers chatting in the seat in front of her. For a moment she thought about her own aunt, Aunt Chat, but she wasn't traveling much these days, pleading old age, which gave Faith a pang. Her mother loved to travel, though, and she thought how much fun it would be to do something like this together, but reality quickly intruded. Jane Sibley's idea of a perfect dinner was a nice piece of fish and a salad or alternatively a nice salad and a piece of chicken. Faith's father never seemed to notice what was on his plate, whether due to a lack of interest the invariable fare had produced over the years or because his thoughts were elsewhere—on divine, not mortal, matters—she did not know. She did know that Jane was more likely to look forward to a root canal than an epicurean holiday like this one. Now shoe shopping in foreign locales was another matter.

She tuned in to what the Culvers were talking about. It wasn't shoes, but it was shopping.

"As soon as we finish with the group," Hattie said, "we hit the jewelry stores on the Ponte Vecchio and go find the place for gloves on the other side. Madova, I'm pretty sure that's the name. Maggie Sue Crawford told me about it and you know how particular she is."

Faith had a friend who'd grown up in New Orleans who'd told her that even though it happened almost fifty years ago, people were still talking about the fact that Lynda Bird Johnson had worn *nylon* gloves not kid to a Mardi Gras ball. Gloves apparently still mattered in Louisiana.

They were coming into the city and Francesca was giving a brief history of the market and the area.

"The Mercato Centrale was part of what we would now call 'urban renewal' that took place in the last quarter of the nineteenth century. The Mercato Vecchio, the Old Market, was demolished to create the Piazza della Repubblica and relocated to what had been a very poor area of the city, the San Lorenzo quarter. You will see how large the market is, a city block. For its time, the building was very high-tech. The architect modeled it on a cast-iron and glass *galleria* he had built in Milan. If you can tear yourselves away from looking at the food, there is much beautiful ornamental ironwork, and of course the two stories are filled with natural light from the windows and the ceiling. After we visit some of the stalls, I would encourage you to explore on your own, and you may also want to visit the outside ones, very different, that sell typical Florentine souvenirs—decorative wooden boxes, scarves, leather goods. If you want suggestions for specific shops for these items and others elsewhere in Florence, just ask me. I can show you on your maps. I have a friend, Sylvia, who sells high-quality, Italian silk ties and scarves at good prices in the Mercato Nuovo near the Palazzo Vecchio, the city hall, where the copy of Michelangelo's *David* stands outside. Just say to any vendor, '*Dove* Sylvia?' and tell her you are my friend. You may know of this market because of *Il Porcellino,* the famous brass statue of a large piglet—a copy there now like the *David*—but the saying is that if you rub *Il Porcellino*'s snout, you will return to Florence. It is *very* shiny."

"Well, I'll give it a pat," Sally said. "I'm already in love with Florence and I definitely love anything pork, especially barbecued. But if we keep going to all these places with customs like this, I may never see the rest of the world. I tossed a coin over my shoulder in Rome, so I have to go back there, too."

Francesca laughed. "I think there are many things like that in many countries. There are several opinions about throwing coins in the Trevi Fountain. Some say you have to throw with your right hand over your left shoulder, facing away; others that it doesn't matter how you do it. Also they say if you throw two coins, you will have a new romance, and three means marriage. I think it was because of an old movie."

"Yes," Terry Russo said. "I love it—*Three Coins in the Fountain*." She started to hum the song, made famous by Sinatra.

"Cool it," Len said.

She flushed. "Maybe I should have thrown in more than one," Faith heard her mutter. Fortunately they had arrived at their destination, so the group was spared further bickering from the Russos.

"*Andiamo,* we're here!" Francesca said. "It is always very crowded both inside and outside the market, so mind your personal belongings."

Gianni pulled the van over and everyone got out. He told the group he would pick them up at the same spot at three o'clock. Now he would park a ways off, return to shop with them, and then he and Francesca would bring the food back to the house while the students toured on their own.

As they passed what seemed like miles of merchandise outdoors—Faith wondered how much was from Italy and how much from China—Francesca pointed out the nearby Basilica of San Lorenzo.

"You may be surprised by how plain it looks, since it was the church of the Medicis."

Faith *had* been expecting something more elaborate than the crude-looking, unfinished brick facade. She hadn't had time to read up on Florence, just as she hadn't about Rome. Freddy would approve, she thought, and resolved to leave her guidebook in her purse. Besides, Francesca was proving to be an extremely adequate source.

"Brunelleschi designed the basilica, which replaced a smaller Romanesque church. Later Michelangelo was commissioned to complete the front. He spent three years searching the quarries for the right stone for the statues and columns he'd planned, but the work was postponed and finally abandoned when the then pope, one of the Medici popes, wanted to use cheaper marble from nearby and Michelangelo refused.

"I like the way the outside looks, although some people say it's a *biscotti* that has been overcooked. Now there is a proposal by the mayor to finish it. All the plans, the drawings have been saved. He is looking for big money sponsors, hard to find these days, but you never know. It could happen—five hundred years later what Michelangelo intended would be completed. In any case, you will see a great contrast with the interior, the final resting place for the family. Michelangelo's Medici tombs are very beautiful and very elaborate. They are very sad, too, not because of Lorenzo's and Giuliano's deaths, but because the artist was worn-out and ill when he did them. Maybe all that arguing with the pope. The last member of the family to rule, Anna Maria Ludovica de' Medici, continued to adorn the inside and is buried with all her ancestors, but with her, it ended. Still we feel their presence all around us. This is a favorite place of mine, since I am often here at the *mercato*. Now I am talking too much! No more wasting time! It has been open since seven!"

If the market at the Campo de' Fiori in Rome had been like the Elysian Fields, then, Faith thought, Florence's Mercato Centrale was like walking into Ali Baba's cave; except better, since the riches were edible.

Having parked, Gianni joined them, and they followed the Rossis down the aisles, where they were warmly greeted by the various merchants. Soon the group was sampling slices of ripe melon, fresh figs, sips of wine, and bites of cheeses. Faith recalled the feeling of being drunk on Rome, and now she felt high on the flavors and atmosphere of what was undoubtedly the best market she'd ever visited. Upstairs and down, the wares were displayed like jewels, each fruit and vegetable polished in their crates, the fish and meat temptingly spread out in the refrigerated cases. A straw *porcellino* hung over the counter offering his products, and they stopped to taste shavings of proscuitto, pancetta, salamis, and *soppressatas*. Faith's favorite was *finocchiona,* strongly flavored salami with fennel seeds, which the group selected with some prosciutto *crudo* for panini and to wrap around *grissini,* the thin bread sticks, for a quick snack or antipasto. The Rossis had planned a picnic alfresco for Wednesday's trip to Montepulciano, and they were picking up supplies for that along with what they'd need to make dinner tonight.

Francesca led them to her favorite mushroom stand and urged them to get dried porcini, which the Baronis, the next stop, would shrink-wrap for them. The aroma was again nothing short of intoxicating, and Faith knew she'd be sorry if she didn't take any home. The Culvers bought some, too.

They had passed numerous displays of zucchini blossoms and even to Faith's educated eye, they all looked fine, but Francesca didn't stop until she reached a spot tucked into a corner presided over by an elderly man wearing a bright purple sweater and matching cap that proclaimed his allegiance to the Florentine football team—soccer loyalties were sacred in Italy, Faith knew. He stepped into the aisle and kissed Francesca on both cheeks. *"Ciao, bella."*

She beamed and they exchanged a few words in rapid Italian before she turned back to the group.

"For *Il Secondo* tonight I thought we would do *porchetta* stuffed with zucchini blossoms, some fennel, herbs, garlic, of course, and maybe figs. *Porchetta* is a boneless pork roast—you will use a boneless pork shoulder to duplicate it at home. My friend Antonio here will supply the fennel bulbs and the blossoms. We'll get extra flowers to stuff with ricotta and fry for an antipasto."

"It's the male flowers that we have to use, right?" Sally Culver said. "I mean I think I heard something about this somewhere."

Curiouser and curiouser, Faith thought. Either the woman was watching a hell of a lot of the Food Network or she knew a hell of a lot more about food and cooking than she wanted people to know.

Francesca nodded. "That's right. The females have a little bulge at the base of the flower that will become the squash, so we don't want to pick those or we won't be able to make frittatas and other dishes! She needs the males—they have a regular stem—to pollinate, so we have to leave some, but we can pick most of the others. If we don't they just dry up and fall off."

"Sounds familiar," Terry Russo said with a venomous glance at her husband, who walked off toward a stand selling tripe sandwiches, returning with just one, which he proceeded to eat with gusto virtually in her face.

Francesca bought the produce, adding several varieties of tomatoes and *ceci,* chickpeas, that she told them they might use today and if not, definitely tomorrow, for salad. The lettuce would come from the Rossis' garden, as would the herbs.

The Nashes were waiting for everyone at Baroni Alimentari. Faith was very glad it was a few minutes before ten o'clock, giving the couple no cause to complain of the group's tardiness. She was beginning to regard Constance Nashe as a sort of horrible headmistress like Frances Hodgson Burnett's Miss Minchin in *A Little Princess.* No cake for you.

They were all here now except for Luke, Jean-Luc, who had stayed home. Coming to the *mercato,* and Florence itself, was an everyday occurrence for him.

Francesca introduced the group to the Baronis, and soon Paola, a lively, striking brunette, was lining up samples of Parmesan cheese.

"Wow!" Tom said. "Which one is this?"

"That is the Parmesan that has been aged in wine," Paola told them. "The other is the fresh Parmesan. A big difference, no?"

"A big difference, yes," Tom said. "I want them all."

"Try the fresh one with a drop of this balsamic vinegar. The real kind, from Modena. I will give you tastes of a number of different ones. The flavor of the vinegar depends on the age, to be sure, but also the kind of wood used to make the barrels."

Faith noticed that as soon as they entered the market, the Culvers were once more taking pictures of all the food in sight. Olivia seemed just as enthusiastic, or what passed as such for her, but wasn't taking many photos, instead jotting things down on her phone. Her fingers flew. Faith was reminded of the way Ben and his friends texted, members of the Thumb Tribe. Texting even when a few feet away from one another.

So far Jack and Sky had trailed behind everyone but were now getting into the tastings. They stopped holding hands long enough to sample the vinegars and then the olive oils.

"Who would have thought they would taste so different. I mean E-V-O-O is E-V-O-O, I always thought," Sky said, sounding more than a little like Rachael Ray.

Faith had made a small pile on the counter in front of Paola— some Malpighi Saporoso balsamic vinegar, she could already taste it on the strawberries they'd pick this summer; several kinds of honey, including acacia and fennel; tubes of black and white truffle paste; and cards with the Baroni Web site, so she could get more of everything when she was home. Francesca, she noticed, was busy buying cheese, including several kinds of pecorino, that delicious Italian sheep cheese. Another tasting back at Cucina della Rossi?

They said *arrivederci* to Alessandro and Paola, as well as the Rossis, who were lingering to talk with their friends. Once outside the market, the Fairchilds, Olivia, and the Russos headed for San Lorenzo. Faith presumed the Culvers were going straight to the Ponte Vecchio, maybe stopping to find Sylvia and her scarves on the way. Sky and Jack left with a "See you later" and headed toward the center of town—maybe to get a room, who knew? The Nashes hadn't had much time in the market, but it was apparently not of sufficient interest to capture their further attention and they left also—without a "See you later."

After an hour in San Lorenzo, Tom turned to Faith and said, "It's too much for now and I'm hungry."

She nodded in agreement. Donatello's bronze pulpits with the anguish of the Crucifixion and other scenes portrayed in realistic bas-reliefs; Michelangelo's massive somber figures on the tombs—*Dusk* and *Dawn, Night* and *Day*; and the interior's stark white walls and gray stone, *pietra serena,* were overpowering. They had been walking in silence, oblivious of other tourists and even of each other. She had come back with a start at his words.

"Yes, we need to go outside. And yes, it's time to eat."

Francesca had included a number of suggestions in the packet for all kinds of places for food ranging from gelato to a full-course meal. They were not far from one of them, Cantinetta del Verrazzano. It sounded perfect from the Rossis' description—one side a coffee bar and bakery—*pasticceria*—the other a wine bar with Chianti from the family's vineyards. A place to stop in for a quick bite, but not too fast.

"I like the Verrazano Bridge, so let's give it a try," Faith said.

They had missed the lunch rush and were able to get a table near the enormous, venerable wood-burning oven. The smell of freshly baked bread was enticing.

Standing at the display cases, Tom said, "I think I want one of everything, but that one for dessert definitely." He pointed to an almond-studded *torta della nonna,* dusted with plenty of powdered sugar. "I loved her dearly, but I'm afraid my grandmother's gingerbread, which tended to be a bit heavy, wouldn't have stood a chance in any Italian grandmother Bake-Offs."

Because you can never have too many artichokes, too many zucchini blossoms, or too many truffles, Faith completed their order by selecting two kinds of pizza topped with the flowers and *carciofi* plus a hefty wedge of focaccia made with chickpea flour and stuffed with prosciutto, ricotta, and shaved white truffles. They decided to sample the Verrazzano Rosso Chianti, which turned out to be as excellent a choice as the rest of the menu. By the time they left the wood-paneled, marble space, they felt as if it had become their "nabe," everyone had been so friendly—pressing some biscotti on them when they left to eat as they roamed the city.

"Italians are so nice," Faith said. "We need to come back with Ben and Amy."

"Absolutely," Tom said. "But this trip it's just you and me, kid."

However, when they reached the Piazza del Duomo, they decided to separate for a while. Faith knew Tom would be totally bored by the Ferragamo shoe museum and store and the window-shopping she wanted to do on the rest of Via Tornabuoni. She also thought she'd try to find some little gifts for Amy—maybe something covered with the marbleized paper so typical of Firenze.

"Go on," Tom said. "I want to gaze on Ghiberti's *Gates of Paradise* on the Baptistery right here and then sit doing nothing at all and people watch. Why don't we meet at three back where Gianni dropped us off?"

The *Gates of Paradise,* copies now, but burnished to soft gold, reminded Faith she wanted to check out the jewelry on the Ponte Vecchio, too. You never knew what you might find . . .

"Perfect. Give me a kiss and I'll see you later."

On the way to Via Tornabuoni, she passed a *farmacia* and ducked in. How could she not enter a place with such pretty bottles of fragrance and soaps in the window—and a place that looked as if it had been in the same spot since medieval times, surviving the city's man-made and natural disasters: the Arno flooding, fires, pestilence, Savonarola, the occupation during World War II?

Another friendly Italian immediately greeted her and showed her the testers for fragrances, lotions, and soaps made there. The bottles had labels decorated with famous Florentine paintings, and each sported a different-colored grosgrain ribbon tied around its top. The combinations were intriguing: Rose and Blackberry, Camellia and Coriander, Olive and Sunflower, Fig and Poppy. They smelled as luscious as they sounded. The perfect gift for Amy, and maybe her mother-in-law, too. Marian Fairchild, mainstay of her garden club, The Evergreens, would love the notion of wearing the contents of her trug on her person. The young woman rang Faith's purchases up and filled the bag with samples, which Amy would be as excited to get as the perfume.

Pleased with herself, Faith decided not to consult the map and started walking toward where she thought Ferragamo was, ending up first at the Uffizi and then the riverbank. She followed it toward the Ponte Vecchio, which was in sight, happy the Germans had not blown it up when they retreated from the city, the only bridge spared. Why didn't they destroy it? Someone in charge had realized what it would mean to demolish the ancient span, parts of which had withstood floods and other invasions since the fourteenth century? She'd have to ask the Rossis.

She took a quick look at the glittering stalls lining the bridge, giving a sigh at a trio of gold mesh bracelets—a deep wishful sigh—and then felt a shiver, looking at another offering—who would buy one of these copies of Lucrezia Borgia's poison ring and why? She crossed back and actually found herself on Via Tornabuoni after only a few turns.

Florence was very different from Rome, not as exuberant. It felt older, although it wasn't; the streets were narrow, the buildings looming over them obscuring the sky. There was less open space, and the colors were more sepia and of course, *pietra serena*. It was beautiful, but a very different kind of beautiful.

The weather had been warm when they stepped out of the

market, even warmer when they left San Lorenzo. The wine at lunch had added to the temperature, and now it was almost too hot. Before she went into Ferragamo, she needed to get something cold to drink. Some cold San Pellegrino. *Limonata* or, better, *aranciate*—orangeade. There was a cart near the end of the street and she made her way toward it. A man had just purchased something, and when he turned around, Faith realized it was Jack. She smiled and started to greet him. He smiled in return and came toward her, but then the expression on his face turned to pure horror. She stopped, amazed. What could be wrong? The street was filled with tourists. Nothing out of the ordinary. She didn't think there was anything about herself that could be causing his reaction. Maybe some powdered sugar from lunch, but nothing that would provoke what was now clear panic. He looked frantically to his right and left, then rushed toward her. He threw an arm around her shoulders and abruptly pulled her into the doorway of a shop that had gone out of business.

"I'll explain later," he said and put both arms around her, burying his head against her in an amorous embrace.

She gasped and was so astonished she didn't move. If she'd thought about something like this happening on the trip—and maybe she had—she'd pictured someone who looked like Marcello Mastroianni not Malibu Ken.

"Jack," she managed to say. "Jack, what . . ."

"Sssh," he said, raising his head a few inches to peer over her shoulder.

"Jack," she repeated and gave him a slight push. She didn't want to offend the man, but really . . . There was also the fact that they'd be cooking, and living, together for the rest of the week.

"It's okay," he said, straightening up and brushing his hair out of his eyes. "An old college buddy of mine was leaving one of the shops and seemed to be coming this way. He's gone now. He was, and is, a total jerk. If he saw me there'd be no way Sky and I could escape having to get together with him and his wife, who is even worse. I am truly grateful to you, Faith—and very sorry. I cannot imagine what you thought, but I can assure you I do not go around tackling females, even pretty ones like you, on the spur of the moment. This was an emergency."

He had a charming grin. Very charming.

Faith didn't believe his story for a New York minute. There were any number of excuses he could use to get out of having dinner or whatever with the couple—he and Sky were leaving Florence that afternoon sprang first to mind. How would the couple know otherwise? No, what was more likely was that this was an old college—or other time of Jack's life—buddy to whom he either owed money or had cheated. Or, *most* likely, a buddy whose girl Jack had poached. Then she realized she didn't know what Jack, or Sky, did for a living in LA. The man could be a more recent acquaintance—business deal gone sour?

"Let me buy you a cold drink. That's where you were headed, right?" She quickly decided a cold drink right now would make up for it, and also decided to put the whole thing out of her mind. What happened on the Via Tornabuoni . . .

"Yes," she answered. "And then I'm headed for Ferragamo. Not Tom's thing."

She still thought it politic to mention her husband.

"Not mine either, and that's where Sky is. Maybe you can pry her loose. This could turn out to be the most expensive trip we've ever taken, what with all these vowel endings—Prada, Valentino, Armani, Gucci."

Faith laughed and followed him to the stand, where she gratefully accepted a cold *aranciate*.

It was getting close to three. Faith had been able to pry Sky away from the shoes earlier but now found herself lingering, completely captivated not just by the finished products for sale but also by the exhibits in the *museo* of the lasts and shoes for all those famous feet—Marilyn Monroe's high-heeled spectator pumps for *Some Like It Hot,* Audrey Hepburn's ballerina flats, which Faith's mother said were all anyone wore when she was a teenager, Rita Hayworth's wedges. Equally fascinating were the drawings and photographs that accompanied the displays. Salvatore Ferragamo's shoes were works of art, dazzling colors, styles reflecting the surrealists, other artists, and the past—all the way back to the gladiators, although they would have been severely challenged attacking the Christians in the high-heeled sandals they'd inspired. She bought some postcards for her mother—shoes were out of the question. The ones Marilyn had worn that sold for $39.95 in 1961 would set Faith back $1,200 now.

She rushed back through the streets, using the map, and when she got to the meeting place outside the market, she turned out to be early. There was only one person there—Terry Russo, who was carrying some shopping bags. Faith presumed the couple had separated for the same reason she and Tom had, but as she drew closer she wasn't sure that the decision had been mutually agreeable. The woman had been crying, crying a lot. Her mascara had run, giving her a look more at home on Olivia.

"Hi," Faith said. "Did you find some nice things? Any bargains?"

Terry dabbed her eyes with a sodden Kleenex, which made things worse, but Faith was not about to comment.

"The woman—Sylvia—Francesca mentioned was great. I got a bunch of scarves. She told me which people to go to for other stuff and I've pretty much done all my Christmas shopping—lots of those leather boxes and picture frames."

Faith always intended to shop early, but somehow Thanksgiving invariably arrived with her list still in her desk drawer and still blank. Maybe she should bring some gifts back, too.

"I guess we're the first," Faith said. "Tom isn't much of a shopper, so he decided to hang out near the Duomo. Len, too?"

"Len isn't much of an anything," Terry said bitterly and lapsed into silence. Then she dug into one of her bags and pulled out a small wooden Pinocchio key chain, one of the ones with a very long nose. "I got this for my husband."

What to say? TMI, Faith thought to herself, wishing desperately that some of the others would arrive. Someone, anyone.

Her wish was granted and soon everyone except Olivia and Tom had gathered on the sidewalk. Gianni pulled up just as Olivia joined them. For a moment Faith didn't recognize her. Somewhere during the time apart she'd found a sink and thoroughly washed her face. Her hair was combed back, and she'd also bought a long rose-colored scarf that was now wrapped around her neck. Yes, she still had multiple piercings—ears, one eyebrow, and a tiny stud in one nostril, but she looked, well, normal, and very pretty.

But where was Tom? He'd been raised in the rigorous Fairchild School of Punctuality. She still struggled to make him understand that a dinner invitation for seven o'clock did not mean standing on the host's doorstep at 6:59 with one's finger poised over the bell, even after repeated episodes over the years with hosts still in the shower, putting out hors d'oeuvres, and one notable occasion when their hosts hadn't arrived yet themselves.

They all got in the van.

"Does Tom have a phone with him?" Gianni asked. "Maybe we should call him."

Faith shook her head. Both their phones were packed in their luggage. Now that they were at Cucina della Rossi, a number that everyone had from their itinerary, Tom had said they didn't need them. Faith suspected this was to keep her from sneaking in a call to her sister, but she saw his point and had agreed.

"This isn't at all like him. I'm sure he'll be here any moment," she said.

And there he was, sprinting toward them, much to her relief.

"Sorry, everyone," he said, climbing into the van. He sounded out of breath. "Thanks for waiting, Gianni."

"*Prego,*" he said. "No problem, *mio amico.*"

Tom slid into the empty seat next to Faith.

She started to ask him where he had been, but before she could, he leaned over and whispered urgently in her ear, "I saw the man who attacked Freddy, but I lost him."

"No!" She gasped.

Tom nodded gravely. "And Olivia was with him."

CHAPTER 6

It was a strangely silent group on the return trip. And the trip seemed much longer, Faith thought. She knew why she wasn't feeling chatty, but what about the rest? Tired from too much walking and too much sun? Renaissance overload?

The Russos were sitting together, but Len was asleep, or at least his eyes were closed. Terry was staring out the window. All Faith could see was the back of her head. Sky and Jack were across the aisle from the Fairchilds, and their body language was different from usual. That is, they weren't all over each other. Jack looked surprisingly resolute, like a man who has just dodged a bullet and is ready to stand up to another. Sky, on the other hand, looked worried. No, Faith amended, the woman looked scared.

The Culvers were also quiet, and she chalked that up to "Shopping 'til You Drop" syndrome. Olivia, the person Faith most wanted to observe, was up front, out of Faith's sight line, next to Gianni in the passenger's seat. Francesca had stayed behind at the house. After she'd put the food away and prepared what would be needed for the next lesson, Faith imagined she'd gone to see her children. It was hard to wear so many hats at once—parent, teacher, host, even tour guide; but so far her friend seemed to be managing well.

The Nashes were off on their own. Again Faith wondered why they had signed up for Cucina della Rossi. If they were indeed such die-hard food lovers, why not take some day classes? There were plenty of them in Florence. If what they had primarily wanted was to tour the countryside, it would have made more sense to stay in the city and use it as a base. Oh, she'd almost forgotten. They already "know" Florence. Well, they could have chosen someplace else to know—Siena or Pisa. Except, she realized, there was a kind of reverse snobbery at work here. Sign up for a course like this and then not participate. They would regale their Surrey neighbors with tales of the "too dreadful" week with "such common" people and a teacher who didn't know beans—favas *or* cannellinis.

Her speculation had so occupied Faith's mind that she hadn't noticed they'd turned off the main road. The Rossis' home was in sight.

After they stepped out of the van, every atom in her body wanted to hurry Tom up to their room, but common courtesy demanded first thanking Gianni and Francesca, who came from the kitchen to greet them, for the market tour and great Florentine suggestions. The others, milling about in the hall, echoed the sentiment, and Faith started for the stairs. At last! But then Francesca started speaking.

"We will start with drinks on the terrace at five, and then cook after that. Until then enjoy the pool or do whatever you like. For those of you still with some energy, there are some nice walks. Just ask us—and remember if you are hungry, or thirsty, there are always things set out on the sideboard in the dining room."

The group went its separate ways. Faith noticed Len Russo head for the pool and fervently hoped if he was going to swim that he had trunks on under his clothing. Olivia apparently was one of those with energy and disappeared out the French doors to the rear, where Faith saw her start to climb the path the Fairchilds had taken that morning. Everyone else went upstairs.

Faith shut their door firmly behind her. It was solid oak, no question of eavesdropping, but she locked it and left the key in the keyhole for good measure. The only living creatures that could listen in on their conversation through the open windows were the doves from the dovecote on what had previously been the barn. Yet, in tacit agreement, the Fairchilds moved to the middle of the room and sat down on the bed, well away. When Tom spoke, his voice was hushed—and intense.

"It was definitely the same man."

"Why are you so sure?"

Even if the killer had been wearing the same outfit, that wasn't the kind of thing her husband would remember, or notice in the first place. There had to have been something else about him.

"I saw his face more clearly and longer than you did. Aside from the funny sort of eyebrows he had, like a straight line across his forehead, his mouth drooped at one side, almost as if he'd had a stroke at some time. Odd because he's young, but there could be other reasons. Drugs maybe. Anyway, it was the same man, Faith. I'm positive. And besides, if it wasn't, why did he take off like that as soon as he saw *my* face? I know he recognized me, too."

That clinched it so far as Faith was concerned. "But Olivia? How does she figure in all this?"

Tom rubbed his hand through his hair, causing it to stand up on end. It was a familiar gesture and meant he was upset. "I don't know. There she was . . ."

"Wait, start at the beginning and tell me everything you saw."

"Okay." He leaned back on one elbow. "After you left, I went to the Baptistery—and, Faith, you have to go see the doors, even if we don't go inside any of the other buildings in the piazza. They're extraordinary. I could preach any number of sermons on the way I felt looking at them—"

"Tom! Later!"

"Yes, yes, I guess I'm still a little rattled. I'll try to stick to the point."

She moved closer to his side and put her hand on his.

"Go on."

"It was getting very hot, so I got a cold drink and sat down on one of the benches. It was away from the front of the cathedral and all the tour groups back by Giotto's Campanile."

Faith interrupted, fearing another digression. Tom loved Giotto.

"So you were out of the way a bit?"

"I guess you could say that, although there were plenty of people around. Nothing was going to happen."

Hearing Tom's last words, with "in broad daylight" implied, Faith knew they were sharing the same thoughts, seeing the same scene, the one in the piazza obscured by the dark night.

"You're thinking what I'm thinking. About what Freddy said just before he died: 'You have to stop them. They're going to ki . . .'?"

They'd reported Freddy's last words to the police in Rome, who did not seem to regard them as important—just a plea to try to prevent what was occurring.

Tom nodded. "Ever since I saw the guy I keep coming back to what Freddy said, or was trying to say. We know he took one life, Freddy's. I'm sure the word he was struggling to get out was 'kill.' He was trying to tell us about another attack, and one that involved more than this person, 'them.' But Italy's a big place— who, when, where, and how?"

His face was anguished. His job was to provide help, comfort, even preserve life where he could.

"Since the killer's here in Florence, that has to be the 'where,' and the 'when' must be soon. Freddy knew we weren't going to be in Italy long. But go on."

"I was watching a class trip. The kids were about Amy's age, and they all had bright orange caps and knapsacks. They were sitting in the shade, eating sandwiches."

Not peanut butter and jelly on Wonder Bread, Faith thought hastily. Italian children lucked out in the lunch department.

"The group left after a while and when they did I noticed a man standing off to one side. I could just see his back. He seemed to be waiting for someone. Pretty soon a girl came running up to him, and they began talking. I could only see her face and after a moment I realized it was Olivia. She didn't look like herself—you saw her on the trip back here—so who it was didn't register at first."

"How did she look? Happy to see him? Like he was a boyfriend, a lover? Or angry? Or . . ."

"Nothing. Her face looked pleasant. She was smiling a little, but nothing special. I couldn't tell what they were talking about from the way she looked. Just seemed like an ordinary conversation. They started walking toward my bench, and that was when I knew who he was. I couldn't believe it, but I was positive it was the same man instantly. I stood up and when he saw *me* he took off like a shot. Without thinking about it, I ran after him shouting, 'Stop!' What is that in Italian, by the way? I may need it again," he added grimly.

"I think 'stop' works, but today I heard someone call out the name 'Carlo' and what sounded like '*basta*'; the guy ahead stopped, so that could be it. We'll ask. Could you tell where he was going? Toward or away from the river? And where was Olivia? With him?"

"I don't know the city well enough for that, and anyway I was concentrating on keeping him in sight, not where he might be heading. As for her, I'm not sure she noticed me when he did. I was chasing him seconds after I recognized him. At that point, all she would have seen was my back. I never looked around, so I don't know if she was following, too. He was a pretty fast runner. I'd say he's had a lot of experience."

Tom was wearing jeans and a navy tee shirt, untucked. Faith had taken the small knapsack they'd brought that morning to hold any purchases, so he wouldn't have been holding anything. From the rear, there was nothing to identify him as Olivia's fellow classmate. He could have been any one of the number of male tourists crowding the streets.

He continued. "I was gaining on him and then suddenly we were in the open, pounding across the big square in front of the train station."

"Very smart of him to head there," Faith said. "People would assume you were both trying to catch your train. Nothing that would draw the attention of the police or anyone else."

"He went into the terminal, but by the time I got through the door—you wouldn't believe how crowded the place was—he was gone. I looked around for a while, but it was hopeless."

"Besides jumping on a train, it would have been easy enough to come back out another door and take a bus. Or just walk away."

"And if he's a native Florentine, he would know the area surrounding the station."

"You didn't see Olivia there?"

"No. The next I saw her was in the van."

"She didn't look out of breath, as if she'd been running," Faith said. "Although her cheeks were a little red, which could just be her natural color under that white makeup."

"You can see why I had no idea who she was at first."

"So, what do we do now?"

"Swim, shower—and keep an eye on Olivia," Tom said.

Excerpt from Faith Fairchild's travel journal:

I feel as if we have been in Italy for weeks rather than days. And here at Cucina della Rossi it's only been a little over 24 hours. Time has become elastic and there has been so much happening that it's stretched almost to the breaking point.

Am going to start carrying my notebook with me. Don't want to leave it lying around. Is that what Freddy did? And is that why his is missing?

I believe Tom. When he's sure, he's sure. So we know Freddy's killer has turned up in Florence and equally sure we don't know where he is now. Probably long gone. He'd been recognized, crazy for him to stay. He'd assume Tom would go straight to the police. We talked about whether he should or maybe tell the whole story to the Rossis and ask them what to do. But there's no point. I doubt the police here, or in Rome, would believe that Tom could have identified the killer. It was dark etc. We'd hear again that Freddy was the victim of a mugging gone wrong. And no point in upsetting the Rossis. What could they actually do?

The big question mark is Olivia. Was she simply asking the man for directions? He's not bad-looking. Or is there a closer connection? A connection back to Rome and Freddy? She was staying in the same hotel at the same time as he was—and the same time he was murdered. For that matter, everyone here was. Although I never saw Sky and Jack there, they seemed to be every other place we went with Freddy. Francesca suggested the hotel in the materials she sent out, so it's likely they were there, too. Spending a lot of time in their room?

Tom doesn't think the group has secrets. He got a rude awakening today when he saw Olivia. And the others? It's no secret that the Russos are having major marital problems, but why? What did he do? What lie, or lies, did he tell that made his wife buy the Pinocchio? Was it the same ol', same ol'—an affair? Maybe she found out just before the trip and the plane tickets were nonrefundable? Can't imagine traveling with someone under those circumstances, sharing a room, let alone a bed. The matrimoniale in our room is big, but not that big.

The Culvers seem to be just what and who they are—aunt and niece of certain ages intent on bargains, even if that means a little skulduggery.

But Jack? Haven't quite figured out how to tell Tom what happened. You never know with men. He might demand pistols at dawn—or he might just laugh. Why did Sky look so frightened on the way back? Jack must have told her who he saw and whoever he was, he's somehow a threat. The contents of the bags she was carrying could pay off the debt of any number of small nations. Where are the Californians getting their funds?

Tom's in the shower. The pool is wonderful and we had it to ourselves. Len had disappeared, thank goodness. Swimming under the Tuscan sun with the smell of jasmine in the air is just what we needed. It would all be so perfect if it wasn't so not perfect. That's the only way I can describe it. Far from perfect. The water stopped. Time for cocktails on the terrace.

Faith stood sipping a Campari and soda with a twist of lime, trying to figure out how to introduce the question of Jack's and Sky's occupations into the flow of conversation when Len Russo beat her to it.

"So what do you do out there in California, Jack?"

Len was on his second martini. When Terry had objected, telling him that he could get those at home and why not try something Italian, he'd shut her up with, "What do you think the name 'Martini' is? Polish?"

Faith was liking him less with each passing moment and was tempted to tell him that the cocktail was born in the USA, prompting H. L. Mencken to call it "the only American invention as perfect as the sonnet."

"So what do you and the little woman do?" Len repeated.

"Well, Len, we both like to surf. Sky's better than I am."

He was drinking Prosecco, as was she.

Len didn't let it go. "That's nice, but you didn't answer my question. What's putting the bread on the table?"

His wife shot him a warning look, which he ignored.

"We're both in PR," Jack said. "What about you? What's your line of work?"

Grinning like the Cheshire cat, Len said, "I'm in waste management." Whatever either was going to say or not say was forestalled by Gianni's appearance with a tray of antipasti. Tom said softly to Faith, "Isn't that what all those Sopranos were in?"

She shook her head in a "not now" gesture. She was pretty sure Len Russo was no wiseguy and was just putting them all on. She'd be willing to bet he was an insurance salesman or if he did have something to do with waste management it was managing a business that cleaned people's septic tanks.

Francesca had sent out the *grissini* wrapped in prosciutto, roasted peppers, olives, marinated artichoke hearts, wedges of pecorino, some caponata, and the zucchini blossoms stuffed with fresh ricotta, floured and fried—delectable. A basket held small slices of several kinds of focaccia, lightly toasted.

Food is magic, Faith thought, not for the first time in her life. Oil—in this case, olive—upon troubled waters. The mood had changed instantly as everyone began to eat. Even the Nashes unbent, and Constance started asking the Culvers about what they had done in Florence that day. Of course it was no doubt so she could tell them all the places they'd missed and that they had gone to the wrong shops, but it was at least a step toward amiability. Gianni freshened drinks and Faith reached into her pocket for her camera. A nice scene for her trip album.

It was as if she had pulled out a Beretta. Every head save Tom's and Gianni's ducked.

"No pictures! I haven't done my face," Hattie said.

"Roderick and I do not like to be in other people's snaps,"

Constance said. The others said nothing, but their actions spoke louder than words. Len put a hand, fingers spread out, in front of his face. After ducking, Sky and Jack turned to enjoy the view to the rear. Olivia actually left the terrace, leaving her drink, so far untouched, on the table.

"Sorry," Faith apologized. "Maybe some other time."

But there wouldn't be another time. For whatever reasons, and each was bound to be different, no one in the group wanted to be photographed.

"Time to go to work!" Francesca said gaily, coming out the door. "Or we won't be eating until midnight!"

After Faith was sure that everyone else had gone into the kitchen, she told Tom she wanted to "freshen up a bit." She'd had an idea and she might not get another chance. Olivia had rejoined the others as soon as Francesca had come out onto the terrace. Judging from what the girl had been carrying on the train, Olivia packed as lightly as the Fairchilds; and Faith wanted to take a quick look at what was in her knapsack, mainly her passport. Hotels and other places routinely requested them, recording the information, but she didn't feel comfortable asking the Rossis for a peek at a guest's private information. Plus they'd wonder why Faith didn't ask Olivia outright.

She was sure Olivia's room would be locked, but she also thought the key to her and Tom's room would work—all the locks were the same vintage. She walked to the end of the hall where she'd seen Olivia's name on a door, slipped the key in, and turned. It was almost too simple. Yes, she should not be doing this and yes, she wasn't going to tell Tom, but she was doing it for Freddy. There was a tangle of loose ends surrounding Miss Olivia and it was time to tie some together.

The room was a smaller version of theirs—no balcony, but a

spectacular view across the valley and walls painted the color of lavender honey—gold with a slight amethyst sheen. Olivia was tidy, or it may have been because she didn't have much with her. A quick look in the bath revealed a minimum of shampoo and other beauty products, but a separate makeup bag was jam-packed. Then Faith went to the armoire and opened it. A few shirts, a jacket, and jeans hung on hangers, along with what looked like a Liberty-print bathrobe. A surprise—Olivia had struck her more as the deadly nightshade floral type as opposed to multicolored tiny posies. Rubber flip-flops, a pair of sandals, and Reeboks were lined up beneath. There were underwear, socks, sweaters, a bikini, and some scarves in a pile next to the shoes. The knapsack was there and it was empty.

Faith turned to the small desk by the window. Guides to Rome, Florence, and a general one for Italy plus maps were stacked in a pile. There were a few new postcards and a pen. The drawer was empty.

She was running out of time. On the nightstand next to the bed, there was an unopened bottle of water and a book—a Lindsey Davis mystery set in ancient Rome—half-read from the bookmark. She opened that drawer. Pay dirt.

A gun small enough to fit in the palm of one's hand was lying neatly next to a package of tissues and a tin of cough suppressants. Small, but deadly. The same as Olivia herself, Faith was beginning to think.

The vibe in the kitchen upon her entry could only be described as hilarious. Len wasn't even pretending to cook but had opened the wine that Faith was sure the Rossis had intended for the meal and taken it upon himself to dispense it liberally. Her eyes went to Olivia immediately. She was joining in, but alcohol had nothing to do with it. Save for the welcome Prosecco aperitif last night,

Faith hadn't seen her drink anything except Pellegrino. There hadn't been a passport, euros, or credit cards in Olivia's room. Now that she knew to look for it, Faith saw the string around Olivia's neck. She must have everything in one of those traveler's pouches. Her loose black tee would conceal it well. Her phone was clipped to her belt. It was camera, notebook, everything all in one. She'd have no need of a purse or other satchel, except when she was traveling from place to place.

Again they had been divided into groups and Faith joined the threesome of Hattie, Luke, and Constance, assuming that was where she'd been assigned.

"We're making panna cotta for tomorrow night," Hattie informed her. "It has to be chilled for at least five hours and it's even better overnight, you know. I just love it. We're doing a pure heavy cream version, no yogurt. Too bad about the calories!"

The vino had definitely loosened the woman's tongue, and now she, like Sally last night, was revealing that she knew far more about food, Italian food in particular, than she had let on. But then this was the sort of easy dessert that was sure to have been featured on the cooking channels numerous times. It was one of Faith's standbys for dinner parties. She looked at the sheet Francesca had given the group. It was the classic recipe, literally "cooked cream": gelatin, sugar, heavy cream, and a bit of both vanilla and almond extracts (see recipe, page 237). They had progressed to the stage where they were dissolving the sugar into the mixture. Mario had set trays with small ramekins out on a counter. There wasn't anything for Faith to do at this point, but she got a large pitcher ready. Easier to pour the liquid than ladle it into the ramekins.

"Very digestible," Constance said. "And when our summer fruits come in—neighbors joke that Roderick and I could be supplying Tiptree, they have a Royal Warrant from the queen, you know—I simply mound each portion with berries on top or some of the preserves that haven't been put up."

This was all getting quite jolly. Faith looked over to see what Tom was doing. He was in the *porchetta* group with Olivia, Sally, and Len. Even coming in late, Faith could see that the two women had taken charge and the men were happy to look on as they deftly rolled and tied the pork.

"What's in the stuffing?" she called over to them.

Tom answered, glancing at the sheet. "Sautéed onions and garlic, rosemary, stems and all, parsley, those zucchini flowers, figs, wild fennel, salt, pepper. Francesca sometimes uses sautéed chicken livers, too, but she wants us to taste the meat by itself tonight. I cut up one of the onions." He was clearly proud of himself.

"And into the oven it goes," Sally said with a flourish as she shut the door. Her face was red either from the heat in the kitchen or the glass Len was refilling.

He appeared to have appointed himself tonight's cruise director. To make up for his earlier sour behavior toward his wife?

"The meat will take an hour and a half or so," Francesca said, "which gives us time to make the risotto for *Il Primo* and do a vegetable to go with the meat."

What had the third group been making? Faith went over to the table where Terry, Roderick, Sky, and Jack were busy making what was probably *Il Dolce,* dessert.

"Olive oil cake," Terry said in answer to Faith's questioning look. "I've never heard of it, but I'll try anything once."

"I've had it," Faith said, not revealing that it was Francesca who had given her the delicious recipe, one of her grandmother's. Italian grandmothers were responsible for most of the best recipes the country had produced, it seemed. Besides the olive oil, which had to be extra-extra-virgin, the *torta* called for the juice and zest of an orange, flour, sugar, milk, eggs, and ground almonds. It was extremely rich. She'd have to pace herself, reflecting that she'd been saying this at every meal so far on the trip.

She went back to her group to finish the panna cotta and put it into the refrigerator.

Constance had a spoon in her hand and was dipping it into the large saucepan. She blew on it slightly and tasted it. The spoon flew from her hand and she screamed at Francesca, "Your cream is sour! Get me some water immediately!"

Mario dashed to the sink with a glass.

"Not tap water, you fool!"

He ran to get bottled.

"How can this be? I bought it yesterday and we had it this morning for the *colazione*?"

Francesca walked over and tasted the mixture herself. From her face it was obvious that Constance had been right.

"Do you have more in the fridge?" Faith asked, thinking she could quickly make another batch.

"Yes," Francesca said, and Faith followed her. Meanwhile Constance was in fine fettle, proclaiming she'd almost been poisoned. Her stomach was a delicate one and she'd often found that notions of hygiene and safe food preparation were "vastly different" abroad than at "home."

Faith took a spoon and tasted the container in the refrigerator. Sour as well.

She shook her head, and Francesca whispered, "I got it from the same place I get it all the time. Many of us had it earlier, including Mrs. Nashe. She had a lot of it on her fruit. Nothing was wrong."

"These things happen," Faith reassured her. "I can make a new batch in the morning when you get more cream. There will be plenty of time for it to get cold enough for dinner tomorrow night."

"We can do it together; I'll send Mario early."

But these things *didn't* happen. Not in Faith's experience. From now on she'd be keeping a close eye on all the ingredients. Unless she was very much mistaken, someone was tampering with them. To close Cucina della Rossi down before it even got started? Or for some other darker reason?

Len was pouring Constance the wine equivalent of a double and she appeared to be calming down somewhat, uttering only a few asides about salmonella and mad cows.

"Why don't we combine all our groups and make the rest of the meal together?" Francesca said. "I need people to clean and chop the mushrooms for the risotto and more to prepare the vegetable *contorni*."

The vegetable turned out to be cannellini beans with tiny new carrots from the garden, garlic—always garlic—fresh thyme, chopped tomato, and diced *pancetta,* the bacon cooked to a crisp. It involved much chopping, and increasingly, much laughter. Once again, food had done the trick, and the panna cotta mishap was soon a distant memory, if a memory at all.

What wasn't a distant memory was the gun she had seen in Olivia's room. Why would she leave it there, somewhat in plain sight? Faith assumed whoever made up the rooms didn't open drawers, but there was no way of telling that. Maybe Olivia was packing during the day. She'd been wearing light cotton cargo pants with plenty of pockets. Once they were back from Florence, she might have placed the gun in the drawer so it would be out of the way while she cooked, figuring the room had already been made up. Maybe the reason she had it at all was simply because she was a woman traveling alone? A habit honed by growing up in the Outback?

By the time they sat down for *Il Primo,* the risotto prepared with wild mushrooms and truffle oil, Faith was hungry again. Smell played such a crucial part in cooking—and appetite. She doubted she'd be this ravenous if she hadn't been immersed in the kitchen's aromas.

It was close to midnight when they finished the last course, the olive oil cake served with mint gelato, the fresh tang a perfect foil for the rich *torta*. What was the name of the Florentine *gelateria* Freddy had told them was the best in the world? The Rossis would know.

"Your gelato is fantastic, Francesca, but I'm trying to remember the name of a place in Florence especially known for their unusual flavors that our friend Freddy told us about. Something like Serafina?"

Luke answered instead. "It's Carapina and whoever gave you the tip must be a connoisseur. It is the best place in Italy and I think I have tried them all from the tip of the boot to the Alps. It's easy to find. They have two stores. I'll mark your map."

"We need to put it on the list," Gianni said. "How could we forget? It's all made by hand, no mix. I like to get a *doppio,* ricotta and chestnut. And any of their chocolates."

No one seemed in a hurry to go to bed, except for herself, Faith reflected. People drifted out to the terrace. It was a warm night and the stars were out blanketing the sky with tiny points of light. Much as she longed to crawl beneath the sheets with Tom, she followed the Russos and sat down. This was one of the times that she knew might occur more frequently as the week progressed, when she would have liked not to be part of a group, but on her own with Tom and maybe the Rossis.

Gianni was offering grappa. Faith had had enough to drink and the meal had made her thirsty. She got some water and noticed that Constance was doing the same. Like Olivia, she wasn't a big drinker, Faith had noticed. Roderick—and seriously, did she always call him that, even in the throes of passion?—had as usual partaken freely of the grape all night and was continuing to do so. He could hold his liquor, though, or perhaps he was just used to holding his tongue. He was no more talkative than he ever was.

"What's the schedule for tomorrow?" Jack asked.

The next day was a full one. Luke had invited everyone for

lunch at his villa. Afterward, the Rossis had arranged visits to several wineries and the place that pressed their olives.

"I thought those of you who wished could join me in the kitchen after breakfast and make several kinds of biscotti. I mean the kind you think of as a biscotti. We use the word 'biscotti' to mean all cookies, or what the British call biscuits."

Sally, who was feeling no pain, said, "Whoa, doesn't 'biscotti' just mean 'twice baked'? Because you bake them again after you slice them?"

Her aunt looked perturbed and said quickly, "We learned this from Giada's Food Network show."

"Well, wherever you learned it, it's correct and I will show anyone who wants to join me how to do it tomorrow. We will have them later for dessert with the panna cotta and a glass of vin santo from one of the wineries. After the biscotti come out of the oven, we'll go to see Luke's house and have lunch, then visit the places on the list in your packets. We should be able to get to most of them."

"And," Gianni added with enthusiasm, "we'll have time to detour to a few of the *pievi,* the area's Romanesque parish churches. We can't let poor Tom go too long without being in one, but we won't make him do a service!"

Cat's out of the bag, Faith thought and saw the dismay on Tom's face as well. It had only been a matter of time, though.

"But how is it that you are a *prete* when you are married to this *bella donna*?" Luke asked.

"I'm a Protestant clergyman, not a Roman Catholic priest," Tom explained. "And I'm very definitely on vacation, so feel free to behave as if I were any other profession."

"Waste management?" Jack said slyly, looking at Len, who appeared to find the remark hysterically funny.

Faith tapped Tom on the hand, their signal for "Let's get out of here." She had had enough of her fellow classmates for now. A very long day.

"Good night, everyone," she said, standing up. "And thank you, Gianni and Francesca, again for everything. I don't think I've ever eaten so well on a single day before."

Tom rose also, but before he could follow his wife into the house, Sky put her hand on his arm and stopped him. "Wait a minute. You're not a priest, but isn't it the same? The secrets of the confessional. I mean you can't tell anyone what someone tells you," she asked.

"That's the idea," Tom said affably. "Fortunately no one's confessed to murder."

It was an unfortunate example; the group went dead silent.

This early rising thing was in danger of becoming a habit, Faith thought. Even Tom wasn't awake when she crept out of bed, dressed, and went downstairs into the kitchen.

Francesca was, though, and most important, had been up long enough to make coffee.

"Let's do two kinds of panna cotta," Faith suggested, virtually inhaling the strong cappuccino—the Rossis' morning favorite and, unlike Americans, something Italians never drank later in the day. "The traditional kind and something a little different—lemon, maybe a spice like cardamom or"—she took a sip—"coffee."

"Do the cardamom and we can add the flavor easily at the end," Francesca said.

They got to work. Soon trays of ramekins were filled, ready for the fridge. Mario had put the new container of cream straight into Francesca's hands, but both she and Faith tasted it to be sure before they prepared the dish. It was fine. Mario was helping put out the breakfast things and Gianni joined him.

"Sit down and eat something, Faith," Francesca said when the two men were in the other room. "I hate for you to work this way. It's your time to relax."

"I *am* relaxed," Faith said, adding silently, at least now. There was always something calming about finishing food preparation. She knew everyone would love the dessert, topped with a little fruit or drizzled with one of the local honeys. Maybe the notion of feeding people something tasty was why she always felt this way when she'd taken something from the oven or plated a course.

"How do you think it's going?"

Francesca handed her a plate with slices of melon, fresh figs, and two warm *cornetti* on it, placing some preserves within reach.

"I think it's going beautifully. You and Gianni have thought of everything. I'm sure you haven't had any complaints about the accommodations, even from Constance Nashe, and you know the food has been great. But what is going to set you apart from other places—besides the fact that you're both so nice—are things like the excursion to the market yesterday. Without you we would never have met the Baronis, or been able to taste so many different things. It's a culinary education without the pressure of a classroom. No grades, just fun."

Francesca nodded. "This is what we are hoping. We want to attract those who know a lot and those who know nothing. Today will be similar. They are all our friends. And wait until you see Jean-Luc's house. It makes this look like the poor relations! But Faith"—a shadow crossed her beautiful face—"the spoiled cream. I can't explain it. You don't think it's some kind of omen, do you?"

Remembering that as a younger woman Francesca had been somewhat superstitious, Faith put every ounce of conviction she could muster into her reply. "Absolutely not. It could have been on the point of turning, or something like vinegar accidentally got splashed into it. There are any number of logical explanations. The only omens I've noticed have been favorable ones—the stars that looked like the whole zodiac had settled in just above your terrace last night and when I woke up I saw a ladybug on the windowsill, always a good sign."

Francesca seemed reassured, and since noise in the next room indicated that some of the guests had arrived for breakfast, she shooed Faith out of the kitchen, pausing to put more coffee on before going in to take orders.

A few hours later, the biscotti (see recipe, page 238) were cooling on racks and Faith went upstairs to change before leaving for lunch. Tom had drifted away shortly after they started the dough, and she suspected the pool had proved more of a lure than baking. Both Culvers had been involved in the entire process, clicking away at the biscotti with the camera and taking copious notes. Constance drifted in and announced that Roderick and she were going to get the paper but would be back in plenty of time for lunch. Francesca told them the nearest place for the *International Herald Tribune,* which is what she assumed they wanted, was in only one spot in the village, but more in Chiusi. Sky and Jack showed up just before breakfast ended and disappeared immediately after, saying something vague about going to look at the olive groves. Faith wondered what the Italian equivalent for a "roll in the hay" was, thinking the idea of one in the fields of poppies and wheat not an unattractive one. Olivia had reverted to her Goth Girl look, which Faith was now beginning to regard as a disguise, just as the freshly scrubbed Cover Girl look was one, too. The woman with a thousand disguises, or was that faces? She had deftly shaped the dough into the long thin loaves, leading Faith to think once more that Olivia was no stranger to cooking techniques. Terry Russo was, however, but eager to learn. Len was conspicuously absent, sleeping in, his wife said. Sleeping it off, more likely, Faith thought.

Up in her room, she quickly changed into a light pair of crop pants and white tee and tied a brightly striped cotton Missoni scarf by way of Target around her neck. The maid had closed the windows, and Faith decided to open them, even though they weren't screened. They dealt with mosquitoes and blackflies in Maine.

So far she hadn't seen any similar pests, and the room would be sweltering when they returned if she left them shut. The Rossis had installed central air, but knowing what electricity cost in Italy, Faith hadn't wanted to turn it on.

She stood at the window facing the pool and rear of the house. There was a small garden house, like a gazebo, farther down the slope where Faith assumed they kept extra chairs and other outdoor equipment. They'd trained wisteria over it, which was in full bloom, sending cascades of blossoms over the doorway. As she stood there, Faith saw the door open, and a head popped out. It was Sky and she seemed to be looking about, looking for someone? It was definitely a furtive gesture. She stepped out, and Faith thought it was a shame there weren't people around, especially males, to see how gorgeous the woman was. A white bikini set off her light tan, and her hair almost seemed to have been sprayed with gold leaf. She let the door close behind her and rapidly headed toward the house. Faith started to turn away to pick up her bag, but stopped when she saw the door open again. Jack?

It wasn't Jack. It was Tom. The Reverend Thomas Preston Fairchild, her husband.

Luke's house was everything Francesca had intimated and more.

The villa, much larger than the Rossis', also looked more formal from the outside. The circular drive cut through an extensive, well-tended garden with boxwood hedges and statuary. Their host was waiting for them at the door and came forward, hands outstretched in welcome.

"*Benvenuto!* First we eat, then the guided tour," he announced, ushering them down the wide center hall, which offered tantalizing glimpses of rooms to either side, before he led them through one of a series of double glass doors to the outside. Beyond was what amounted to an open-air dining room, a lovely loggia. There was a fireplace set into the wall at the far end, and Faith had a sudden desire to give a late-night party here. The table was set with an eclectic mix of antique silver and bright linens Faith recognized from a shopwindow in the nearby village, resolving to pick some up for herself. The long table easily accommodated everyone, and with a flick of a switch Luke activated an awning to provide shade.

Tom had not come up to the room before they left and when Faith joined the group, he was already talking to Len, who seemed to have recovered after his "beauty" sleep. Although they sat next to each other in the van, Faith had resisted saying what was uppermost in her mind, namely, "What exactly were you and Sky, aka Bo Derek, Miss Ten, maybe even Miss Twenty, Miss California, Miss any number of titles, doing in the shed just now?"

She was afraid she'd shout instead of whisper and she was even more afraid of what he might say—something like "What are you talking about?" "Nothing" "She had a thorn in her paw," all unsatisfactory answers. So, she kept quiet. With difficulty.

Now he was at the other end of the table, laughing at something Hattie was saying and—maybe she might be reading into it, maybe not—ignoring Faith's eye.

In her heart she knew Tom would never cheat on her, no nookie—or gnocchi—having occurred, she was sure, but it was still a shock. And, she'd immediately thought, what if someone else had been looking out at them? The suspicion of a rendezvous was as dangerous as the reality of one in some ways. Dame Rumor.

Luke, or his housekeeper, had prepared a perfect summer meal. They started with an Italian version of gazpacho—a cold tomato soup with chunks of the ripe vegetable and zucchini instead of cucumber, with fresh parsley, a hint of garlic, all of it thickened slightly with bread crumbs. Instead of a first and second course, they'd been combined: cold rice salad with roasted red peppers, diced red onions, blood orange segments, parsley, toasted pignoli, a simple olive oil and balsamic vinegar dressing topped with shaved pecorino; alongside slices of cold chicken dressed the same with a hint of rosemary on a bed of field greens.

"While some of you have dessert—some pears poached in one of the red wines you will be tasting today—I'll take one group around and then we will switch," Luke said. He had entertained them throughout the meal with humorous tales of all the crises he had weathered before the house was finished. Tales that were probably, no definitely, not at all funny at the time. Faith jumped up to go with the first group and motioned to Tom to join her, but he seemed intent on continuing his conversation with Hattie, mouthing that he'd go with the next group.

Short of dragging him from his chair there was nothing Faith could do but shoot him a look that she hoped would convey her mood. It did and he seemed genuinely surprised.

"It's a pretty big place for just one person," Terry whispered to Faith as they trailed after their host down the hall, painted a warm cantaloupe color. Framed antique prints of Florence and Rome lined the walls. "Do you think he has a lady friend?"

Was that a note of hope in Terry's voice? Hope that he didn't and hope the job might be available for her? The rooms displayed the same combination of old and new, formal and informal, as the tableware. Both the living and dining room furniture could have come straight from this year's Milan Furniture Fair—contemporary designs in glass, metal and plastics—but the walls and ceiling were decorated with trompe l'oeil frescoes that would have been at home in an ancient Pompeian villa. The one on the dining room ceiling pictured an orange grove with a mix of doves, swallows, and other birds.

"And this is my favorite room," Luke said, opening a door at the far end of the first floor. They'd already oohed and aahed over the kitchen, twice the size of the Rossis' and outfitted with not only state-of-the art appliances but also antique tile backsplashes and marble countertops from Carrara, Michelangelo's preferred quarry, Constance noted for them, beaming at her host as if she had selected them for him herself. Faith had been amused to see the way the woman fawned on the admittedly attractive Frenchman, sticking so close to him that she'd stepped on his heel twice when he'd stopped to tell them something. She'd reddened only slightly and gave what some would call a girlish laugh, but what Faith regarded as being closer to a member of the animal kingdom, say a hyena?

The room was indeed lovely. And not at all what Faith would have expected to find in the heart of Tuscany. It was a wood-paneled library that would have been at home in an English country house—bookshelves to the ceiling lined with gleaming gold-embossed leather-bound volumes. A spiral library ladder made from the same rich mahogany provided access to the tomes out of reach. The floor was tiled, as was the rest of the downstairs, but was almost entirely covered by a plush, deep blue Oriental rug with red and gold medallions. The furniture, however, reverted to the same clean, modernistic design as elsewhere on the ground floor: the sofa and chairs were slip covered in white with the exception of two antique Empire side chairs upholstered in dark green with tiny gold bees woven into the damask, a nod to the country of his birth? But the focal point of the room was an Empire writing desk complete with lion's-paw feet and ormolu trim celebrating the emperor's Egyptian campaign. Luke gestured toward it.

"When I sit at my desk, I can see the entire valley. And the desk itself was made for the space by a craftsman you may meet tomorrow in Montepulciano. It is an exact reproduction of one Napoleon had."

Terry Russo was obviously impressed. "I went with some of my girlfriends to the Biltmore Estate in North Carolina and they had a lot of his things. Real ones, but this looks just like them. This is just as nice," she added hastily, lest her host think she was criticizing the copy and stumbled on. "He was short, right? They kept referring to him as 'The Little Corsican.'"

Luke looked amused. "An affectionate term for my fellow, that is, the fine fellow . . ."

Constance, never one to shy away from interrupting to talk about what she wanted, did so. "Ah yes, Napoleon. Well, what I want to know is who did all these divine ceilings? Surely not some little man in the village."

Uninterested in hearing Constance enthuse, Faith moved to examine the desk more closely and then closer still, riveted by what was on top. She'd know it anywhere. One corner worn, but more telling, the discoloration from the wine that he'd spilled when he'd poured some into their glasses. Into their glasses at Hostaria Giggetto, a scant four days ago.

It was Freddy's notebook.

CHAPTER 7

Normally there were few things Faith Fairchild liked better than seeing other people's houses. She shared this trait with her mother-in-law, who admitted as well to a secret passion for looking into a home's lighted rooms at night—"just like watching a play." Together they had enjoyed many a house tour, and Fairchild Realty, the family business, had provided additional fodder. Faith often thought she should have gone into real estate herself, although recently a Realtor friend had pointed out that there was much more to it than opening closet doors, and some of it not so much fun.

Now, in one of the most spectacular houses she had ever been in—they were on their way to a wing that included a screening room and home gym—Faith might just as well have been viewing the Port Authority Bus Terminal.

How did Freddy's notebook get from Rome to Luke's house? Her immediate thought was that the Frenchman had to be involved in Freddy's death, but as she walked blindly behind the others it occurred to her that this could be a case of hiding in plain sight. She had mentioned Freddy's name last night at dinner, she realized, thereby establishing the relationship. Someone, say Olivia, might not have known the connection and, knowing it now, decided to quickly get rid of anything linking herself to the dead man, especially since she had been spotted with the killer. Granted it hadn't been in Olivia's room when Faith had searched it, but the young woman had been wearing those pants with all the pockets down in the kitchen and the notebook was small, easy to fit in one. Why not throw the book into a field or the trash? Things like this often had a way of inconveniently turning up again. And besides, putting it on someone else's desk where Faith or Tom would surely see it this morning pointed a finger another way.

But how? Or rather when?

They were climbing a staircase to the second floor. Faith had a fleeting impression of walls the color of polenta passing by as her thoughts churned. In fact, any one of the people here could have done it. When they'd arrived, Luke had indicated a door and said if anyone needed a bathroom, that was the closest to where they would be lunching. It was next to the library. Easy enough to excuse oneself and slip the notebook onto the desk while ostensibly using the facilities. And, Faith thought back, everyone had. Whether from necessity or curiosity, each guest save Faith herself had made use of the bathroom before sitting down to lunch or during it, Len Russo going so far as to announce, "Have to see a man about a horse," before heading indoors.

They were all at the hotel in Rome. They were all here. They were all suspects.

She realized that Terry Russo was tugging at her elbow. "I know it's spectacular, but we're leaving now."

Faith had been standing stock-still, lost in thought. She focused on the room. They'd been in and out of bedrooms and baths—she'd registered that much—but this was undoubtably the master, and it *was* spectacular. One of the largest beds she'd ever seen was set against a wall decorated with another trompe l'oeil fresco, this one floor to ceiling. In between Corinthian columns cerulean blue swags hung above a series of vistas, like those in the background of Renaissance paintings—tiny hill towns, misty embankments, shimmering lakes. The bed itself was covered with a white spread so pristine that Faith imagined someone whose only job was to wash and then iron it in situ every day.

"Are you okay? I mean you seem a little out of it," Terry asked anxiously, steering Faith out of the room and into the adjoining one.

"I'm fine. The heat sometimes gets to me," she said.

Terry looked skeptical. The temperature inside the house was almost too cool. Possibly central air or just the thick several-hundred-year-old walls. "Oh my God!" Terry said. It was her turn to stop in her tracks.

Faith, now tuned in to her surroundings, was tempted to echo the woman's words.

They were in the master bath to end all master baths. A master bath easily as big as the First Parish parsonage's entire downstairs. The fixtures were the most twenty-first century she'd ever seen: the high-tech Japanese toilet that did everything for you except the actual act of elimination; as well as a glass-enclosed shower large enough for two, or even three, with a rain forest showerhead plus jets that she'd read about—they misted parts of the entire body with one's preferred scents; and then the tub itself, sunken of course, and carved from Romano travertine. She'd seen a photo of a similar one in a suite at the Rome Cavalieri in her wanderings online looking at hotels before Francesca had sent the information on the hotel where they'd stayed. Like the luxury hotel, there was a large picture window in this bath. Instead of St. Peter's, Luke's seemed to overlook all of Tuscany. And a Swarovski crystal chandelier hung from the ceiling. But it wasn't the view, the fixtures, the stone, the tile work, not even the fireplace, but the aquarium that wrapped around the bathtub on three sides, extending all the way to the top of the room, that took Faith's breath away. It was alive with exotic fish and gently swaying aquatic plants, yet what made it so extraordinary was the concave glass. Luxuriating in the tub, you'd feel as if you were immersed in a tropical sea.

"When can I move in?" Terry said.

Luke laughed. "You are welcome anytime. I admit this room is over-the-top, but ever since I was a little boy, I've dreamed of being a merman and this is the closest I'll get."

The group left quietly to change places with the others, who had progressed to coffee. The bathroom had literally left them speechless.

As usual, Jack and Sky had stayed together. Tom jumped up and walked into the house with them. A threesome. Not a three-way, surely! Suddenly Faith was back at the window in her room. Sky was wearing a sundress now that didn't cover much more than her bikini had.

But her thoughts quickly went back to the notebook sitting so tantalizingly near, and she wondered whether Tom would notice it, too. Or did he only have eyes for something, or someone, else?

One thing was cheering her up though. Luke had said they were "welcome anytime." He may have been talking about a soak in his bathtub, but Faith was choosing to interpret it as a more general invitation—and one she intended to take him up on just as soon as she made sure he wasn't home.

Compartmentalize, Faith told herself. Create some mental storage containers, fill them up, and seal the doors. And do it now. What was that quote, something like "We may pass this way but once"? And who knew when she'd pass the breathtaking scene outside again—it would be a crime to miss it. The van seemed to be climbing to the top of the world and as the road wound ever higher, the view of the valley below became more enchanting. The vineyards and olive groves had begun as well-defined straight lines, lush green with spots of color from the wild yellow broom and red poppies. And now it was all one soft color, like layers of organdy in pale hues. This was her dream trip after all, she reminded herself, taking her husband's hand and kissing it.

Once again Francesca was providing the commentary while Gianni drove.

"The first place we will visit is a small family-owned vineyard, as we are, except they bottle their grapes themselves. We hope to do that someday, but at the present we are selling them to a cooperative. As you know, we are in the Chianti Classico region, which has a very long history and we think produces the best wine in the world."

"What kind of grapes is this place growing and when do they harvest?" Hattie asked, pencil and pad in hand.

"Like us, the Sangiovese variety, which matures in early October. The grape harvest, La Vendemmia, is a very special time in Chianti, and it is something no one who loves wine should miss. All the villages have *festas* of some sort. You may know the most famous one in Impruneta, La Festa dell'Uva, a huge all-day celebration of the *uva,* the grape!"

"I was there last year," Luke said. "I'll bring my photos over tonight for you to see if you like. Parades with floats, amazing food, and wine flowing everywhere."

"Sign me up," Len said.

"To be a float?" his wife said archly.

He ignored her.

"Every year," Francesca said, "especially these last years, we watch the weather as the grapes grow. It has been very dry, a major problem, which affects the sweetness of the grape, also the flavor of the olives."

"Global warming," Olivia said.

Ah, Faith thought, an environmentalist. But she was right. The signs of it were all over the world. Even in Aleford. No one could remember a spring coming as early as it had this year. Daffodils and forsythia had bloomed in March.

"So when do you harvest the olives?" Hattie asked.

"Our Tuscan valleys can have an earlier frost than other parts of the Mediterranean where olives are grown, so we must pick well before then, again mid-September to mid-October. Hard to predict now. But you will hear more about this later in the afternoon when we go to the mill."

Gianni pulled up to the front of a farmhouse that was surrounded by several other buildings. They were in sharp contrast to Luke's villa. The age of the structures may have been similar, but that was all. No statuary, no landscaping of any sort, except for several clay pots of geraniums. A man and a woman who both appeared to be in their forties came rushing out, greeting them with smiles and a hearty welcome in Italian that needed no translation. The tour did, however, and the Rossis and Luke served as interpreters. The vintner was telling them that grapes had been cultivated on their land since the Etruscans. Maybe before, he added with a shrug. Luke, whom Faith remembered had a particular interest in these early Italians, broke in to tell them that the Etruscans were, in fact, believed to be the people who happily introduced vinoculture to the area, bringing grapevines from Asia.

"You just have to look at what they left to know how much they enjoyed good food and wine—the banqueting frescoes and the pottery—wine casks and vases, urns for all kinds of food storage."

"I don't know about your Etruscans," Roderick said, "but it was a Roman, Horace, who wrote 'No poem was ever written by a drinker of water' and I say amen to that and when are we going to get to the tasting of this stuff?"

It was the most Faith had heard him say, and amid the laughter that greeted it, she wondered at the cause of his seemingly constant need for alcoholic fortification. Something in addition to being married to Constance? The farmers looked a bit puzzled at the sudden merriment, but after Gianni spoke to them, obviously translating, they burst into laughter, too, and waved everyone into the first building.

An hour later they climbed back into the van, sated not only from tasting the winery's excellent Chiantis but also from samples of the pecorino they produced that had been served on a platter filled with olives, several kinds of salami, and bread.

"Maybe it's the wine, but I think I'm beginning to understand Italian, and if I'm right I've committed us to returning in the fall to help pick grapes," Tom said. "Well, the kids should enjoy it."

"I hear it's very hard work," Faith said, amused at the way this tried-and-true New Englander was taking to la dolce vita. However, her amusement, as well as the pleasant time she'd just had, wasn't keeping those storage container doors closed, especially the one containing Freddy's notebook. Faith could keep the news to herself no longer. It was like a canker sore. Despite knowing it still hurts, your tongue keeps going there.

She and Tom were at the rear of the van, which was full. The Nashes had joined them for today. Even they wouldn't have insisted they could make their own way to the places the group was visiting.

"Tom," Faith whispered in his ear. Maybe the others would assume the anniversary couple was indulging in some sweet nothings. "I saw Freddy's notebook on the desk in Luke's library."

He looked startled. "On Napoleon's desk?"

She nodded. "A copy."

"Of Freddy's notebook?"

This was descending to a Who's on First.

"No, the desk is a copy. The notebook is real."

"How could you be sure?"

"The corner was bent just like Freddy's and remember he spilled wine on it? The stain was there."

"Honey, lots of people spill things on books and corners wear."

He stopped whispering and started nuzzling her ear instead. She sat up straight.

Her own husband didn't believe her!

Whether to give them time to digest, and in some cases sober up, or because it made sense geographically, the next stop was the mill where the Rossis brought their olives to be pressed into oil.

Francesca put on her tour guide hat again.

"Like with the winemakers, there are large *frantoii,* olive pressers, and small ones. This small mill, as you will see, uses traditional methods to grind the olives and extract the oil. If you are interested, we can arrange for you to visit one of the big places where they are using modern machinery and computers. It's very interesting to us, but since we have a relatively small harvest, we come here."

"We would anyway," Gianni said firmly.

Francesca smiled. "My husband is a little old-fashioned, but I do agree with him on this. It's the way I've always known."

The Culvers had their questions ready once more.

"Can you walk us through from when you pick to what we're going to see?" Sally asked.

"Of course. We harvest in the fall again. Everything with the grapes and olives happens one after the other in Tuscany! It's a rush to pick the olives because the timing has to be just right."

Gianni picked up the thread. This was obviously a passion for him, even more than the grapes, Faith realized.

"It cannot be wet and the moon has to be right. You can't stop in the middle, and we bring the olives to the mill in batches. If you store them until they are all picked, they lose their flavor. For us, the concern is the taste of our oil, the quality. It is nice to get a large yield of oil, but better to have less and make it the best. This is also why we pick by hand. The big growers use automatic rakes to shake the olives from the trees, or other machines to harvest them."

"He treats his trees like children," Francesca teased. "The way he prunes them, checks them for pests. I think he even sings to them. And by the way, the leaves of the olive tree do not change color or fall. It is an evergreen."

"How much oil does each tree give you?" Sally asked.

Gianni was apparently not trusting his wife to answer and scowled at her playfully. "About one liter for each tree is a good estimate."

Jack seemed surprised. "But that's nothing! All that work for something the size of a bottle of Coke!"

"Worth it, I'd say, if the oil we've been enjoying is your own," Terry said.

"It is and *grazie*," Francesca said. "The color of the oil varies with the kind of olive, and ours is the typical Tuscan green, like the first grass growing in the spring. We are permitted to label it 'extra virgin' since it is cold-pressed, no heat or chemicals used, and has an acidity of less than one percent."

Sally and Hattie were both scribbling away.

"Okay. You pick, bring the olives to the mill, and then what?" Sally asked.

"I will let the owners tell you, but basically after the olives are washed and any twigs separated out, they are crushed by three granite millstones," Francesca said. "In the old days a donkey provided the power, walking round and round. The mashed-up olives, a paste, are spread on layers of round straw mats and piled up, then the press pushes the oil out. You will not see this today. But you will come back for this, too. There is nothing more delicious than fresh oil!"

Sally was insistent on the details, though. "How does it get into the bottles from these straw things?"

"The oil drips down the sides of the stack into a tank and a centrifuge spins the water out and then it is bottled. Never store your oil in anything plastic, by the way. I can't remember what they are called in English, but it will affect the flavor and also may be bad for us."

"PVCs, polyvinyl chlorides," Faith called from the back. "Both things are true—bad for taste and for health. What isn't true is that you have to store olive oil in the fridge. I keep mine in a cupboard, away from light and heat. I only buy E-V-O-O that's dated, and although I've never kept any this long, unopened it's fine for two or even a bit more years."

"Faith is right," Francesca said. "We use a dark green bottle like most growers to protect the oil from sunlight. For cooking, I keep a virgin-grade oil and I buy it in gallon tin containers. I transfer what I need into a smaller glass or ceramic one."

"We're here!" Gianni cried, swiftly pulling in next to what looked like an oversize garage. Faith had expected something with more character, but that came when they entered the building.

Two men got up from the lawn chairs set up next to a Rube Goldbergian–looking machine where they had obviously been waiting for them. They were both young, both very good-looking, and it soon became apparent, both fluent in English.

"Welcome, American and English people! Welcome to our *frantoio*! I am Sandro, like Sandro Botticelli, except I cannot paint, and this is my partner, Maurizio, like Maurizio Pollini, except he cannot play the piano, just what do you call it, 'Chopsticks.' I have so much English because I was one summer in Nebraska picking corn."

With a flourish he grabbed the nearest person—it was Jack— shook hands, and then much to Jack's surprise kissed him on both cheeks.

"You must excuse him. He is alone with only me too much," Maurizio said. "Come. This is a slow time in the *olio* business. Of course we find much to do, but compared to the fall . . ." He rubbed the side of his face, the universal hand gesture for extreme boredom. "Your visit is a blessing."

The tour expanded the Rossis' information, and there was no question about enjoying the mode of delivery. Faith hadn't laughed so much in years, let alone on the trip. The two men were definitely what the Italians call *personaggi*.

"We use hemp for the mats," Maurizio said. "And I try to keep Sandro from smoking them. We do not weave them ourselves. We would like our mothers to do this, but they are modern women and have important jobs. Mine is a lawyer, which she says she chose as soon as I was born because she had the feeling I would need her services sooner or later. My papa is an accountant. Botticelli's namesake over there has two high-powered parents; journalists in Milano."

"Enough," Sandro said. "It's time for them to judge whether our oil is as appetizing as we are."

They had set up the tasting outdoors under a large oak on a picnic table covered with a checked cloth. Chairs had been scrounged from the house, which Faith saw was an old farmhouse farther down the road.

"It is like a wine tasting. But better," Sandro instructed once they were seated. "I will give you a taste in these glasses. Smell first. Inhale deeply. Three or four times. Closing your eyes is good. Then a tiny sip, swish it around your mouth. Swallow, or spit it out on the grass if you must, but then wait, drink some water, and try the other two. You are going from last year's harvest, the newest, to oldest. See which you like best. Then we will have some wine and you will be our best friends forever, isn't that what you say?"

Faith already was beginning to think of these two charming men as her BFFs, and after she tasted the oil they were producing, she knew they would also be her suppliers for small quantities to use in special dishes. She'd order some oil now and some in the fall.

The afternoon was stretching out lazily. Everyone was happy

and relaxed. Even Olivia was smiling and asking Sandro questions about being on the farm in Nebraska, possibly so she could laugh at his answers, which were very funny and involved many puns.

"But although there was much food that I was not sad to leave—many, many sweet green, orange, and red gelatins they called salads with canned fruit and cheese trapped in the middle that looked like ricotta but tasted like overcooked gnocchi and all the other salads, the ones that had lettuce, were smothered with sweet mayonnaise dressings, also orange—they liked that color, those happy smiling peoples. I cried to leave their steaks. Cover your ears, Rossis, but even Chianina beef doesn't come close to what I had in Nebraska."

"Tonight is the night for *Bistecca alla Fiorentina,* so they can decide for themselves," Francesca said. "I thought we would be tired from today, so we will grill. Sandro, Maurizio, come join us. We will eat at nine, but come early."

"You are all so nice. Of course we will come. We can do *bruschetta* on the grill, too. We will bring the oil, and garlic from our garden," Maurizio said.

The final stop of the day, at a vineyard, was a marked contrast to the two previous ones.

A long drive lined with well-tended cypresses led to the *castello* that was the grower's home. Gianni turned in front of it and parked in a lot near the equally impressive old buildings that housed the winery and tasting room. The gardens were overflowing with specimen blooms, and when someone came out to greet them, it was a guide, not the owners themselves. It didn't matter. The guide, whose name was Mia, was well informed, and even though the scale was so much larger, she conveyed the deep appreciation all involved had for their craft and product as she gave them the tour, an appreciation apparent at the other winery and the olive mill, too. As she spoke she passed out sheets explaining how wines are classified—the meaning behind those letters following all the names; DOCG, Designation of Controlled Origin Guaranteed, being the highest. The Culvers were in heaven. Handouts!

This was where Francesca had said they would purchase some vin santo to go with the biscotti they had made earlier for tonight's *dolce*. And since she was sure this process would be completely new to most of the students, when they emerged into the sunlight, she asked Mia to speak to them about it.

"At our *cantina* we are making Vin Santo di Montepulciano DOC from white grapes," Mia explained. "Seventy percent of the grapes must be the Grechetto, Trebbiano, and Malvasia varieties. The other thirty percent can be local varieties, and we have some we use that give our wine a very special taste. Unlike the processes for other wines, vin santo is made from dried grapes. We spread them out on straw mats after the regular harvest in a warm room, which causes the moisture to evaporate and the sugar to become very concentrated. The amount of time we leave them is important, but it is many weeks. Some people add yeast afterward to speed fermentation. Instead, we take some of last year's vin santo saved for the purpose to add to ours. Then it goes into oak barrels where it ages, for us, at least four years. Methods vary. Some places hang the bunches of grape to dry, but basically it is the same process—a wine made from the raisin. Some use a different wood for the barrels. Originally all the barrels were made of chestnut."

Earlier they had passed through a room filled with the enormous barrels lying on their sides with bright red rims and polished steel hoops. Very impressive.

"Please follow me to the tasting room and I think today it would be nice to sample some vin santo even though the Rossis have said you will have some later. Although ours is the traditional amber, you will notice a slight difference in each color, and in sweetness. I will be interested to hear which one you prefer."

She led the way out into the bright sunlight and across another flower-filled courtyard to a building that was a shop and tasting room. Faith wondered how she managed in the elegant high heels she was wearing, but she must have been used to navigating the cobblestones and never even teetered.

"Mia, tell them the story of how the wine got its name," Gianni said. "Tom here is a priest. Not like ours. A Protestant one, but I'm sure he will want to know."

"I do want to know," Tom said. "And I may have already heard at least one story, but please tell us yours."

"First the official version, then the apocryphal, which is much more interesting," she said, her face lighting up.

Mia really was darling, Faith thought, her hair a tumble of dark curls and face dominated by golden brown eyes. With her heels, stylish short skirt, and a Gucci scarf gracefully tied around her neck, she exemplified what the Italians call *la bella figura,* a hard-to-define philosophy that means the whole way one presents oneself, especially in public. Not just how one looks but one's attitude and behavior, a striving for perfection, with no apparent sweat.

" 'Vin santo,' which means 'holy wine,' takes the name from being used for mass," Mia said. "That's the official story, but many of us believe another is the true one. In the fourteenth century a Franciscan friar from Siena began to use the wine that was left over after mass to soothe the pain of those suffering from the plague. It was a miracle! They were cured! The sweet wine began to be used for many kinds of sickness, and we still think of vin santo as having medicinal properties."

"Definitely more believable," Tom agreed. "And it's the story I've heard before."

Since Roderick was looking longingly at the table with the glasses and bottles, Faith thought she'd do her good deed for the day and steer the conversation that way.

"Is all your vin santo sweet? I've heard some kinds are more like a dry sherry."

Mia nodded and, much to Roderick's obvious delight, started to open the bottles and pour samples.

"I should let you decide for yourselves, but yes, we only make a dessert wine. Now, please enjoy. And we do ship to the United States and United Kingdom," she added.

Everyone appeared to like the wine. As they sipped, Luke added to their vin santo lore by reciting the phrase "a holy wine for a hell of a day," which he said he'd often heard people say.

"Another kind of medicine for another kind of illness," Terry observed. "I've had days like that. I think I'll order a case!"

"Although until today I've never heard about the wine being for a bad day as such, in Italy we also call vin santo, *vini da meditazioni*—'a wine to meditate with,'" Mia added.

After consulting with Tom, Faith decided they should order some, too.

"And not just to help you think about your sermons," she said. "This has a very different flavor from others I've tried. You taste the raisins, of course, but it also has a nutty flavor and isn't cloyingly sweet."

It was an ebullient group that piled into the van, to head back to Cucina della Rossi. The brilliant late afternoon sun lit up the landscape like klieg lights from a Hollywood film set.

Gianni turned the radio on as they plunged into the valley, or at least that's what it felt like to Faith. After what was obviously an announcement of football scores, greeted with groans from the driver and causing an alarming sudden swerve, the station started broadcasting a series of American and British oldies. A number of people were humming along, and when the familiar opening of Don McLean's "American Pie" came over the airwaves, Terry Russo shouted, "I love this song!" and started singing. Her enthusiasm was contagious, and she had a great voice. Soon the whole group was joining in on the chorus, although Constance did say loudly at the start that the song made no sense whatsoever and she could never understand why it was so popular.

"No levees and precious few Chevys in your part of the world, darlin', " Hattie said before belting out the chorus.

It was a nice moment and Faith felt herself caught up in the mood. That is until they came to the famous last line—"This'll be the day that I die."

Possibly because of a full day of close proximity, the group went their separate ways as soon as Gianni pulled to a full stop back at the house. Faith decided to take a swim in the pool and then dry off in the sun while relaxing with a book. She was trying to distract herself and keep from marking time. Tom's reaction to her revelation about the notebook had convinced her that what she was planning to do as soon as it was dark enough and as soon as she was sure Luke was not going to run home, she'd be doing solo. On her way outside, she stopped to look at the assortment on the bookshelves in the Rossis' lounge and found a copy of Elizabeth David's *Italian Food,* much to her delight.

Olivia was doing laps, and Faith decided to read for a while. The pool was more than large enough for both of them, but she didn't want to disturb the young woman, who was churning up the water with a very authentic Australian crawl. She was wearing goggles and a black tank suit. Lean, not thin, Faith was surprised to see how toned Olivia was. Muscles that could only come from many hours at the gym.

She turned to Elizabeth David's section on *carni*—meat— reading her description of Florentine beefsteak, *Bistecca alla Fiorentina,* which praised it as the best in Italy, "similar to an American T-bone steak." A woman with extremely firm opinions, and one of Faith's culinary idols, David went on to say that since the cut is so big there is "no room, nor any necessity" for vegetables on the plate. Faith wondered what Francesca was planning. Her fellow Americans would expect side dishes, if not on the plate, on the table. The Italian way of eating in small stages throughout a meal was indeed foreign to them.

Soon she was completely engrossed in the book, and the sound of the chaise next to her being moved made her drop it.

"Sorry, I hope I didn't make you lose your place. I just wanted to get into more sun," Olivia said.

"Not at all, and with this book"—Faith picked it up, displaying the cover—"the point is to lose one's place and wander through it." Much, she thought with a pang, like Freddy's travel advice.

"I love her books. She's one of those people I've wished were still alive, so I could meet them in person, not that I would bother her by actually doing it," Olivia said. "Growing up, everything we ate was frozen or from tins. The notion that one should only eat what was in season never occurred to me until I read Elizabeth David. She was also a rebel, and I was drawn to that part of her, too, especially when I was younger."

It was an opening. Olivia had rebuffed any inquiries about her personal life, but this shared admiration for the food writer, who was indeed a rebel in her day, might provide an opening. Faith started slowly.

"Thackeray said somewhere that next to eating a good dinner, the best thing was reading about one, and I've always liked to read cookbooks and food essays, like M. F. K. Fisher's, too. Another woman who marched to her own drummer."

"I'll have to track the Thackeray quote down. Anyway yes, *How to Cook a Wolf* and the rest of Fisher's are favorites, even though I've never cooked a thing from them."

"The point is that we don't have to cook from these books. I think of them as novels with a whole lot of food."

Olivia laughed. It changed her face, free of any makeup after the swim, markedly. She was very pretty, and very young, despite her remark about looking back at her youth, Faith decided.

"You definitely know your way around a kitchen," Faith said. "From all this reading? Or have you worked in them?"

Olivia reached for her shades, literally and figuratively, putting on dark glasses and leaning far back in the lounge chair.

"Oh, I've been here and there," she said. "This sun is so delicious. My sunblock is waterproof, so I think I'll doze."

Well, it was a start.

Tom was in seventh heaven. He'd never made it to the pool, but after waking up from a nap in the room, went to ask Gianni if he needed help with preparing tonight's cookout and became the sous chef, or Italian barbecue equivalent. Mario was also on hand. When Faith had changed and came down to see what she could do, she followed the noise. She found her husband behind the house by the large brick-and-cement grill that Gianni had built when they'd remodeled for just this kind of occasion, starting to prepare the coals. He was both grimy and ecstatic. This was the man, she reminded herself, who had never gotten the hang of a toaster oven. Now he was a grill master. She clearly wasn't needed and went inside. Francesca was in the kitchen alone.

"Where is everyone and what can I do?" Faith asked. She'd expected that some of the class would be there.

"Those naughty boys Sandro and Maurizio have arrived and brought big pitchers of Italian sangria—Campari and Prosecco instead of Rioja and brandy, but still with fruit floating in it. They took everyone down to the pool for drinks. I just hope no one falls in. I'm putting together an antipasto similar to what we had Sunday night to soak up some of the alcohol. We have the wines we bought today for dinner still to come! I thought some people might help with the *contorni* and then later we must unmold the panna cotta, but I'm afraid it will be you, me, and Mario. Except he's being very macho, with our husbands getting ready to grill the meat."

"What do you want to serve with the steak as side dishes?"

"Not very much. We'll be doing the *bruschetta* soon while we wait for the coals to get hot enough to sear the meat, and with what I have here"—she motioned to what looked like enough cold cuts, cheeses, roasted vegetables, and olives for a whole village— "it should hold them until the *carni*. For the meal, first a Caprese salad—slices of tomato, fresh mozzarella, and basil from the garden. I'll put some of our olive oil out for people to add themselves. It's all plated. With the meat itself, just sautéed spinach with garlic. I have both the Caprese and spinach recipes in the recipe binder. They are so easy, the students don't need to do them with me, but I do need some help now. While I finish the antipasto and get the steaks ready to go on the grill, could you wash the spinach leaves—and cut off any stems? Once that's done, cooking it won't take any time at all."

Sautéed fresh spinach, especially the new young leaves, was a standby of Faith's (see recipe, page 236). Washing it took longer than cooking it; it would literally be done in minutes. She liked to squeeze a little lemon on top of hers, as well. They could put some wedges out.

She had barely put an apron on when the Culvers and Olivia came rushing into the kitchen.

"What are you making? Did we miss anything?" Sally was panting slightly and her face was red from haste, sangria, or both.

Francesca explained what they were planning and asked Olivia to cut up some fresh strawberries to use as a garnish for the panna cotta and some to boil for a quick coulis while she brought the antipasto down to the others. The Culvers and Faith made short work of washing the spinach. They'd wait to mince the garlic until just before they were ready to sauté it.

"What next?" Faith asked when Francesca returned.

"Not much. Sandro and Maurizio have their oil and cloves of garlic prepared for the *bruschetta* down by the grill. All we need to do is cut up these loaves of bread. They would be offended if we added a topping to their oil, like herbs, or even a little cheese."

"I like to experiment with different ones—vegetable purees, cured meats, even shrimp—but I'm looking forward to eating the real thing, plain and simple," Faith said.

Hattie had her pad out and was taking down Faith's every word.

"You need to tell me more about what to put on top of the *bruschetta,* but I have a question first." She paused for effect. "Now we love our beef, but what makes this kind so gawdalmighty special? I've been hearing about it ever since we stepped off the plane!"

"I can tell you," Francesca said, "but why don't we join the others and start the *bruschetta,* so everyone can hear? It really is whatever-that-word-was special."

The sky was still quite light, but the coals were sending up sparks, which would be more dramatic as the evening wore on. The two young men from the olive mill grabbed the bread from Francesca, and Sandro proceeded to instruct the class on the proper way to make *bruschetta.*

"Listen, *bambini,* this is the true Tuscan, and only, method. First"—he placed slices on the grill—"we char the bread lightly on each side, or more if you like a little taste of the fire."

It didn't take long and he transferred the slices to a tray.

"All of you take a piece of garlic and rub one side with the cut clove. Put some muscle into it!" Sandro said. "And now the best part—pour our *favoloso* oil on top and eat it right away!"

The oil was indeed fabulous and Faith knew it was running down her chin, but she didn't care. All she wanted was more—immediately.

While everyone was merrily preparing the *bruschetta,* much in the manner of overgrown Boy and Girl Scouts around a campfire, Francesca asked Gianni to tell everyone about *Bistecca alla Fiorentina.* The explanation, and preparation, were apparently his domain.

He stood on the low wall next to the grill, silhouetted against the horizon, speaking seriously—a culinary sibyl.

"You may have seen photos of the Chianina breed, one of the oldest in the world. We have recorded descriptions of them going back many thousands of years."

"I'm beginning to think that everything food-related started here," Jack called out. "The grapes, olives, now the beef!"

"Ah, now you begin to understand and appreciate who we are, the importance of our past," Gianni said. "But back to the Chianina. They are pure white with a black tail, the switch, and are not just big, but gigantic! One male can weigh as much as three thousand pounds and stands almost six feet tall, taller if he is a *castrato.*"

Jack interrupted again. He was in a very good mood. Faith reminded herself she had yet to discover what Tom and Sky were doing in the garden shed earlier. Would Jack be so jovial if he'd seen them?

"Do those Chianina bellow at a higher pitch than the rest of the herd?"

Gianni joined the general laughter, relaxing his stance for the moment. "I will ask my friend who raises them near Arezzo, in the Val di Chiana region, which gives them their name. Besides their history, the way we prepare them is key. We will be grilling them over very hot coals. First we sear them close to the heat to get a nice mark, then we raise the grill slightly, flip the meat, seasoning the steaks with salt and pepper. Nothing else. For rare, the only way I will permit you to eat this beef, it will take in total, ten to twelve minutes."

Wait for it, wait for it, Faith told herself. And bam, it came.

"Roderick and I do not eat bloody meat," Constance said, and possibly the use of the word referred both to the British expletive and appearance of the dish. "You will have to cook ours longer."

Gianni took it in stride. "This meat has been aged for twenty-one days, so it will not be bloody even when rare. You can try a taste, and if you insist I will cook yours longer, but I know what a fine appreciation for food you have, so I think it will be to your liking."

Constance looked slightly placated and said something that sounded like "harrumph" but didn't object further.

"When in Rome, dear lady," Luke said and that was all that was needed.

Constance flashed him a toothy smile. "Well, we might just try a small piece."

A few hours later, everyone had tried everything except dessert, and there was an unspoken consensus that waiting a bit to make room for it was desirable. The steaks had possibly been the best Faith had ever tasted—incredibly tender and buttery, a superb beefy flavor. She knew some ranchers in Texas were raising the breed and she was sure that her butcher in Cambridge, Ron Savenor, could get some for her. A treat for a special celebration. But now she had something else to think about.

Francesca had urged everyone to linger at the table that had been set up outdoors for the meal. Mario was clearing. Sandro and Maurizio were telling jokes and threatening to sing some of their favorites from Puccini.

"I'll come help unmold the panna cotta," Faith said and followed Francesca indoors before she could object. Once in the kitchen she kept going, saying "I'll be right back" as she went out the rear door. Mario could help Francesca with the dessert.

There was no time to waste. Faith had been running through her plan all afternoon, and she had to go now. She only hoped Luke was like the Rossis, who, when the Nashes had asked how they might get in if they were out late, mentioned they never locked their doors and didn't have an alarm system. "By the time anyone came, the robbers would be long gone," Gianni had said.

She ran down the drive. When they'd arrived on Sunday, Francesca had pointed out several bicycles for the use of guests by the quarters occupied by the Rossis and Mario. Faith had checked to make sure the bikes were still there earlier, and they had been. She grabbed the closest and as they say, riding one was, well, just like riding one. She sped off, switching on the headlamp once she was away from the house. Luke's wasn't far, but it would have taken too long to walk there and back. During conversation at dinner about employment in Italy, she had managed to discover that his housekeeper didn't live in, a topic she'd introduced in the hope of finding out this crucial piece of information.

The fear of discovery was pumping adrenaline through her body. She soon reached her destination and wheeled the bike out of sight in the back of the house. The door they had used at lunch yielded, and she was in.

The house seemed even grander at night. The only sounds she heard were the ticking of a clock somewhere and her own heart beating. Luke had left a few lights on and she had no trouble finding her way to his library. She opened the door and walked in, leaving her flats in the tiled hall to avoid leaving any traces of the outdoors on the carpet.

The moon had risen, but she didn't linger to look at the view out the large windows, moving swiftly instead toward his desk. Nothing had been moved. She grabbed the notebook. Freddy's notebook. A Moleskine with the top corner worn off and the wine stain squarely in the center of the cover. As she retraced her steps, she slipped off the elastic that had kept the book closed and opened it eagerly. She turned the first page, then the next, and the next—more rapidly with each one.

They were all blank.

CHAPTER 8

Faith didn't realize she'd finally gotten to sleep until a hand clamped tightly over her mouth awakened her. She struggled for breath and tried to scream as she sought to identify her attacker in the dim morning light. The shutters they had closed over the windows before finally going to bed last night were preventing all but a few rays from seeping in. Just as she was about to push the person away and connect a punch, a voice whispered, "Sssh," in her ear. It was a voice she knew. A familiar voice. It was Francesca's

"Come quick. I need you."

Faith slipped out of bed and followed Francesca out into the hall. "What's going on?" She assumed not much. It was only a little after six o'clock. Help with breakfast? Or the day's plans?

Francesca's words tumbled out in a panic.

"Olivia came down to the kitchen to tell me that there was a *serpe*, a snake, in her bathtub. I told her I was sorry and I would come get it out. That it was certainly not a harmful one. She told me she was sure it wasn't and would have taken it outside herself, except it was dead in an odd way—the head chopped off and left next to it! She wanted me to see it."

"The cat? You have one, right? Or some other predator?"

Francesca nodded. "I told her that and went to clean it up, but I was feeling uneasy. Oh, Faith, I checked your bath before I woke you now and there is one in your tub, too! Exactly the same! The head cut off and put next to it."

Faith gasped.

"Who could be doing such a thing?" Francesca was twisting her hands together, an agonized expression on her face. "We have to check the other baths and get rid of any more before the others see one. I can't tell Gianni. It would make him too nervous. He is already worried that we will fail."

And, thought Faith, this is just the kind of story that would cause Cucina della Rossi to go under if it got out. The snake, probably a nonvenomous grass snake, common in the area, would become a black mamba, and the decapitation, dismemberment or worse.

"Let's think. Since you slipped in here, you have the master key for the rooms with you, right?"

"Yes. But what excuse can I give for waking them up?"

"First let's get a trash bag to put the snakes in and then I'll think of something." They got some bags and paper towels, and as an afterthought, Faith grabbed a pair of rubber kitchen gloves.

"Everyone is most likely still sound asleep," she said. "You'll knock and explain that you need to do a quick check on the hot water in the bathroom. That there might be a problem. You dispose of any snakes, rinse the tub, and tell them it's fine. I'll wait in the hall."

She wasn't sure why she thought Francesca might need backup, but it seemed like a good idea.

They returned upstairs. Francesca took a deep breath and started to knock on the Russos' door. Faith grabbed her hand.

"Wait! Listen," she whispered.

The snores coming from the room were so loud it was a wonder they hadn't woken everyone up. The two women started to giggle—nerves, plus the noise was truly comical, a human buzz saw.

"It's the two of them," Faith said, again softly, although there was little reason to think anything short of a bomb going off would wake the Russos. "We'll both go in. If by some slim chance they do wake up, you can give your speech about the hot water and I'll climb out the bathroom window onto the ledge. Is it like ours?"

Faith always liked to have a plan, an escape plan. Francesca could come around with a ladder if need be.

"Yes—and you are okay to pick up the *serpe*?"

"Snakes, yes; mice, no."

They were in and out in under a minute.

And there had been another decapitated serpent in the bath.

It was a typical grass snake, very thin and long—at least three feet. With its dark rings, including the bright yellow one just behind its severed head, it looked much more dangerous than it was. Had Faith not known what it was, it would have caused her more than a moment's consternation—she'd have run out of the room screaming. Using the gloves, she'd accomplished her task swiftly and left the oblivious Russos in the Land of Nod.

"Now Sky and Jack," Faith said, doubting they would hear any snoring, predicting something more in the nature of panting.

Francesca put her ear to the door. "Too thick. I can't hear anything."

Faith stepped to the side and Francesca knocked. After a moment, Jack called out, "Yes, what is it?"

Francesca did her number, leaving the door slightly open. Faith thought it sounded convincing, and in a few minutes, Francesca was out in the hall again. "Another one?" Faith asked.

"Yes! Someone must hate us very much! What am I going to do!"

"For now, get the last ones, if there are any, and then we need to dispose of the one in our room. For the rest of the day, and what remains of the week, we'll be keeping a very close eye on everyone until we can figure out who our Madame Defarge is."

"How could someone get into the rooms? I keep my key in a drawer in the kitchen pantry, out of sight."

Faith decided now was the time to tell her the Rossis had to come up with more secure room locks, although she didn't tell her how Faith had found this out.

"You can replace them before the next group comes. Tell Gianni I suggested it. And meanwhile, carry the master key with you or put it someplace secure in the other house."

They had arrived outside the Culvers' door.

"Just do what you did with Sky and Jack. It will be fine," Faith reassured Francesca, who was beginning to look pale. It *wasn't* all right, but she had to get her friend in and out of this room with her grisly find plus one more, the Nashes'—and that could pose a challenge.

She knocked and Faith heard a sleepy voice say, "Come on in, y'all." It could have been either Hattie or Sally.

Francesca went inside and Faith heard the voice say, "Speak quietly if you don't mind. Sally has to get her eight hours or she's as mean as a snake."

The bag for the *serpi,* gloves, and other removal implements were in a larger canvas satchel slung over Francesca's shoulder. Peeking through the door hinge, Faith watched it slip to the ground as Francesca looked startled and appeared about to say something. Faith needed to do something quick. She darted into the room.

"Sorry, but I was passing and saw the door open. Is everything all right? I was on my way downstairs to find you, Francesca. I think there's something wrong with the hot water."

The relief on her friend's face was palpable.

"I was just about to tell Hattie that. I don't think it's every room, but I will check this one and then look at yours."

Sally snorted and rolled over but didn't wake. Hattie held a finger to her lips. Both women were firm believers in hairnets and liberal applications of face cream. Hattie was also wearing a chinstrap. Beauty did not come without effort. Faith smiled and went back out.

"Phew," Francesca breathed out, closing the door behind her. "That was close. I thought she was talking about the snake in the *bagno*."

"I know. That's why I went in. 'Mean as a snake' is an expression. In this case, Sally would be in a bad mood if she didn't get enough sleep."

Francesca looked dubious.

They had come to the Nashes' room. The last hurdle.

"She'll be very upset at being waked up. But imagine what she would be like if she sees the *serpe*! You don't think she has, do you?" Francesca said.

"There are few things in life that we can be sure of, but this is one. If Constance Nashe saw a snake several feet long in her bath, dead or alive, the entire village would hear her shrieks."

No one answered Francesca's first knock—or the second. Reluctantly, she opened the door and walked in.

"But they are not here!"

Faith went into the room. The bed had been slept in, and unlike Olivia, and the Russos also, the Nashes were not tidy. Clothing was strewn around, and evidently both Roderick and Constance liked to eat in bed—candy wrappers and other empty packaging was mounded on their nightstands next to used glasses from the bathroom. Road maps scattered on the table by the window attested to their wanderlust.

Francesca headed straight to the bath while Faith stood watch, and they were able to leave almost immediately with yet another headless reptile. Afterward they cleaned up in the Fairchilds' room and, carrying their gruesome burden, walked outside to get rid of the remains.

Faith had had a great many unusual experiences in her life, but this one would be hard to top.

And where were the Nashes? Up at dawn for a constitutional, what ho? She looked out the window; their car was there, so they must be on foot.

Tom was still sound asleep. Unusual for him, but it had been another late night. He was going to have a hard time readjusting to his Aleford decidedly noncontinental schedule—one that found him in bed before ten and any phone, or other, calls after eight meant an emergency. She got dressed and decided to go downstairs to have her breakfast in the kitchen. She was hungry—and needed coffee, much coffee. She also wanted to be around to provide silent moral support for her friend when Gianni came for his *colazione*. The episode had been profoundly disturbing—and disgusting. The question was who had the stomach to do such a thing in the first place? Someone who didn't have a problem with snakes, clearly. The big question was not so much how as why?

Excerpt from Faith Fairchild's travel journal:

Snakes. All I'll need is the word to remember this morning whenever I go back and read this journal, which is not the one I thought I'd be keeping. Took a lot of pictures yesterday at the wineries and the olive mill, so those will have to serve instead of writing here about them. Before I left, Ursula gave me a big leather-bound, very fancy album for photos of the trip with spaces for descriptions and she'll be sure to ask to see it, so unlike every other trip and the best resolutions, I'm going to actually use it, or forever feel guilty. Not that Ursula would ever intend this. She and Pix, who I sometimes think is a clone of her mother, not simply the offspring, religiously keep albums of all their trips near and far. I'm rambling. Don't want to think about the snakes.

Or the notebook.

Travel is disorienting, yes, but could I be going mad? Freddy was writing in it when we joined him at the restaurant in Rome and the page was almost filled. The page opposite was completely filled. I can see his writing now. Tiny, almost microscopic. And the pages were past the middle of the book, so presumably those were filled, too. He was writing with a fine-tipped Sharpie-type pen. Not his fountain pen, come to think of it. Afraid of blots in his copybook? I can hear him saying this.

I can't tell Tom about the blank book. Aside from breaking into someone's house, although the door was open, he already thinks I've imagined the whole thing, and this would clinch it.

Have I?

No. I saw it! And what I saw last night wasn't the same book.

Why did I put it back? It felt almost as if it was burning my hand. I just wanted to get rid of it, but I should have taken it, then I'd be able to see for sure that the wear and stain had been recent. Someone faking a new one to look like Freddy's. It has to be Luke, Jean-Luc—whoever he is. But it still could be any of the rest of them. Everyone scattered when we got back from the vineyards and the mill. Plus later someone could have done what I did and snuck in. Luke was here all the time, or was he? Maybe he went home for a while before the barbecue. A quick shave in that fantasy bathroom? (Remember fish tank bathtub and the rest. Write more about it at home. Think I'll be doing a lot of catching up after the fact. Too much else going on here.)

I'm by the pool, but sitting in the shade. My eyes may have been playing enough tricks on me without adding sunspots. Everyone must still be at breakfast. It's very nice to have some time alone.

Can't really enjoy it though. Why was Olivia up so early? Well, she could be an early riser and wanted a bath. And certainly made of stern stuff. No hysterics when she found the snake. How does she fit into all this? How do any of them? Now if the snakes had been shot . . .

After breakfast we're leaving for Montepulciano, a longish drive, and other than Florence, the big outing of the week. Then back here for pasta making. Can honestly tell the Rossis they have a success. Just so long as the cream doesn't turn again and the snakes stay in the grass.

Francesca's an incredible actress. Gianni came in for his colazione while we were having ours together, and there was no way he could have sensed from her that anything was wrong. But then she'd been able to pull this sort of performance off all those years ago in Manhattan. She fooled me. Is she playing a role again?

Damn, Sky is coming to soak up some rays. Wish I looked this good in a bikini. Must remember to ask Tom what they were doing in the shed. Cannot believe have not done so yet. Cannot believe other more important things keep getting in the way. Husband possibly fooling around should shove all else aside.

Faith closed the book and tucked it into her bag. To keep writing seemed a little antisocial, and besides, she had some questions for the golden girl from the Golden State.

"Beautiful day," Faith said. Start slow.

"Every day has been. We're so lucky."

Sky sat in the chaise next to Faith and stretched her extremely shapely legs out. Looking at her face, though, Faith thought that the woman didn't look as if she was feeling lucky. She looked tense, almost fearful. It was the same expression Faith had noted earlier. And glancing at her hands, Faith saw that Sky had been picking at her cuticles—definitely not a pageant queen habit.

"As you know, we're friends of the Rossis and I hope you've been enjoying the week so far," Faith said. "They want suggestions from us, especially as we're their first group, about things they can do to make Cucina della Rossi better."

"I can't imagine how." The woman sounded sincere. "They

seem to have thought of everything. The place is great. Our room is extremely comfortable, and we have a gorgeous view. I wasn't sure about a cooking class, but Jack is such a foodie. Now I'm thankful he pushed. I'll definitely use what I've learned."

"I'm glad. That's what I think, too, but I'm biased. After the course will you be going back to Rome or on to someplace else?"

Sky shook her head. "We could only snatch this week. I'm excited to go to Montepulciano today because we'll be seeing more of Italy, but mostly because I'm a huge fan of *Twilight*—the books and the movies."

Faith had heard of the series by Stephenie Meyer—you'd had to have been living in a cave not to, although that might have been an appropriate location, given the books' vampire and werewolf characters. She knew that although they were YAs, adults were also big fans of the romantic series—true love with more than a little horror thrown in. But she had no idea what they had to do with Montepulciano.

"I haven't read them, but I thought the books took place in Washington State," she said.

"Mainly, but scenes in *Twilight Saga: New Moon* were filmed in Montepulciano. It was supposed to be Volterra. I don't know why they couldn't shoot there, but anyway there's an evil vampire coven called the Volturi who live there, and Bella, that's the human girl who becomes a vampire to be with the vampire she loves, Edward, has to go there to stop Edward from killing himself, because he thinks she's dead. Really dead. It's before she becomes a vampire. Oh, you just have to read the books. Anyway, when I heard we'd be going to the actual spot where they filmed, I was thrilled."

The woman shed ten years as she gushed, and Faith glimpsed the teen she must have been. Then she put her grown-up face back on, and once more Faith wondered what could be worrying Sky. She was picking at her nails and looking toward the house as if she was expecting someone. Jack? Tom?

"I'm going to get ready. They want to leave at nine," Faith said. "Francesca is packing a picnic, and we'll buy wine, the famous Montepulciano Vino Nobile, when we get there for tonight's dinner."

"Do you think she needs any help?" Sky asked, clearly hoping for an answer in the negative.

"Mario is there, and she's probably finished by now. If she does, I'll let you know, but I'm sure she's fine."

When she got inside, Faith looked back out. Sky was standing up, peering anxiously at the house. She was definitely waiting for someone.

"We know the way to Montepulciano," Constance had said firmly before they got in their car and drove off. No one had shed any tears. Sky and Terry Russo, another *Twilight* fan, were sitting next to each other in the van. Faith could hear snatches of their conversation—"I always liked Jacob" and "Don't worry, honey, childbirth isn't like that." This last remark from Terry was truly puzzling, and Faith made a note to ask the Millers' daughter, Samantha, to explain the reference. She'd gone through a Bella phase.

That left Len and Jack, who seemed to be bonding over golf. Olivia was seated with Luke across from the Culvers, who were uncharacteristically quiet. Olivia and Luke were getting along quite nicely. Faith wished she could hear what they were talking about so intently. He was much older, but May/December, or rather *maggio/dicembre,* romances had been known to work out well. Look at Carlo Ponti and Sophia Loren. Luke was leaning close to Olivia, but then he may just be wanting to see out the window better.

Everyone was accounted for, which left Tom and Faith herself. She'd deliberately picked the seats in the rear. It was a long ride, and he'd have plenty of time to explain himself.

Except he didn't, or rather wouldn't.

She'd spoken very calmly, merely stating a fact.

"I was looking out our window yesterday morning and saw Sky and you coming out of the shed in the garden. Or to be more precise, she came out first and then you did."

He hadn't responded and she'd ramped things up—"Looking for a rake? A shovel maybe?"

This had done it. Even more calmly, he'd answered, "I'm sorry, but I can't share this with you."

"You mean it's one of those times?"

"One of those times" meant that someone had told something to Tom as the Reverend Thomas Fairchild. It was one of the drawbacks to being married to a man of the cloth. You never got to hear the good stuff.

"Let's enjoy the day, okay?" he said.

Which translated as "Subject Closed."

Faith wished she'd brought something to read. Something about vampires maybe.

As soon as they pulled into the Montepulciano information center's parking lot, Faith quickly made her way off the van. She'd had a lot of coffee for breakfast, and it had been a long trip. She hoped the office would have a restroom or would direct her to one close by.

"Be right back," she called to Tom over her shoulder.

There was no one at the desk and she didn't see any signs indicating a lavatory. The only occupants were a couple examining a rack of postcards, which reminded her that she had to mail the ones she'd written to various people, especially the kids. A slight pang of guilt hit as she realized Ben and Amy had been far from her thoughts of late, but it passed as she reminded herself that if anything were wrong, she'd have heard. It was also unlikely that her two children, very much wrapped up in their own lives, were overly missing their parents.

The couple was speaking a language she didn't know. It sounded like Italian, but she recognized some French words. A dialect? She was about to leave—there must be portable toilets outside, since no facilities were evident here—when the man turned around and she realized it was Roderick Nashe, with Constance by his side.

"Hi. We just pulled in and I was looking for a restroom. I didn't know you spoke, what was that, some kind of Italian?"

If looks could freeze, Faith would have instantly become a Popsicle. "When I was a girl"—Constance seemed to be trying out for the role of Miss Jean Brodie—"it was considered impolite to eavesdrop. What you may have heard was our own patois, a little pet language. There is a restroom that you enter from outside. The key is on the desk, clearly marked. It is cleaner than one would have expected. Come, Roderick. We will join the others."

The woman really is insufferable, Faith thought as she grabbed the key and followed them outdoors. And again she wondered why they had signed up for the course when they clearly preferred to go off on their own, although they wouldn't want to skip this. The Rossis had arranged a Vino Nobile tasting at Contucci Cantina right on the Piazza Grande in the Palazzo Contucci. Faith was pretty sure Roderick would never turn down a free glass of anything bibulous, and Constance no doubt wanted to be able to boast that she'd visited parts of the Renaissance building not normally on view to the public, which the Rossis had arranged.

As Faith rejoined the group, Gianni was speaking. "It's a short walk to where we'll be having our picnic. Francesca will lead some of you, and I'll lead the rest. We'll be passing by the church of Sant'Agnese, which you may want to visit later to see the Simone Martini Madonna."

Feeling vaguely like a nursery school class, as if she should be holding on to a clothesline, Faith trailed after Gianni on the narrow sidewalk as typical Italian traffic—tiny cars, scooters, bicycles, trucks, buses—went speeding by. It was another perfect day. Not a cloud in the sky and not too hot. They passed a combination Upim—the very affordable department store chain—and Conad grocery. Maybe she'd be able to lure Tom in with the promise of hardware. He seemed to be able to spend hours contemplating lightbulbs, nails, screws, and especially tools at Home Depot, so an Italian version would be a treat. She could check out the food and maybe find fennel pollen or some other spices to take back.

Gianni opened a weather-beaten wooden door in a high brick wall, and suddenly they were transported into a *giardino segreto*. You would never have suspected a paradise of lush grass, flowering shrubs, and trees was hidden behind the walls, which muffled the sounds of the outside world. Birds were chirping, bees humming, a few butterflies fluttered prettily. Faith half expected them to turn into Disney-like creations and start singing aloud.

"This house and garden belong to a relative of Francesca's father," Gianni explained. "And they are happy for us to use it. Unfortunately they are not able to welcome you today, as they had to be somewhere else, but please come in, and while we eat we can talk a little about Montepulciano. We have picked it as one of our destinations not because of this nice spot for a picnic, although that may be reason enough, but because it has an interesting history and beautiful buildings. The center is also closed to cars, so you can stroll and imagine what it was like before the invention of these useful but unattractive necessities."

Everyone pitched in to spread the ground cloths, and Faith noticed both she and Francesca seemed to be making sure no snakes were slithering underneath. Faith immediately decided to get Tom to share so she could taste both the mortadella, *finocchiona,* and pecorino panino and the one with roasted eggplant, zucchini, and *robiola*. She'd helped Francesca and Mario finish making them, as well as others with tempting salamis and one featuring huge portabella mushrooms. There were also an assortment of olives, a salad with tiny, thinly sliced artichokes, and another with tomatoes and basil. Mario had fetched the fresh rolls from the village early that morning. To go along with the meal, Francesca had packed bottles of sparkling and still water, wine for those who wished, and to finish, fresh fruit and almond biscotti.

Half-reclining in the fashion of the ancient Romans, Tom said, "Tell us about Montepulciano, then. It's so much fun to say." He repeated the name of the town, clearly enjoying the lilting syllables.

Gianni grinned. "Like everywhere else around here, the Etruscans were the first inhabitants, or I should say the first we know for sure. One of the things you may have time to explore are the underground tunnels, some of which connect to grottoes that were Etruscan tombs. The tunnels once were a network among the palazzos and other buildings. Now they are for the wine, and also in some, you'll see cheeses aging.

"We'll go into town by way of the Porta al Prato near where we parked and where we'll meet later. Here you will see the first sign of the Medicis—their crest cut into the stone. You always know the Medici one. It has a varying number of balls—seven during Cosimo's time. When painted, they are red on gold, and I leave it to you to decide what they mean. There are theories about what they represent ranging from dents in a shield to pawnbroker's coins and also the name itself, 'Medici,' which translates as 'doctors,' their ancient profession. The balls in that case are thought to be cupping glasses. You know them?"

"They were used both in the United States and England, too, and even now as an alternative medical treatment," Hattie Culver said. "Although I think they are famous for doing more harm than good, burning the patients or causing them to bleed to death." She shuddered.

"There are also some ruder interpretations of the Medici balls,"

Luke interjected. "But I think that you should skip that part, Gianni."

Everyone laughed and Gianni continued with a quick rundown of Montepulciano's greatest hits, urging them not to miss the interior of the duomo with its beautiful triptych by Bartolo and the famous well, so often photographed opposite the cathedral on the Piazza Grande with again the Medici arms flanked by Florentine lions and Poliziano griffins, symbol of the famous philosopher and tutor to the Medici children. Faith thought it was rather lovely that there should have been a tribute to a teacher, the equivalent of an edifice on Aleford's green honoring someone like Mrs. Fine, a longtime middle school teacher, adored by students, parents, and colleagues alike.

It was so pleasant in the garden that everyone moved slowly, putting some of the food away and then sitting back down to eat one more fig or munch one more biscotti. Faith looked at the bucolic scene. It could have been from any number of Italian films—a rustic feast—and like those films there was much going on beneath the jovial surface. Who was trying to destroy the Rossis' business—since what else could be behind an act like this morning's *serpi*? Someone here, or someone creeping in from the village or elsewhere? In Florence there had been commedia dell'arte masked street performers, and for an instant she pictured the people in front of her hiding behind those intricately sculpted disguises. Masks. Jack was concealing something, so was Sky. The Russos most likely their own misery. Olivia? Many possibilities. Luke as well. The Nashes? The only couple that seemed to be exactly what they were was the aunt/niece one. Except there was that odd remark she'd overheard in Rome . . . Faith's head was spinning, and she moved over closer to Tom. Here was certainty. Usually.

The Rossis handed out maps and told the group the time to meet for the tasting.

"You will get a good workout," Francesca said. "The streets are steep, also narrow. Do not miss the view from the Piazza San Francesco. It is my favorite—and not just for the name. There are also many places to buy ceramics. I know you were interested in this, Faith. They will ship, as will other shops. Montepulciano has been an artistic center during its whole history." She started to laugh. "It is also known for the Bravio delle Botti. Again you will all have to come back to see this. You know about the Palio in Siena, but here the *contrade*—the sections of the town, the neighborhoods, I think you might say—do not race horses, although the tradition started this way back in the fourteenth century. In the twentieth it changed to *botti,* the big wooden wine barrels as a way to celebrate—and publicize—the wine! Anyway, two men on each team roll a *botte* about a kilometer uphill along the streets leading to the duomo. They train hard for this. The competition is held on the last Sunday in August, but the celebrations go for the whole week before. There are postcards and souvenir books that show it better than I am describing it—all the costumes and each *contrada*'s banners."

"I'm beginning to think we should just move here for all these festivals," Jack said. "We certainly don't have anything approaching this back home. What's the prize for the winners?"

"The *bravio,* a banner painted with the image of San Giovanni Decollato, John the Baptist, Montepulciano's patron saint."

"You mean they do all that for a piece of cloth!" Jack said.

"Hey, buddy, it's a holy article and they're bringing honor to their *contrada*." Len was bristling. The subject was obviously a touchy one, close to his heart. "That's exactly it. Honor," Francesca said hastily.

Sally had been writing down what they had eaten for lunch. She was clearly adding the *Bravio* information. "What's '*decollato*' mean?"

"I know that one," Tom said. "'Beheaded,' possibly because

Salome demanded it on a silver platter and her father, Herod, was a parent who needed to learn how to say no. Anyway, 'decollation' is another word for 'decapitation.'"

Faith and Francesca looked at one another. There had been quite enough *decollations* for one day. Both started folding the cloths, and soon the group returned to the van to stow the remnants of the picnic before starting up the steep main street. It had gotten considerably hotter, and Faith was glad she had both her sunglasses and visor.

They hadn't progressed very far before she heard the hour strike and, looking up, saw a life-size metal figure of Pulcinella strike a bell on a tall clock tower. Pulcinella, the commedia dell'arte character, crafty, mean, even vicious, dressed in white with a black mask—the representation of life and death. Was everything today going to be fraught with meaning?

Gianni pointed upward. "This is the medieval Torre di Pulcinella. You will see many articles for sale reproducing this not so very nice fellow all over Montepulciano."

They lost the Culvers to a shop with a display of handbags with vintage Vespa logos in the window. Others fanned out into the steep side streets.

Terry and Sky were determinedly staying on course, making their way straight to the Palazzo Comunale, the town hall, and the Piazza Grande, where the *Twilight* movie had been filmed. Faith wanted to start there, too, in the duomo, and Francesca had mentioned a shop selling pottery near it that was her favorite.

It didn't take long to reach the piazza, and it was delightfully cool inside the cathedral. Faith and Tom sat in silence and then took time to look at the artwork. A large Della Robbia baptismal font drew Faith's eye. She had always loved the deep blue and white glaze of the master's ceramic bas-reliefs, but it was the bright green, yellow, and orange fruit and flowers encircling the pieces that made them her favorite.

"Let's go find that pottery shop," she said softly. If she kept to one place and didn't spend too long looking, she could get him to shop, an activity he normally avoided like the plague, filling sartorial needs from L.L.Bean and clerical sources online and leaving all other purchases to her. When it came time for her birthday, anniversary, and Christmas, he went with Sam Miller to the Jewelers Building on Washington Street in Boston. Sam's father had been a jeweler and it was in the blood. Faith had often blessed the happy chance that placed the parsonage next door to the Millers' house, or vice versa.

The potter at BAE ceramiche was throwing pots on a wheel, and a young woman, whom they learned was named Roberta Rocchi, was sitting close by, beautifully decorating the ones that had been fired. There was plenty to occupy Tom, including a basement down a short flight that Roberta told them had a window in the floor looking into part of an Etruscan grotto complete with some ancient pots. Tom eagerly went to look, giving Faith plenty of time to buy a large platter decorated with red poppies, sheaves of wheat, a line of cypresses, and the hill town itself, as well as similar patterns on other pieces that she would give as gifts. Meeting the people who had made the pieces gave them special meaning. She also bought a reproduction of the Medici crest in glowing scarlet and gold for Tom to hang on his study wall. In her eyes, her husband *was* a Renaissance man.

"I love this place," she exclaimed out on the street, which was little more than a sidewalk, after arranging shipment. "And not just because we're going to have that lovely platter. But the colors of the stone—the houses glow—and everyone has a green thumb. I want some of those pale lavender geraniums like the ones in that window box and the deep red roses climbing up the wall over there! Maybe we could try a climbing variety in Maine on a trellis outside the cottage."

Faith Fairchild was not known for her gardening skills. In fact, she had even managed to kill some fake flowers—realistic silk ones a friend gave her that Faith, thinking them fresh, promptly put in water, spritzing them as well, which she'd heard made blooms last longer. But today anything seemed possible, and she was ready to reproduce the entire White Flower Farm catalog.

"Oh, Tom, look at this view!"

They had come to an opening between houses; the panorama was spectacular. Small white petals from a fruit tree were blowing toward them, like rice at a wedding.

"We're on the top of the world," Tom said, putting his arms around his wife from behind, holding her close.

They spent the next hour before they were due to meet for the wine tasting strolling up and down the streets. Faith found a whole new collection of door knockers to photograph, elaborate ones with the Medici crest and others with smiling bearded faces that looked remarkably like some of the men they were passing. They stopped for coffee at a charming place, Al Tocco, on Via San Donato, and sat outside, contentedly watching the pedestrians pass by—mothers pushing strollers, older people out for a walk, and a few business types clutching laptop cases in a hurry. There was an art gallery with striking photos on display across from them that she wanted to check out.

"I could live here," Faith said. "Couldn't you find a church nearby?"

"Not sure about that—plenty of churches, but perhaps not the same denomination—but if it will make you happy, I'll try. Montepulciano could get pretty crowded in the summer, though."

They were ahead of tourist season, Gianni had told them, and there had been no sign of the hordes that he told them would soon flood the streets during the daytime. The Rossis planned to adjust the schedule to make the visit to the town a late afternoon one. Faith wanted to return immediately, imagining sitting in the long light before dusk at one of Al Tocco's small tables with a glass of

Prosecco, a few *crostini,* olives—how could she be hungry again? And wine? Which reminded her.

"Tom, we have to hurry. It's time for some Vino Nobile. We're not far."

Nothing was too far in Montepulciano, she noted, which was much of its charm. A small place where you knew everyone and everyone knew you. Wait, wasn't that Aleford? She was walking past an imposing stone building that a plaque identified as a *fortezza,* a fortress. It was surrounded by more of the vegetation she had come to expect—rich greens, cascades of blooms. Tufts of wildflowers, small daisies, and others had seeded themselves in the remnants of the old wall. It was a Medici fortress from the times when the town was caught up in the bloody rivalry between Siena and Florence. Aleford boasted no fortresses of any kind but did have an old wooden belfry that sounded the alarm on that famous day and year, surrounded by a few sad yews and not much else. The town had seen its share of rivalries—ones that pitted their football team against archenemies like Lexington each Thanksgiving—but nothing even vaguely fifteenth century. Unless you counted the pep rally bonfires, which would have made Savonarola proud.

After a tour of the Palazzo Contucci, which was designed by Sangallo, the man also responsible for the Porta al Prato and the well in the Piazza Grande, which Faith was beginning to feel was as familiar as the Boston Common, but infinitely more interesting, the group descended to the *cantina* far below the palace for a tasting.

Down, down they went on stone stairs worn smooth from centuries of use, passing a honeycomb of rooms on each level until finally they stopped at what Faith assumed must be the bottom and followed their guide through labyrinthine corridors with row upon row of *botti.* Not for the claustrophobic, Faith thought, enjoying the slightly musty fragrance of the wine cellar. Old presses and other antique tools were displayed on the walls. The low lighting suggested the torches used in bygone eras.

While they waited for everyone to catch up—Hattie, for one, moved a bit more slowly than the rest but had been proving she was up to anything—"Plan to get my money's worth for this new knee"—Faith found herself in an alcove with the Nashes. Searching for a polite topic of conversation, she asked them nicely, "Did you have a good walk this morning? We went the first day. Lovely to be out so early."

They regarded her with total astonishment.

"Walk, what walk?" Constance said. "Roderick and I never exercise before breakfast. Wreaks havoc with one's digestion."

There was no way to contradict them without revealing that she had been in their room and why.

"I thought I saw you. It must have been another couple."

"I'm sure it was," Constance said firmly. "Now I believe the guide is telling us about the wine we are to sample. Roderick."

He heeled, and they moved away from what was obviously a seriously deranged person.

The wine more than lived up to its noble appellation, Faith decided, swirling some in her mouth before swallowing. As before, some of the group was partaking more liberally than others. Olivia's glass was barely touched, nor was Constance's. Not so with all the other men, save Tom, although his cheeks were getting rosy. He was having fun. What a wonderful idea this trip had been, his idea. They should travel more on their own, now that the kids were older. But that also meant the kids would be off to college soon and the nest empty, so she needed to spend as much time as she could with them! What to do? It was all going so fast—this child rearing. Although Pix had assured her, sometimes more ruefully than others, that you are never finished rearing your children.

Faith spied what she thought was a room used to age cheese

and went to investigate. It was, and there was another one off it with even more shelves. Large rounds of pecorino were nestled on top of what looked like very large bay leaves. She'd have to ask Francesca about it. The cheese, made from sheep milk, was at different stages. There were fresh white rounds that she knew would be soft as butter inside and taste of the meadow. Others had an orange rind and some a russet one. One of the Parmesans at Baroni had been aged in wine, perhaps this had been, too? It was all she could do to keep from slicing into one or more with the small Swiss Army knife she carried. It had had to go in her checked suitcase for the flight, but she'd put it in her bag as soon as she'd unpacked in Rome. Besides a handy knife for picnics, there was the equally handy corkscrew.

She looked at her watch. Time to rejoin the group. She turned the way she had come and found herself in a room she didn't recall, one lined with barrels. She retraced her steps and was in a cheese room again. But this one had only a few on the shelves and they looked very aged, perhaps forgotten?

Feeling ridiculous—how could she get lost in such a short time?—she picked another corridor, and then another. Ah, there were stairs leading up at the end. It wasn't the way she'd come, but it would get her out of here.

The stairs led to a door. Faith opened it, expecting to see another flight in front of her.

Except she didn't.

It was one of those grottoes, a cave carved into the soft earth, the corners filled with pottery shards and small metal vessels. The door slammed behind her. Air currents from the surface. Quickly she went to open it again and go back down the stairs.

Except the door didn't budge.

She was trapped in an Etruscan tomb.

CHAPTER 9

Of course she would soon be missed.

And then what? She tried to keep from panicking as she envisioned the search. They might imagine she had left the *cantina* and gone back to the pottery shop or for another cup of coffee. Failing to locate her at either of those places, the hunt would fan out all over Montepulciano and beyond. She tried to concentrate on taking deep breaths. There was plenty of air. The door had blown shut. Hadn't it?

But she was far underground. There weren't any ventilation shafts here. No wind either that could have moved the heavy door. So how did it close?

Faith had come full circle. Many years ago when Ben was an infant the two of them had been locked in a basement preserves closet by a deranged murderess. There had been little air there either. And no way out. All Aleford searched for them, and it had been the redoubtable Millicent Revere McKinley who had saved them, forever putting Faith uncomfortably in the woman's debt. Yet what she wouldn't give to see that interfering, overbearing pillar of several historical societies and the DAR come through the door now! The Revere family started out as Rivoires, French Huguenots. No Italian connection, and given Millicent's lifelong membership in the Cold Water Army it was extremely improbable that she would be anywhere near a wine cellar, whatever the country.

Her mind was wandering. She needed to focus. That other time she recalled going through the diaper bag she was carrying in search of anything that might save their lives. There had been diapers and all the accoutrements babies need and some other necessities for herself—lip gloss, blush, folding hairbrush, sandwich . . . Why was she reminiscing when she could be looking at what she had in the bag she was carrying now?

Nothing to eat—and because of that she was suddenly starving; a half-filled bottle of water—that was good, and she took a tiny sip; room key; updated version of old hairbrush; lip gloss again—when they found her body at least she'd look presentable; some euros; her American Express card—the slogan "Don't leave home without it" was extremely irritating at the moment; a tiny flashlight—Tom kept buying them for her, bless him; a pen; her journal—she could record the experience for posterity; antacid tablets; Tylenol; the camera—when the flashlight gave out she could use the flash for what exactly she wasn't sure, but it would be light anyway; Kleenex—she could blot her tears; a few neon-colored gelati spoons she thought the kids would like; and of course her trusty Swiss Army knife. She switched on the flashlight and opened the knife. The ancient door couldn't be a tight fit. She might be able to pry it open.

No such luck; the door *wasn't* a tight fit. Light was seeping in around the edges. But it was shut tight because it had been locked. From the outside. She could see the bolt. The door was not going to budge.

She sat down with her back against it.

She stood up and pounded on it.

"Help! Someone, help!"

What was it in Italian? French was *au secours,* but the Italian wasn't anything like that. Damn! She couldn't remember.

"Help!" She screamed louder and banged harder.

After several minutes, she sat back down on the cold dirt. It was hopeless.

The caves were carved from tufa, the limestone the town perched on. Even if she had something more sturdy than the plastic ice cream spoons, something like a backhoe, all she would be doing was digging deeper into the mountain. The grottoes were connected by a series of tunnels, but this one was obviously at the end of one or some sort of way station. The only thing she could do was wait. She turned on the flashlight and looked at her watch. The group would be gathering back at the van in twenty minutes.

She would never make it.

What she had to do was to establish a routine. Like prisoners or people stranded on a desert island. Sip water, stand up, stretch, bang wildly on door, and scream. Sit back down, lean against door.

"Bye, bye, Miss American Pie"—she couldn't get the song out of her head and found she was pounding in time to it.

Would Tom remarry? Of course he would. He was still young. Well, youngish. But she didn't want it to be anybody she knew. Anybody from Aleford particularly. And the kids couldn't call her "Mom." If she did get out of here alive, she would have to tell him this. He'd ventured once—marrying a native from the Big Apple, no McIntoshes please with all the flavor bred out these days—and he should do it again. Hope would find someone. She'd network. Hope! The hell with the roaming charges. She needed to call her sister. Now. Except the phone was back at the Rossis' and wouldn't work here anyway. The Rossis! Gianni had mentioned these grottoes. They would surely steer the searchers to the caves. Wouldn't they?

Maybe they'd think she'd been kidnapped. That happened in foreign places. Hitchcock's *The Man Who Knew Too Much,* only that was Morocco. Not all that far away though. Well, as Doris Day sang in the movie, "Que Sera, Sera."

She was beginning to feel a bit light-headed. She took a deep breath. Although, maybe that wasn't a good idea, shallow breaths so she wouldn't use up what oxygen there was? At least it was cool. Cold, in fact. Like the place it was. Now she couldn't get the "We Three Kings" Christmas carol of her head—the verse ending "Sealed in the stone cold tomb." She'd be very happy for a little frankincense to send up some smoke signals right now and hoped she'd be following stars in the sky again, shooting stars, "Star Light, Star Bright." Focus, focus, Faith! For a brief moment she was back in Aleford at the kitchen table helping Ben with his homework. Stay on task!

She got up, repeated the routine, and sat back down, leaning heavily against the door. It was the only solid thing around and oddly comforting. She felt herself falling backward and for an insane moment felt annoyed, which immediately changed to a feeling of extreme elation.

She was free!

She crawled out and stood upright on the stairs.

Notebooks with words that vanish. Locked doors that open themselves. Again, was she going mad? Had she simply imagined it was locked when she couldn't open it?

No. It had been secured. It was an old-fashioned mortise lock, and the bolt had been shot. Someone had turned the bolt to shut the door and someone—the same person?—had turned it to open it.

However compelling it was to find out, the point now was to get aboveground.

She went back down the stairs. At the bottom she heard footsteps coming from the corridor to the left and ran after them. As she increased her speed whoever was in front of her did also. Was it her rescuer? Someone who didn't want to be identified? Faith concentrated on keeping up and soon she was back in the tasting room—empty now. She easily found the way up to the piazza level, then took off down the treacherously steep street she'd climbed with Tom only a few hours earlier. Her heel caught on a cobblestone. For a moment she thought she was going to roll the whole stretch like one of those *botti* they raced with, but she regained her balance and took both shoes off, running the rest of the way barefoot. She headed straight toward the Porta al Prato and the parking lot where the van was parked. Tom, and the Rossis, must be going crazy with worry.

They weren't. In fact, the van was pulling out and Faith could see her husband sitting by the window, laughing.

She jumped in front of it waving frantically as Gianni stopped before pulling onto the main road. He looked completely surprised to see her. Francesca came out the front passenger door.

"Faith! But you were going back with the Nashes, who are staying longer. We thought you must want to do more shopping."

"I . . ." Out of breath and slightly in shock, Faith was having trouble finding the words. Something along the lines of "I've been buried alive?" Instead she asked, "Who told you I was going with the Nashes?"

Francesca looked puzzled. "We were all coming out of the Contucci Cantina and I'm not sure who it was. But you're here now and I'm glad you made it! We were waiting for several people, so didn't leave on time."

Faith wanted to pursue the matter further, but she could tell that Gianni was eager to get going. She'd wait until later.

Tom had been sitting next to Olivia. She immediately got up and moved to a place farther back, giving Faith her seat.

"Thank you," Faith said. She really, really wanted to sit next to her husband. It was all she could do to keep from throwing her arms around him and sobbing in relief.

The moment passed almost immediately as she remembered he apparently hadn't noticed she wasn't with them. The van was leaving. Why didn't he try to get it to wait for her?

"Honey," she said slowly, "didn't you wonder where I was? I almost got left behind." Now was not the time to go into detail.

"Someone said you were staying on and I figured you wanted to do some more browsing without me underfoot. We all left the tasting at the same time and the stairs were so narrow I thought you'd gone on ahead of me."

"Well, I didn't."

"Sorry, but everything's fine now." His expression clearly indicated "No worries." At all.

"Who said I was staying and going back with the Nashes?" Maybe Tom had the answer.

"Francesca told me."

No luck here. Yet she couldn't let the subject drop.

"Why on earth would you think I'd drive back with the Nashes? Spend all that time in the car with them?"

"It never occurred to me you wouldn't want to. What's wrong with them? I mean, they can be a little difficult, but no more than some of the others. And you're the one who's such an Anglophile, got me to like brussels sprouts, plus face it, Faith, I'm not the person who ordered the Diamond Jubilee commemorative mug that's sitting in the china closet." He gave her a playful poke and leaned over for a kiss.

Whatever energy remained from her precipitous dash down the streets of Montepulciano immediately began seeping from every pore. Faith felt very, very tired—and utterly baffled.

Walking into the kitchen to join the cheerful group in their aprons ready to make pasta, Faith felt decidedly out of synch. As soon as they'd returned from Montepulciano, she went to their room for what she hoped would be a nap. Tom followed her but left for the pool almost immediately while she was still deciding whether to tell him what had just happened or not. In the past, he'd tended to overreact to things like this. She hadn't mentioned the snakes either. Part of her was annoyed at his eagerness to go, and part of her was happy that he was so clearly enjoying what was a rare treat—yes, the leisure time, but even more the setting: a sparkling pool in an Italian villa under sunny skies. He wasn't in New England anymore. He did urge her to join him when she woke up and the kiss he gave her suggested he'd like to join her in bed. Suddenly she desperately wanted to make love, an act so very life affirming. She wanted to be transported away from all that had been occurring, safe in her husband's embrace, but the fact that he had changed into his trunks so quickly and was halfway out the door killed the mood.

She didn't sleep.

Feeling grouchy and weary, still shaken from what now seemed like an almost out-of-body experience—could she really have been trapped in the tomb?—the last thing she wanted to do was cook anything. Something on a plate, a glass of wine, and she was ready to call it a day. The glass of wine part was forthcoming. Gianni was pouring glasses of the Vino Nobile purchased earlier.

"We are going to be making *pici* (see recipe, p. 234), the pasta of Montepulciano, so it means we must also drink the wine of Montepulciano," Gianni said. "*Pici* is thicker than spaghetti and traditionally made without eggs. It holds the sauce very well. In Italia we say that we have three *picis*—the pasta; PCI, which is the Communist Party; and PCs, our computers! All pronounced the same."

"We will never eat if you don't stop with the jokes," Francesca said and addressed the group. "This time, no teams. Each person will be making *pici*. I want you to learn how easy it is so you will do it at home."

Sally Culver had the camera out and Hattie had her pen poised. "This is what we came for," Sally said. "Nothing is more Italian than pasta making!" Soon everyone was measuring flour.

"I use a mix of half-semolina flour and half–*doppio zero,* double-zero flour," Francesca explained. "In Italy this is the grade of flour that has been most refined. You can feel how soft it is, like talcum powder. But that doesn't mean it isn't good for you, overrefined. You are using it tonight, because you are here. When you make this yourselves, you don't have to search out this flour. Pasta can be made as well with all-purpose flour. When I worked for Faith, we used King Arthur's. I always remember that name. It seemed so funny, like if we called our flour 'Julius Caesar's.' " She laughed.

She continued to walk them through the steps, making a mound of the flours with a well in the center, adding water, and kneading. Faith felt her mood improve. She was on her second glass of wine and everyone was having so much fun. They'd moved on to the kneading stage—kneading, the rhythm and feel of the dough becoming a smooth mass, was always comforting.

"How are you doing, sweetheart?" she asked Tom. It wasn't the gnocchi he had said he wanted to make, but it was close. She'd teach him to make gnocchi when they got back home if he wanted.

"This is great, but hard work. Do we really have to knead for so long?"

"If you want good *pici,* yes," Faith said.

"We could have a peachy *pici* party in Maine this summer," Tom said. "And challenge the guests to say it ten times?" She decided to indulge her husband. Just so long as he didn't bring up gnocchi and nookie.

"What kind of sauce are we making for the pasta?" Hattie asked.

"The dough will need to rest for thirty minutes or more—up to an hour—so I thought we would make three sauces then and also *Il Secondo*—a pan-seared veal chop with sage and balsamic vinegar that gets finished off in the oven. But for now, why don't we take our glasses outside—you know Italians live outside whenever we can—and Mario will bring a few things we made for the antipasto?"

"*Perché no*—why not?" Luke said. "This is a very useful Italian phrase, like *andiamo,* so let's do it, let's go!"

He had certainly adapted well to the Italian way of life, Faith thought. She wondered whether he had roots in the country. The French people she knew would consider it high treason to leave their native *pays* except for vacations. No matter how old or rich a culture, what language was spoken, the scenic splendors, and above all the cuisine, there was no place for them that came close to La Belle France.

It was still light out, which made the days seem to go on forever. Tom looked slightly bronzed, the result of all the sunshine. There had not been a drop of rain the whole trip. Faith knew the growers needed it for the grapes and olives, but was thankful bad weather hadn't spoiled their precious time here. As for the other things, the things that were not at all precious, she packed them up in the storage containers of her mind and reached for a *crostini.* Francesca had made some with different toppings from those of the other night. Faith picked one thickly spread with olive pesto, made tangy, Francesca had explained, by adding capers and a squeeze of lemon to the garlic and olive puree. Faith loved the traditional pesto with EVOO, basil, and pignoli, but liked to vary it with pestos made from parsley, mint, arugula, or cilantro—but always lots of garlic. She followed the pesto *crostini* with lardo, a succulent sliver of that heavenly fat on the toasted bread—why were all the things that tasted so good so bad for you?

They were talking about cookbooks. Olivia mentioned Elizabeth David, which seemed to find favor with Constance, who then brought up the person who she declared started it all—Mrs. Beeton.

"It's been *the* food bible for over a hundred and fifty years. I can tell you it's on my shelf—right next to that adorable Jamie Oliver."

Clearly Constance had a weakness for attractive men. As usual she was sitting next to, and close to, Luke. It made Faith think more kindly of the difficult woman, so she didn't correct her. Poor Isabella Beeton was dead at twenty-eight, never knowing she would become quite literally a household name and also never hearing the criticism that most of her recipes were copied from other sources. Not that she had claimed they were original, but Faith kept her mouth firmly shut as she savored one more *crostini*— chicken liver this time. No need to smash Constance's kitchen idol.

Luke had no such compunction, offering up his own lares and penates. "*Cara signora,* I'm afraid your Mrs. Beeton is a recent addition. The honor of the first cookery writer goes to our own Caelius Apicius. *De Re Coquinaria,* 'On the Subject of Cooking,' was written in the late fourth century for professional chefs in Rome."

"Is that the book that describes all those Roman favorites like ostriches, peacocks, and even little dormice?" Sally turned the corners of her mouth down.

Luke nodded. "It was translated sometime in the 1930s, and while not—what do you call it, a page turner?—it's interesting to see how many of the things we prize today, like truffles, as well as cooking techniques, are the same."

"I would like to see a copy of that book," Francesca said. "Perhaps we could duplicate some of the more simple recipes."

Faith had looked through the book a long time ago, and what she remembered was that whoever wrote it, another culinary conundrum, had been an early proponent of letting nothing go to waste. It seemed every part of the animal, and the vegetables, was used as stuffing or was stuffed. She was surprised to hear that Sally was familiar with the book, although Dover Press had a current reprint. She was not surprised, however, that Luke was. He was an epicure obviously. But what was that about "our own Caelius Apicius"? The Frenchman was becoming more Italian with each passing day.

The *crostini* had made her thirsty and she needed some water. She tried to catch Francesca's eye. They should be going inside soon. Sufficient time had passed to let the dough rest before making the pasta, but Francesca, and Gianni also, were deep in conversation with their guests. She had the feeling the Rossis were staging the evening as they had the whole day, the whole week so far. When people were having a good time, they let it go on. The dough would still be fine twenty minutes or so from now. Deciding not to wait for some water, Faith went around the house to the back door of the kitchen and walked over to the sink to fill her empty glass from the tap.

Mario was at one of the stations. He was startled by her entry and dropped the container he'd been holding. Salt spilled all over the floor. He looked horrified, and she wondered what the big deal was—extremely superstitious? And then everything became clear.

It was Mario. Mario spoiling the cream, Mario depositing decapitated *serpi* in the tubs, and now Mario mixing fine salt into the flour that they would be using to dust the tables, and the finished pasta as well. It would ruin the dish.

He started speaking rapidly in Italian and as she was trying to figure out how she could prevent him from taking off and get one of the Rossis at the same time, Francesca came through the other door.

"I think we are ready to finish making the meal." She had a big smile on her face that did not disappear when she saw the mess. She said something that Faith assumed was along the lines of "no problem, get a broom."

"It's Mario! Mario is the one playing all these nasty tricks!" Faith stretched her arm out and pointed her finger at him. How to say "*J'accuse*" in Italian?

"What are you talking about?" Francesca's eyes went to the table and she took it all in. Immediately she rushed across the kitchen, grabbed his arm, and began yelling.

"Do you want me to get Gianni—and Tom?" Faith asked. Reinforcements seemed like a good idea.

She wasn't sure Francesca had heard her, she was shouting so loud, and then suddenly she stopped. Mario was sobbing some words out. A little boy caught, soon to be punished. Francesca pushed him onto one of the stools. He didn't move a muscle.

"What to do? What to do?" Francesca said, looking over at her friend.

It seemed pretty obvious to Faith. If not have him arrested, then immediately escort him off the premises. What had Mario said that was causing Francesca to hesitate, as she clearly was?

"There is a woman," Francesca said, "not too far from here who has a cooking school, has had it for many years. I spoke to her to tell her we were going to be doing this. She wished me luck and said she had more students than she could take. That there was room for everybody."

"She changed her mind?" Faith said. She knew where this was going. Francesca nodded. "It's not that she's losing students. At least that's what Mario says, but when she thought about it she wanted to be the only one."

"That's ridiculous! There are cooking classes and cooking schools all over Tuscany—and especially in this area!"

"I shouldn't have gone to her in the first place. Maybe she wouldn't have known about us."

"So she hired Mario to make sure you failed."

Francesca paused to unleash another stream of invective in Italian at the hapless young man.

"He paid Alberto to quit, which Alberto wanted to do anyway, because he has a girlfriend in Milano and he was afraid she might leave him if he was gone for so long. I'm afraid I have no choice,

Faith. I need someone for the classes, especially for the rest of this one." She paused. "I never told Gianni about what has been happening, so I don't have to tell him now."

"But can you trust Mario? What will he tell that woman, and by the way, she's the real villain here!"

"I think I can trust him now. He has rented his place in the Roma apartment and has nowhere to go, no job. It's not a good time to be without work, especially for the young people. He won't find another one easily and he knows his way around a kitchen. As for the woman, he will tell her he was discovered and if she makes more trouble, we will go to the *polizia*. She will stay away from us."

Faith thought a moment. "If anything more happens, you'll know where to look and he'll have that hanging over his head, so maybe this isn't such a bad idea."

And, she said to herself, now we know it wasn't one of the group. There was an odd sort of relief in that. She'd been so sure there had been an undercurrent. Well, there still was, but at least it wasn't slithering.

"Look, you go and stall people a little more," Francesca said. "Pour more wine. I want to talk to him and be sure."

Mario had stopped crying and now looked completely terrified. Francesca was scary when she was mad. Faith had seen it once all those years ago and if she'd been Mario, she'd be shaking in her boots, too, or rather the chef Mario Batali–like Crocs he was wearing.

Out on the terrace, there was no need to stall. As at the picnic, no one seemed to want to move. Tom was asking Gianni about buses to Siena. Faith knew he wanted to visit the cathedral and especially the adjoining Piccolomini Library with its sixteenth-century Pinturicchio frescoes. He'd confessed to her that he wouldn't mind taking a little time off from the culinary part of the week, and it seemed like tomorrow was the best choice. Friday was the last day, and he wanted to be here for that—everyone would depart Saturday morning and the new group would arrive on Sunday, as they had. Thinking about the new arrivals coming on the heels of those departing, Faith knew Francesca was right. She couldn't fire Mario. Gianni's sister had filled in before, but it had been difficult for her to leave her family, and she only spoke Italian. Faith resolved to have a little heart-to-heart with the young man before she left, however. She might be across an ocean, but she'd be watching him.

"There is a very good bus from the village. I can take you in the morning. Siena is not far. If you like, you could take my scooter instead," Gianni said.

Faith saw her husband's eyes light up. She also saw herself in black throwing a rose on top of a coffin, Ben and Amy clinging tearfully to her. She started to object. It wasn't Tom's ability to manage the Vespa, it was the other guys . . .

"It's very tempting, except Faith wants to stay here, and Gina Lollobrigida isn't available to sit pillion, so I think I'll stick with the bus, but thank you."

"Now *that* was an actress," Len said. "I must have been, I don't know, in my teens and we went to some artsy movie theater in Montclair that was showing old Bogie movies and we saw her in *Beat the Devil*. Mamma mia!"

"Maybe I should get a pail of water from the pool and throw it at you," Terry said, gesturing with her half-full wineglass. It seemed she'd toss that, but instead she drained it and gave her husband a wicked look. "So like you're going to pay for implants?"

Time to change the subject.

"Be sure to bring back some *panforte* for the kids," Faith said. "I know it's sold all over, but it will be special to have it come from Siena."

Hattie piped up, "It's not like Aunt Sister's fruitcake, that's for sure! I think I still have a couple of them from the 1980s."

Again Faith gave a thought to the aunt/niece's food knowledge. *Panforte* was indeed an Italian fruitcake.

"I don't know what your aunt's recipe involves," she said. "And maybe it's one of those fruitcakes that's supposedly been passed around from family to family, trying to get rid of it for years, but *panforte is* quite different from what we think of as fruitcake. It has dried fruit—always lemons and oranges—almonds and honey, but it's moist and chewy, thin with confectioner's sugar on top."

"It sounds delicious," Sky said. "I've never heard of it."

Gianni chimed in, "It is from the medieval time and even though you can find it other places, Siena is the place where it's most famous. Some say that you have to have seventeen ingredients for the seventeen *contrade* in the town."

"Why don't I bring back enough for us to have as dessert tomorrow night?" Tom offered just as Francesca *and* Mario came outside.

"*Grazie mille,* Tom. Now, time to work," she called gaily. "Roll up your sleeves."

First they prepared the marinated veal chops, adding plenty of fresh sage, and then divided into two groups to make the ragus, one meatless. They would both need to simmer (see recipe, page 235).

Afterward, each person's dough was retrieved, and soon all were engaged in rolling long strands out by hand. Faith again felt transported back to nursery school. They weren't going to coil the results into a pot, but the atmosphere was much the same. Roderick, wineglass in hand, wasn't even pretending to try. Olivia, predictably, was the best and soon had a tray of *pici* all the same length and thickness.

"You must be a ringer," Jack called out. "If we're going to eat tonight, you'd better come help me. The darn things keep coming apart."

Sally seemed to be the photographer and her aunt the note

taker. "I want to write down the sauces," Hattie said. "Are all the ones on these sheets going to be in the binder?" They'd finished their trays, a more than creditable job.

"I'm adding one, but it is so simple, you will remember. In any case, I'll put it in with the rest," Francesca said.

As at each lesson, Francesca had passed out the copies of the recipes they were making at the time—and they would get smeared with oil, flour, and other ingredients. It was a great idea to provide everyone with what amounted to a little cookbook, pristine, to take home at the end.

"What is it? I want to write it down anyway." Hattie clicked her ballpoint and started to write something down. "Oh, H-E-double hockey sticks! This pen doesn't work!"

"I think I have one," Tom said and pulled a pen from his pants pocket. He'd changed into his chinos after his swim, the same ones he'd been wearing in Rome. Faith tried to stop him. It wasn't just a pen. It was Freddy's pen. She didn't want to lose it.

Sometimes telepathy works. As Tom was handing it to Hattie he said, "I'll need to have it back, though. It belonged to a friend of ours." He looked over at the Rossis. "Freddy—Freddy Ives." They both nodded. "Anyway it has sentimental value, but please use it tonight."

"Thank you, darlin.' I'll take very good care of it."

Except it immediately slipped from Hattie's hand, which was still slightly moist from rolling out the strands of pasta, and fell on the hard surface of the table before dropping to the ground.

"Oh, I'm so sorry," she said. "I hope it's not broken!"

The old-fashioned fountain pen had split open and Faith grabbed the towel from her waist to mop up the ink before it could stain the flooring. But there wasn't any ink. There wasn't a cartridge either. Just the cap and point, now separated, and the barrel with a small rolled-up piece of paper poking out. Hattie grabbed it.

"Did you know there was a message in here? Like in a bottle!" She sounded excited, and the rest of the group looked over. Faith quickly took the paper from Hattie's hand and bent to pick up the pen parts.

"Oh yes, that's what made it special. His note. Tom, you must have forgotten that the pen didn't work, but I have a pencil. Will that do?"

It would, and the whole incident was over as soon as it began.

But not for Faith. That's what Freddy had been trying to tell them. He'd concealed something in the pen, information of some kind. She wanted to dash up to her room to read it immediately. She was back in the Piazza Farnese hearing Freddy's words, "You have to stop them. They're going to ki . . ." and then once more he had said "pen." Her *pici* were done, yet she stayed where she was. She couldn't explain it, but she felt that there had been a subtle change in the room—a heightened awareness coming from someone that made her decide to bide her time.

Less than two hours later, they were all digging into the fruits of their labor—another memorable meal around the large, now-familiar dining room table. Francesca's three sauces were the traditional Montepulciano one, *Pici Cacio e Pepe*—only three ingredients: the cooked *pici* tossed in a large skillet with a bit of the pasta water, grated pecorino, and a very generous amount of freshly ground black pepper; another simple preparation adding garlic, oil, and parsley to the *Pici Cacio e Pepe;* and finally the two ragus, a meatless one and one with *pancetta*—the bacon from a local farm.

Len was enthusing over the *pici* with the *pancetta* ragu. "I never saw anything for dinner on a plate that wasn't red until I was out of school. We Jersey Italianos called it 'gravy' and my grandmother's was the best. Not that this isn't great."

"The food of our childhood is always the best," Gianni said. "'Ragu' just means 'sauce,' or here in Tuscany we also call it '*sugo*.' And my grandmother's was the best, too."

He ducked slightly as Francesca picked up a piece of bread to throw at him. She put it on her plate and said, "My *nonna*'s was better, and this is her recipe! She used to call the chopped carrot, onion, and celery that we started this sauce with—and that we use for so many dishes—the 'holy trinity'!"

After sampling each of the *picis* and a serving of the tender veal redolent from the marinade and the aged balsamic vinegar used to deglaze the pans, with some garlicky chickpeas, *ceci,* as a side, Faith knew she couldn't eat another bite. Yet when Francesca brought out the limoncello granita she'd made, somehow Faith found room. The cool ice with its rich lemon liqueur taste went down perfectly. Another exceptional meal, and she'd have to remember the term "holy trinity" for what was called a mirepoix in most kitchens, from the French.

By the time they finished, it was quite late. Pleading a long day, Faith told the group she needed to head for bed, bidding them, "*Buona notte.*"

For bed, but first for whatever message Freddy had left in the pen.

Tom was not far behind.

"Stupid, how could I be so stupid?" Tom said when they were alone in their room. "I should have thought of something hidden in the pen immediately."

He had been a big Hardy Boys fan, reading his dad's old books, but there was no need for him to beat up on himself. She was the one who should have thought of it, given her more than passing acquaintance over the years with crime and subterfuge. She'd been over every page of the Graham Greene novel from Freddy's suitcase in vain, hoping for some clue, and here was the pen under their noses—or rather in Tom's pocket—all the time.

They stared at the slip of paper with Freddy's tiny distinctive handwriting. There was precious little written on it:

13/5 Teatro Verdi F.D.

"Thirteen five has to be a date. It's written the way they do here, so that's May thirteenth. Friday! This Friday!" Faith said.

"And the thirteenth on top of everything else," Tom said. "But where is the theater? '*Teatro*' is 'theater,' I'm pretty sure. Look in your guidebook to Rome. Freddy was in Rome, so it makes sense the theater would be, too."

Faith got the book.

"There's a Teatro Verde. It's for kids—plays, musicals. But Freddy clearly wrote an 'i,' not an 'e.' It has to be somewhere else. We need Google. Wait, what time is it in New York? I could call Hope."

"Or I could go back downstairs and tell Gianni I want to look something up for tomorrow. I'm sure they haven't gone to bed yet."

"Better," Faith said. "Do you want me to go with you?"

"No, I'll be right back. You try to figure out the initials. The initials of the target," Tom said grimly. "Freddy was trying to say 'kill.'"

Faith couldn't think of any targets with those initials. She didn't know the names of many notable Italian figures, especially political ones, save the president. Tom was back soon.

"Piece of cake. The Teatro Verdi is in Florence, right here in Tuscany, which has to be why Freddy wanted us to take the pen. He knew where we were headed. I wrote down the address, Via Giuseppe Verdi—no surprise there—but I couldn't read anything else on the site, since it was in Italian."

We *have* been stupid, Faith said to herself. Now they had only a short time to figure out how to stop what could well be an assassination from occurring.

Reaching over to kiss her husband good morning, Faith was surprised to find his side of the bed vacant. She must have been sleeping very soundly. She got up and knocked on the bathroom door. There was no answer, and opening it, she saw the room was empty. She dressed quickly and headed downstairs to find him. He must have been very hungry. The Nashes and Olivia were up early, too, filling plates from the buffet. There had been no more talk about "proper breakfasts" from Constance after the first day, and judging by what she had piled on, she was now a convert to Italian *colazione*.

"Oh there you are," Constance said. "I have a message from your husband, who literally bumped into me in the hall. A terrific hurry. He said to tell you he was off to Siena to that library thingy. Mario, more coffee."

"The Piccolomini Library, you mean?"

"Yes, that's what I said. Milk, Mario. *Latte, latte*—milk."

Faith poured herself a cup of coffee and went back upstairs. She wasn't hungry and she needed to think.

Last night before they had finally gotten to sleep, they'd decided to tell the Rossis everything that had happened and turn the matter over to the authorities. Tom had wanted to go back downstairs to the lounge, where the computer was, and try to find out more about the theater, a schedule for Friday, but they didn't want to wake anyone up.

She went back into the bathroom. His toothbrush was wet, so he'd gotten that far. He'd also obviously dressed—his jeans, a shirt, and his Nikes were gone. He must have decided to get up early and find out more about the theater. Or maybe he went to alert the Rossis? But without her? And then why go on to Siena?

Once more she went down the stairs and checked not only the room with the computer, but also all the other rooms on the ground floor, the terraces, and finally the pool—including the garden shed. There was no sign of him. She went back into the dining room. Everyone except Jack and Sky was up by now. Francesca, who would certainly not look so calm and happy had Tom told her what was going on, was bringing in fresh *cornetti*. Faith scarcely noticed the mound of rich flakey pastries.

"Did you see Tom before he left with Gianni?"

"No," Francesca said. "I've just gotten back from my parents'. I stayed there last night with the *bambini*."

"Gianni, too?"

"No, he was here of course." She gave Faith a slight frown, and Faith was instantly sorry she hadn't watched what she said. Obviously the two would never be away from the guests at once.

"Stupid of me," she apologized, thinking how often she'd been saying that lately. "I just wondered what time Tom left, which bus he caught."

"Gianni was going to Firenze afterward to the Mercato Centrale to get the seafood for tonight. The best is from there. Once everyone is ready we will go to the small village market this morning to get the rest of what we need. You can try him on his cell, but it doesn't always work well."

"No, that's fine. I can ask him later. I'll go get my camera. I know there will be many things I'll want to take pictures of today."

Especially every single person enrolled at Cucina della Rossi.

She packed a bottle of water, the camera, and her journal in her bag, then sat in one of the chairs on the balcony. Another beautiful day. A breeze was setting the fields and groves of olive trees in motion. It had rained in the night and left the landscape sparkling. Totally idyllic.

Her husband had never left in the morning, or any other time, without kissing her good-bye.

CHAPTER 10

There was one thing Faith could do right now. She could call her sister. Her cell was in the suitcase and she had been keeping it charged. Tom's was there, as she'd expected. It was too much to hope that he'd taken it with him. She sat back down, took out her journal, and turned to the back, where she'd written how to dial the States, punching in the numbers that would take her across the miles to Hope's cell.

Hope Sibley did not change her name when she married Quentin Lewis Jr., but did some years later when Quentin III came along. Faith had suggested she add something to her name like "Imperial Mother and Wife I," but Hope had merely stuck "Sibley" in the middle. She was the exception to the rule that it was impossible for a woman to have it all—a lucrative, prestigious job, happy marriage, and motherhood—seeming to juggle the roles effortlessly, and admirably. The phrase "I don't know how she does it" was coined for Hope, but, in fact, Faith *did* know how. Money for a start, which bought a wonderful nanny, who stayed on as a housekeeper. Money also provided a spacious duplex apartment on Manhattan's West Side. And it also paid for romantic, albeit short, romantic getaways with hubby, who was equally dedicated to the pursuit of the next rung until the ladder stopped—where? Some kind of ultimate stratospheric corner office? Hope had been born with advanced organizational skills—sorting M&M's by color had been mere child's play on the way to a BlackBerry and smart phone, with Skype to check in with little Quentin as soon as he came home from school each day.

And on top of everything, it was impossible to hate her because she was an absolute darling.

"What's wrong?" Hope had answered the phone before the end of the first ring.

Since it was 3 A.M. New York time, she knew Faith wasn't calling to chat about Chianti DOCs.

"It's complicated—and I'll explain when I get home—but I need you to do something for me as soon as you get into the office."

Another nice thing about Hope was that she never wasted time with unnecessary questions.

"You have people at work who are fluent in Italian, right?"

"Several."

"I need someone to call the box office of the Teatro Verdi on Via Giuseppe Verdi in Florence and buy me a ticket for whatever performances they have tomorrow, Friday, May thirteenth. There may be both a matinee and an evening concert. I don't have access to a schedule."

"Just the one ticket?"

"Just one and in the front row or near the front of the first balcony, or the equivalent—someplace where I can see as much of the theater as possible. Have the ticket left at the box office under my name." She didn't worry about being so specific. Hope would pull it off.

"I'll be going in at six, so it won't take long after that," Hope said.

Faith had learned years ago when her sister first started working in this totally alternate universe that normal working hours didn't apply. Until she made partner, Hope slept most nights on a couch in her office. Finding an Italian speaker this early in the morning would not pose a problem.

"Thanks. And don't worry."

"Whenever you say this, I know you're in trouble or will be soon. Are you sure I don't need to do anything else?"

"Yes! I almost forgot. I need the address of the British consulate in Florence. I have the American one."

Faith didn't want to use the computer downstairs anymore. Maybe she was being paranoid—or maybe she was just being smart.

"Okay. That I can do immediately. And I'll get you the name of a contact. I'll call you in a few minutes."

"Best to text everything from now on. The address and the performance or performances."

They'd be leaving for the weekly market in the village soon, and she needed to go back downstairs. She didn't want her phone ringing. She didn't want to draw any attention to herself or what she was about to do whatsoever.

"Love you, Hope."

"Love you, too—and be careful, please."

"I'm always careful. Bye."

Her sister ended the call, but not before Faith heard the heavy sigh traveling through cyberspace.

The village market presented the same alluring panoply of food, enticing to eye and mouth, as the Mercato Centrale, but was much smaller. Tables were spread out under an octagonal timbered roof held up by brickwork columns. Francesca told them that there had been a market on this spot for centuries and that parts of the current structure went back to the Middle Ages.

Faith liked the way some tables had set out a few simple offerings—radishes pulled an hour or so ago, spring onions, lettuces, jars of honey—while others were clearly outlets for larger producers that traveled to the various hill town markets. These offered samples of cheeses and salamis. The sellers' cries urging buyers to "*Mangia, mangia*" were hard to resist. All the purveyors were dressed in a layered assortment of aprons, tee shirts that proclaimed team favorites, caps, and bandannas.

She found herself walking with the Russos. She realized she knew very little about them other than where they lived, that Len was in "waste management," Terry a *Twilight* fan—and they seemed unhappy. Normally she would have asked about their family, whether they had kids, and did they grow up in Livingston, New Jersey? Faith had dear friends who had. Maybe they knew them? She was always fascinated by people's stories and she would already have found out this sort of information. The week had been anything but normal, though. Asking now would take her mind off the Teatro Verdi—and Tom.

"Did you both grow up in Livingston?"

Terry shook her head. "Len is from Verona, not far from Livingston, and I was born in Philadelphia, but my parents moved to West Orange, New Jersey, when I was a baby. I'm a Jersey girl, though all these reality shows have been giving people the wrong idea about us."

"I know you don't pump gas," Faith said. "*And* I know why—it's against the law in New Jersey to pump your own gas, male or female."

Terry laughed. "The first time I went to a gas station in another state—it was New York—I sat in the car waiting for a long time, thinking they were on the phone or something. Finally a guy came out and wanted to know if I was going to start paying rent. Then he saw the plates and said, 'Oh, you're from Jersey.' He was nice about it and showed me how to fill the tank."

"Oregon, too," Len said. "Not that I've been there. In Jersey, the law was passed in the 1940s so people wouldn't blow themselves up, like smoke when they were pumping. Personally I like it. Nothing wrong with being waited on, and our gas isn't any more expensive than other states."

"I like it, too, mainly because it's the only time *I* ever do get waited on," Terry said.

Faith quickly interjected, "How about kids? We have two, a teen and a tween."

The couple looked daggers at each other and there was a long pause before Terry answered. "Oh yes, *we* have kids. Three great ones. Len Junior works for Prudential, Jennifer got married last summer—she's a nurse at Saint Barnabas—and our baby, Frankie, has one more year of college. He's at Drew University. They all chipped in to give us this trip for our anniversary. Our thirtieth."

"That's wonderful!" Faith said. "As I think my husband mentioned, it's our anniversary trip, too, although not the thirtieth yet. Congratulations!"

They were still looking at each other with undisguised antipathy, suggesting there wouldn't be a thirty-first.

"Everything was paid for, and anyway," Terry said. "I didn't want to tell them—"

If he could have clapped a hand over his wife's mouth without drawing even more attention to what was an increasingly awkward situation, Faith was sure Len Russo would have. What he did do was interrupt.

"Your husband was in a big hurry this morning."

"You saw him? When?" Suddenly Faith wasn't at all interested in the Russos' marital problems or whether she had Livingston friends in common with them.

"It was early. I was in the bathroom using the, well, I was in the bathroom, and I looked out the window. He was tearing up the path behind the house like there was no tomorrow."

"Was he alone?" The market disappeared from her thoughts. Two people had seen Tom rushing off. Constance and now Len. To Siena? Or someplace connected to Friday the thirteenth, the date in Freddy's note.

"Didn't see anybody else, but I wasn't taking any pictures."

Tom was heading up the path, which meant he was on his way here, to the village, most likely. Buses went not only to Siena but also to a number of other places—including Florence.

Len's phrase reminded Faith that she wanted to get photos of the class, surreptitiously. She left the Russos to their bickering.

How do spies do it? she wondered a few minutes later. She'd been able to get a shot of Sky and Jack, ducking quickly out from behind one of the columns. Olivia was seemingly intent on an array of red, turban-shaped tomatoes, and she sneaked one of her. But the others were proving difficult. Francesca solved the problem by calling, "Everyone, could you gather here by me and we'll decide what to cook tonight, now that you've had a chance to see what's here."

Faith was able to snap the whole group from behind a table with baskets of potatoes, the soil still clinging to the skins—red, purple, yellow, shades of brown—before joining them. They'd added a pair of petite, attractive women to the group, who, hearing English, must have thought it was a tour the village was providing. No one dissuaded them, but realizing their mistake, they tried to leave with blushing apologies. Francesca insisted they stay and quickly gave them cards for Cucina della Rossi.

"Has anything caught your eye?" Francesca asked her students.

"The asparagus looks wonderful and we haven't done a dish with that yet," Olivia said. "Maybe use it in a few ways?"

"I love that idea," Sally said. "A celebration of *asparagi*!"

"We could use it in risotto for *Il Primo*—I want to do another one that you will make," Francesca said. "And then it's so good roasted and wrapped with a slice of proscuitto as an antipasto." She pointed to one of the sellers. "They make an excellent one. We'll get plenty. After that it will be seafood. Gianni will bring scampi for sure. He wants to do some of the shrimp on the grill, and that will be part of our antipasto, too. I won't know the other fish until he gets back. We can have some of the *asparagi* in a cheese sauce as a *contorni*. It will go with any kind of fish. Any other ideas? Remember, this will be the last night we cook together, so you must tell me what you want."

Tomorrow night the Rossis had arranged a banquet for the class at a *ristorante* on Lago Trasimeno. Francesca had told Faith they wanted to make the last night special—no one working hard, just spending time together at what was one of the most beautiful spots in Italy before they all went their separate ways. She'd worked on the menu with their chef and the meal would be memorable, too. Faith thought it was a lovely idea. She pictured the end of the evening with farewells, some fonder than others, and promises to stay in touch, which no one would keep.

"How about grilling some asparagus along with eggplant and peppers?" Jack said. "I had something like that in a restaurant in Santa Monica and it was great, a little charred with a strong garlic flavor."

One of the two women who'd inadvertently become part of the group said, "Did you see the thin stalks of wild asparagus? I only saw it on one table and you might want to try it."

Her friend laughed. "*Stalking the Wild Asparagus,* Valerie? Remember that Euell Gibbons book from the 1960s?"

She explained to the group, "He was doing what was common practice in Italy—foraging in the wild for mushrooms, greens, things Americans thought were poisonous or weeds."

"Come for dinner tonight," Francesca said as they started to leave.

The one named Valerie answered, "That's so kind of you, but I'm afraid we're moving on to Siena. We like markets and only stayed to see this one. Our bus goes in an hour. Enjoy your meal. And thank you for the card. Something tells me you could be our next destination!"

Faith felt an instant kinship with them. They seemed to be having such a good time. The mention of Siena destroyed any vestige of calm for her, though. It didn't make sense. Tom couldn't possibly have gone off with everything that was going on.

Hattie was offering a menu suggestion. "Isn't there some kind of Italian asparagus dish with an egg? *Alla Bismarck,* although why in God's green acre they would name a tasty dish after a Prussian general here in Italy beats me."

"I do not know why either, but it is what we call any dish with a fried egg on it, *Pizza alla Bismarck* is another," Francesca said. "Why don't we make small portions of it, use the wild *asparagi* for a simple *contorni* with butter and maybe a little cheese, with one more dish, an asparagus *sformato,* which is like a soufflé?"

Luke, who seemed an endless font of culinary lore, knew the answer to the question of Bismarck. And it wasn't North Dakota. It was indeed named for the Prussian chancellor.

"Otto von Bismarck was well known not just for his abilities as a statesman and on the battlefield but as a *molto* trencherman who could consume vast amounts of food at one sitting. He was partial to eggs, topping everything from meats to vegetables with plenty of them fried."

"To do the dish well, we need very fresh eggs, so it is fortunate we are here in the market," Francesca said. "You need to keep chickens, Jean-Luc, and then we can have the *uova* and a nice bird, too, once in a while."

"All I know is that with all this asparagus my piss is going to stink," Len said, and after a glare from his wife, "pardon my French, my *urine* is going to stink."

Terry wasn't the only one who didn't laugh, or at least smile, at the remark. Olivia seemed miles away, as if she hadn't heard him.

"Well, *odore* or no, let's select our ingredients and then meet back at the van in an hour. Some of you mentioned you wanted time to explore the town," Francesca said, handing Mario a large market basket. Faith had noticed that the sous chef had not been left behind on his own.

She didn't feel much like exploring, but she did want to sit and look to see whether Hope had texted her yet. The *caffè* where she and Tom had had breakfast a few days ago seemed ideal. She also wanted to pick up a newspaper. The Nashes were not good at sharing theirs. Yesterday Jack had asked to see their *Herald Tribune* and Constance said they weren't finished with it in a tone that really said, "Buy your own."

It was unlikely there would be anything in the paper relating to what was playing at the Teatro Verdi, or anything else going on in Florence unless it was major news, but Faith thought she should check.

She sat at one of the small tables and ordered an espresso. She was going to miss this, she thought, as she looked out over the square, smaller than the one in Montepulciano but pulsing with activity. Maybe she'd try to get Aleford's Minuteman Café to put a few tables on the sidewalk once the weather got good, although that could be late June some years.

Hope had texted voluminously. The Teatro Verdi was large, could seat 806, a historic nineteenth-century jewel—"lots of red velvet and gold" and there was a matinee on Friday featuring Ravel and Debussy. There was no public concert that night, as the theater would be closed for a private event. The matinee was sold out, but of course Hope had scored a ticket in the first balcony, also the other loges, as well as a box, in case Faith felt the need to move around. She added the address of the British consulate, telling Faith she was just in time, since at the end of the year it would be closing its doors after five hundred years, the victim of budget cuts. Hope obviously felt upset writing this—two exclamation marks. Despite her techie gadgets, she was an old-fashioned girl at heart and hated things like this.

She also gave Faith a contact name and a phone number at the consulate.

It was time to join the others. Once again those free-spirited Nashes had brought their own car, but the rest would be returning to the Rossis' for a leisurely lunch before the lesson in the afternoon. Faith stopped at the one and only news dealer, just missing the last copy of the *Herald,* but since she saw Jack buying it, hoped she could get a look at the paper later.

Gianni had returned from Florence in their absence, left the food, and gone off again. Francesca didn't know when he would be back.

"That man! He never tells me anything and doesn't realize that now that we have the business, it's not like the old days where he could go help a friend build a stone wall or prune the trees and disappear on me for hours."

While still not wanting to tell Francesca without Gianni what was going on, Faith was getting increasingly anxious to know when he had taken Tom to the bus and whether Tom had said anything to him. Although if he had, Gianni would most certainly not have gone off. Unless it was to the authorities, in Florence, or here. So she got his cell number from Francesca and tried to reach him back in her room, but the phone was either switched off or not getting service. Nothing to do but wait.

The call from her husband's abductors came at 3 P.M.

Expecting it would be Hope on her cell, Faith had trouble at first understanding the person on the other end, but it all became horribly clear soon. It was a man speaking in a heavy Italian or similar accent.

"We have your husband. He is fine. Tell no one, especially the police, or we will kill him."

Very clear.

"I'll get the money! How much do you want?"

"No money. You just wait. Do *nothing*."

"How do I know he is fine? I want to speak to him!"

She heard the man cover the phone and some muffled sounds. Then Tom came on the line. Her eyes filled with tears of relief.

"Just do whatever they say, Faith. They're hooded, so I'm sure this means they don't plan to harm me. I can't identify anyone." He spoke slowly and distinctly before quickly adding, "So, I'm okay, although I wish I had my Bible with me. I could use the gospel of Saint Luke for comfort, especially chapter fifteen, verse sixteen. And a pen to write my thoughts down."

Faith heard a voice say "Enough!" and the call was terminated. She quickly checked, and as she'd expected the number had been blocked. Without going to the police with their sophisticated tracking equipment, there was no way of knowing where Tom was being held or by whom.

Except for the clues in his own words, and the words of the Good Book. Faith quickly texted her sister: *Could you send me St. Luke, chapter 15, verse 16?*

The reply came back immediately: *He would fain have filled his belly with the husks that the swine did eat: and no man gave unto him.*

"Thought the food was great? Or r u just getting religious?"

Faith wrote: *"Yes and yes. Will explain later."*

Bless Tom's career choice. When she saw him, and she would—any other thought was beyond considering—she'd apologize for all her complaints about parish life. She'd even take on the Sunday school Christmas pageant this year. Just keep him safe, Lord, until she could get him out. Because she now knew where he was and who had snatched him.

Luke, Jean-Luc, the good neighbor with the outrageous *bagno*. And it all was tied to Freddy's pen—and Freddy's murder.

She studied the verse. Tom wasn't telling her he was hungry, although, she thought with a pang, he might be. He was telling her he was being kept in a pigsty, or some other kind of place that housed, or had housed, animals. And it was Tom himself who had told her that Gianni had wanted Jean-Luc to get going with his plans to pull down some old farm buildings far from the main house so the Rossis could rent the cleared space to plant more grapes. Except Jean-Luc was sure there were Etruscan treasures lurking underneath them and wanted a trained team to excavate the site. Etruscan treasures! With his intense interest, Jean-Luc must know about the tomb below the *cantina* in Montepulciano. Easy enough to slip away and lock Faith in. But why let her out? If, in fact, he had been her liberator?

She was due in the kitchen to start tonight's meal soon but thought she'd stretch her legs first. There was something she wanted to check out. Tom never got on the bus to Siena, but Len Russo saw him running up the path behind the house. Unless Len was part of the gang—and at the moment Faith was adopting "Trust No One" as a motto—the path was where Tom had last been seen in the immediate area. She crossed her fingers.

Conspicuously wielding her camera, Faith snapped shots of the pool, the terraces, the gardens, and worked her way up to the hill, stopping to shoot a few of the back of the house and views in every direction. It was hot today and the sun had baked the soil, which would have been wet in the early morning hours after last night's rain. Just as she'd dared hope, Tom's Nikes had left distinctive footprints. He'd been here when the ground was still wet. Yet why had he left the house? Len said he'd been running. Running toward someone—Jean-Luc?—or away from someone—again Jean-Luc? Tempted as she was to follow the tracks, she took a few shots of some instead before strolling with very much assumed nonchalance back down to the house.

She had a plan, but there was nothing she could do now.

Except wait.

❋   ❋   ❋

Faith was the last of the group to arrive in Cucina della Rossi's kitchen and quickly put her apron on, ready to start.

"Sorry. That was Tom. He walked to the village for the bus, but said to thank Gianni and that we'd have to wait for our *panforte*. He met a visiting scholar from Saint Louis University's Center for Medieval and Renaissance Studies who offered to give him a private look at some manuscripts and stay the night at a guesthouse the Piccolomini Library has. What an opportunity! Kind of a Medici-slept-here thing, like the Lincoln bedroom at the White House!"

Neither ignoring, nor seeking out, Jean-Luc, Faith gave the performance of her life, rehearsed on the hill. Pausing, she could swear she heard someone take a sharp breath in, as if he or she thought Faith was going to say something more, something dangerous? For whom?

She was deliberately vague about time. When she expected him back. Tom's captors had been equally vague—saying nothing in fact—but she was quite sure the Fairchilds wouldn't be having breakfast together tomorrow. Whatever was going to happen at the Teatro Verdi would be later in the day.

"He must be so happy," Francesca said. "I'm glad for him. If he calls again, tell him we will save some risotto. It is even better the next day."

"I doubt he'll call again. You know how he is about roaming charges. And yes, risotto is great the next day. I like to make it into cakes and fry them in olive oil. Tom has been known to scoop up risotto straight from the fridge to eat cold." Faith kept her voice light. "Now, what are we cooking?"

While impossible to keep the fact that her husband was being held captive by hooded kidnappers not all that far away, Faith found that the act of cooking, of preparing food, was having its usual soothing effect on her. Gianni had purchased fresh *branzino,* Mediterranean sea bass. Francesca was describing how they would stuff it with lemons, rosemary, and slivers of leeks and either bake or grill, depending on what the class decided.

"You want to try to get a whole fish with the head and tail if possible and also have it cleaned and slit up the side. It is very easy to tell if fish is fresh." She pointed to her nose. "This is the best test, but also look at it. Old fish doesn't have bright shiny skin. If you can, also give it a poke with your finger. It shouldn't be spongy."

The class wanted it grilled, and Faith knew it would be delicious—the skin nice and crunchy.

She began to feel as though she was a sleepwalker, here but not really here, as she listened to and went through all the risotto-making steps, even adding her own favorite professional make-ahead tip—reserve about a cup and a half of the liquid, remove the risotto from the heat when al dente, spread it on a baking sheet or pan, cover, refrigerate for up to two hours, and then reheat it, adding the liquid and whatever else the recipe called for, in tonight's case, the asparagus with grated cheese.

Time marched on at a crawl. The *asparagi* assumed a number of forms, then suddenly the hours fast-forwarded and in succession she was at the table; they were eating; it got dark outside; and now she was standing by the window in her room dressed in a black tee shirt, dark jeans, her hair tucked up into Tom's navy Red Sox cap, waiting.

Then waiting some more.

After dinner, she'd found what she assumed was Jack's newspaper in the lounge and had taken it up with her. There was nothing of note on the front page and inside a page was missing. It seemed to be the one that listed what was going on in various cities—including Florence? Could Jack and Sky be Jean-Luc's coconspirators? Or perhaps the couple was simply planning to do something in Rome before their flight back to the States.

At two o'clock she decided everyone must surely be asleep, and besides, she couldn't stand to wait any longer. All night she had tried to decide whether the feeling she was being watched was paranoia or real. Jean-Luc knew where Tom was, but he didn't know Faith knew. He obviously knew the kidnappers had gotten in touch with her, since he was one of them and he may even have been amused at the story she concocted to explain his absence— whooping it up among illuminated manuscripts in Siena. The story that would reassure him that she was doing nothing. He also didn't know she knew *he* was responsible. She was conscious of not behaving any differently with him, or anyone else, throughout the evening. The effort had been exhausting.

It wasn't raining, but it was overcast, and as she slipped out the back door, Faith was grateful for the lack of illumination. Trying not to think of grass snakes, or especially vipers, she walked parallel to the path in the underbrush instead of on it to avoid being spotted. She had no idea where the old farm buildings might be, but they'd have to be well behind Jean-Luc's house. She remembered coming down the path at what now seemed like years ago, but was only Monday, and not seeing any signs of them when they'd glimpsed the roof of the large villa.

Every once in a while she turned the flashlight on briefly to search for signs of an old drive. Shortly after she passed the villa, she found what appeared to have once been some kind of cart track. If it didn't lead anywhere, she would return and keep going.

The *zanzare,* mosquitoes, now were out in full force, and Faith wished she'd thought to pack a stick of insect repellent back in Aleford. She also wished she'd thought to pack some kind of knockout drops that she could have added to Olivia's grappa— tonight she'd been imbibing, several glasses of wine and then the after-dinner drink. Olivia's trusty pistol would have been a big help, but entering her room, locating it if it was in fact still in the drawer, and leaving without drawing any attention to herself, would not have been possible save only in the worst sort of crime novels.

What kind of mosquitoes were these anyway? Same incredibly irritating whine, but they stung like bees and seemed able to penetrate even her shoes. She flashed the light about in an arc and was rewarded by what looked like a more traveled path, wider and with distinct tire tracks, ahead. When she got to it and turned, she saw it extended in two directions. One, judging from the angle, led to the village road, the other her destination?

What had been a slight breeze began to pick up, and soon an odor wafted in her direction. There may not be any swine there now, but she was approaching a place where they had unquestionably once wallowed. She passed a small brick structure with no roof and the walls caved in on two sides. Beyond it she could make out a cluster of slightly larger buildings. There was a banged-up Ape farm truck, pretty much a tiny cab and flatbed built around a three-wheeled scooter. Tom had been fascinated with the one the Rossis had and was no doubt intimately acquainted with the brand now, if this was what they had used to transport him here. Her spirits lifted. Unless another car had dropped the kidnappers off and left, this meant there couldn't be more than two of them guarding her husband.

Faith circled the darkened buildings, trying to figure out where he was being kept. She was sure he was here. He *had* to be. One of the buildings was in better shape than the other, and she concentrated on that. It seemed to have several rooms, or animal stalls. There was no glass in the windows, if there ever had been, but at the rear, the windows were barred, presumably to prevent escape and performing the same function now. There was no choice. She had to take a chance.

She stood on tiptoe and peered in the nearest one. Flashing her light, she could make out a large blanket-covered lump on the dirt floor.

"Tom?" she whispered.

The lump moved slightly.

"Tom," she said a bit louder and more urgently. His head popped up from the dirty blanket. At least it was protecting him from bites, although there might be predators other than mosquitoes lurking in its folds.

He stood up and came to the window. His hands were tied together in front of him. He looked rumpled, but not hurt.

"I knew you'd figure it out, darling," he said softly.

Faith tried to kiss him, but the windowsill was too wide. She pushed her hand between the bars and stroked his face.

"You haven't done anything? Said anything?" he said.

"No, but I can. It's Jean-Luc, right?"

"Yes. I couldn't sleep last night, so once it was light I went downstairs and was looking online to see whether I could figure out why Freddy had written the theater's name when Luke tapped on the window behind me and motioned me out, pointing toward the hill. He looked extremely agitated. Like a jerk I didn't stop to think he could see what I was doing, although I'm sure he'd figured it all out the moment Hattie dropped the pen. Maybe even before then—but anyway that we were with Freddy when he died."

"Len Russo saw you running. Were you trying to get away?"

"No, but I *was* running. When I got outside, Luke said that he'd come to the house to get help. That he was walking the way he does early every morning and found a woman who seemed to be unconscious. He wanted to know if I knew any first aid."

"Which you do."

He'd even updated his CPR certification last winter. Ah Tom, the Good Samaritan. She didn't have to hear the rest to know what happened.

"He said he'd go get the Rossis and phone for an ambulance. I said I'd see what I could do in the meantime. The next thing I knew I was trussed up and in a burlap sack on the back of one of those roller skate trucks. I saw it when we got here and they took the sack off.

"The guards who are here now have been hitting the bottle pretty heavily from what I could see through one of the cracks in the boards and they're asleep. Unless we start shouting, they won't hear us, but I'll keep this short. They just want me—and you—on ice until sometime tomorrow. One of the guards speaks English, there are always two, but they change. He keeps telling me so long as we don't make trouble, no one will get hurt. But, Faith, some-one *is* going to get hurt—unless we stop them. They're planning to assassinate the French minister of culture, François Dumond, at tomorrow's matinee in the Teatro Verdi!"

Faith's mind was whirling as she walked back to the house, not daring to shine the light after what he had told her. The guards didn't know Tom could speak French, and with that plus a bit of Italian, he'd been able to figure out what was going on. Jean-Luc wasn't French for a start, or rather didn't consider himself French. He, and the others, were Corsican, members of the Fronte di Liberazione Naziunale Corsu, the National Liberation Front of Corsica, a terrorist group. Tom said they were dressed in camo with black hoods showing only their eyes. Faith remembered the fatal attacks by the group—deadly bombings in France and French property on Corsica. In the late 1990s the highest-ranking French official in Corsica had been assassinated, and now they had planned another high-profile one on Italian soil. That was what the initials F.D. meant in Freddy's note: "François Dumond." The Teatro Verdi was home to the Orchestra della Toscana and they were performing a special matinee program devoted to French composers with the visiting minister as guest of honor.

Seeing Tom at the Web site confirmed what Jean-Luc had

suspected—that the Fairchilds, who might be CIA or just very nosey tourists—were on to the plot. He knew they hadn't alerted anyone, since nothing had happened, and he intended to keep it that way until he and the others were long gone after the assassination. At least, Faith thought, she hadn't been seeing things. Jean-Luc had obviously switched the notebooks at his villa after seeing her notice it. They must have been scouring it for information.

It was time to call Hope again. Her sister had friends in high places all over the globe. Then Faith herself had to go to Florence in the morning and find Sylvia with the great scarves in the straw market. How could she have neglected to buy gifts for her mother and mother-in-law? But when she announced this to the group at breakfast she wouldn't add that she also planned to squeeze in a little culture. A concert.

She wouldn't have pegged Olivia as a shopper, but as soon as Faith said that she hoped there would be time for a quick trip back to Florence to pick up some gifts, Olivia announced she wanted to go, too. That she had promised to bring her friends souvenirs of her trip. She seemed like such a solitary figure, no mention until now of friends—or family. The girl remained an enigma in so many ways, shedding her Goth persona and then adopting it again as the week had gone on. Faith never knew who would appear. Perhaps that was the intent.

"I should have picked up the mosaic frames I saw," Terry said eagerly. "Plus I want to get more postcards."

"You'll be home before they get there and you've spent enough of my money," Len said. He seemed more hungover than usual, and Faith wondered if he had a flask in his room. Even now, his speech was slurred.

"*Your* money? I don't think so. Maybe I'll make a stop at Prada, too," Terry snapped back.

Francesca quickly intervened. "We can take the van and every-one who wants to come along is more than welcome."

Faith could have kissed her. Plan B had been sneaking off on Gianni's Vespa, trusting she could find her way back to the city.

The Nashes were off on one of their jaunts. Faith had passed them on her way into the dining room. Constance had looked particularly cheerful and called out, "We're so eager to hear all about your husband's visit to Siena. Such a treat!"

Roderick, as usual, had been mum.

Gianni dropped them in the city's *centro,* arranging to pick them up again in two hours. The Rossis had suggested people use the afternoon to pack so they could enjoy the trip to Lago Trasimeno and the meal without feeling pressured. The group had agreed that a couple of hours in Florence would be enough.

"Although," Hattie said, "can a body ever get enough of Flor-ence? I think it was Oscar Wilde who said 'when good Americans die, they go to Paris' and I'd stick 'Florence' in there instead. For a start Italians are way nicer people than the French!"

No one contradicted her, and it was true, Faith thought, that Italians were incredibly kind and friendly, the exception being when she'd tried to buy stamps, but that could have been her fault. She never had gotten euros straight.

She had sat in the rear of the van, first on, last off, so she'd be able to speak to Gianni out of everyone else's earshot.

"I have to stay longer in the city and won't be here when you pick us up. I'll get back on my own, don't worry. If anyone asks where I am, you can say I ran into a friend from home who will bring me back later."

Gianni did not look happy. "Are you sure . . . ?"

"I'm sure," Faith said firmly. "And don't worry about what Francesca will say."

His brow cleared. "Okay, *a più tardi*."

"Ciao, and see you later, too."

The name Hope had given her literally opened doors, and after giving the condensed version of events to one person in the British consulate, Faith soon found herself sitting across from a distinguished-looking man in a beautiful, well-appointed room directly overlooking the Arno. She couldn't help but notice framed lists of every consul since 1698 and before she got down to business, she thought she should express her sympathy at the consulate's closing.

"Yes, pity," he said. "Probably will become some fancy hotel. But you didn't come here to offer your condolences, however deserved. I've been filled in, but frankly, it all sounded a bit hard to believe until Frederick Ives was mentioned."

"That's why I came here instead of going to my own consulate," Faith said. "I don't know what Freddy's job was, but I was sure his name would mean something to the right people."

"Why don't you start at the beginning?"

So Faith did.

The most crucial thing now was to tighten the net and trap as many of the perpetrators as possible without endangering lives, especially the ministers', both the cultural one and Tom. The hitch was keeping the farm buildings under surveillance without alerting the terrorists that their plan wasn't secret anymore. The same with the theater.

"I'm sure no one saw me come in, but perhaps I should leave by a less conspicuous entrance," Faith said. "I only have about forty minutes to get to the concert hall. I've located the street on the map. It's a bit of a walk."

The diplomat looked shocked. "You must be mad! You can't go and risk putting yourself in danger. And what about your husband? If they see you there, they may—let's be blunt—kill you both."

Faith pulled out a huge pair of sunglasses she had picked up from a vendor on the way and a scarf, not one of Sylvia's, alas—that would have to be another trip. She tied it around her head, a fashionable turban.

"I doubt anyone will recognize me. For one thing, they won't expect me to be there, and people see what they think is going to be in front of them—the minister in this case. All their attention will be focused on him. My husband and I discussed the risks. Unfortunately, we have to take a gamble. We know that Jean-Luc is involved, possibly the leader, but we don't know whether anyone else in the Cucina della Rossi class is. I can vouch for Gianni and Francesca, but during the week everyone else has raised certain suspicions. I'm the only one who can identify them if any of them are in the audience. They should all be back at the villa now."

He gave in but insisted on providing her with an escort.

"One of our agents. And I think you'll approve."

He took Faith out, using a private elevator before opening a door that led to a lovely garden and then another door that he unlocked at its rear.

Olivia was waiting on the other side.

Sitting in the Teatro Verdi in the minutes before the concert was to start, the hush punctuated by discreet coughs and the rustling of programs, Faith reflected she was surprised, but not shocked. It all made sense—why Olivia popped up every place she was, that she had been Faith's tomb rescuer, why she'd been with Freddy's killer near the Duomo—trailing him—and why she would be armed. Faith resolved not to tell her or her superiors how easy it had been for Faith to find that out; she'd already decided she wanted to stay friends with her—a link to Freddy, and moreover the woman could cook!

They were in the front balcony, and of course a seat had opened up next to the one Hope had reserved for her sister. They had a perfect view of the orchestra seats and by looking up could see the other balconies as well. Olivia had morphed into an Italian school-girl with an extremely short skirt, Uggs, which seemed to be worn year-round here as in the USA, and a wig that transformed her hair into a blond cap cut. On the way to the theater, Olivia had tried to convince Faith that she should leave. Olivia knew every-one in the class, too, but Faith had been firm. She had to see it through. For Freddy . . .

She wished she knew the music on the program better. Unless the terrorists wanted to cause a riot, which was a possibility—they'd have chosen a moment when a shot would be obscured by some kind of crescendo. The minister was sitting in a box directly over and to the left of the stage. He couldn't have made himself any more of a target unless he'd pinned a bull's-eye to his chest.

The musicians finished tuning their instruments, there was dead silence, and the first piece began, Ravel's *"Pavane pour une infante défunte,"* "Pavane for a Dead Princess"—heartrendingly beau-tiful and slow. No sudden loud drumrolls or cymbals to muffle the attack. The concert continued with Couperin and Satie—it was bridging many centuries. There was no intermission. Faith kept scanning the seats. She recognized no one except Jean-Luc, and he'd never glanced her way, his eyes fixed on the left of the stage. It was getting late. The concert was almost over. Could Tom have heard wrong? Or had they changed the plan?

The last piece was Debussy's *La Mer.* Everyone seemed to be leaning toward the stage in anticipation. This *was* music Faith knew well. It was one of her father's favorites—and it was tailor-made for the nefarious act the FLNC had planned. If they didn't try a shot during the early staccato punctuations—ones mimicking the crash-ing of waves—the climax at the end would provide the opportu-nity. And it was her opportunity as well. She'd spotted her quarry. They had just entered, poised behind the last row above Jean-Luc.

Insurance? Or was this the plan? That the shot would come from the shadows and the two slip away in the confusion? She saw a glint of metal. It could be a bracelet, or . . . ? No time to speculate.

She stood up as the harp played the opening chords.

"Call yourself an orchestra!" she shouted. "Why, my ten-year-old kid could do better on her kazoo! And as for this place! Hey, how about getting some comfortable seats since we have to listen to this terrible stuff!"

The hisses and boos started to drown her out. Ushers were closing in on her as she continued to scream, "Just ask those people. Over there. She pointed at Jean-Luc, who was scrambling up the aisle. He had certainly recognized her voice. "Ask Constance and Roderick Nashe! They know music."

Admittedly she'd cribbed the idea from Cary Grant in *North By Northwest,* but it worked for her as it had worked for him. Jean-Luc and the Nashes were surrounded by a number of plainclothes police who had been unobtrusively occupying the rows around them and Faith had no doubt others were stationed as ushers in the halls as well.

It was time for her to leave, too. She pushed past the concert-goers in their row with Olivia behind her and Faith felt a woman pinch her arm, spitting out a single word, *"Americana!"*

Sorry to have had to cast aspersions on her native land, Faith nevertheless felt it was worth it. All three had been captured.

Outside on the narrow street, Faith felt herself start to collapse. It was almost over. Olivia was on her phone.

"Tom? Have you heard about Tom!"

"Your husband is safe and sound. He's being supplied with some *panforte* from Siena and dropped off at the Rossis'. His 'friend' drove him back."

There was nothing to do save hug the girl very hard—and Olivia hugged her hard back.

*   *   *

Slightly delirious from the wine, and even more the food—the banquet's *Il Primo* pasta: cannelioni stuffed with prosciutto *cotto* and fresh ricotta—Faith excused herself to freshen up. Their table overlooked the lake and they had been sitting, watching the surrounding towns disappear in the dusk. Stars above, mirrored in the surface of the *lago,* and spots of light from the shore seemed to enclose the group in a celestial cocoon. Of course some of their number were missing.

Olivia had sat the Rossis down with Tom and Faith upon their return and given an abbreviated version of events. It had been no accident that Olivia had signed up for Cucina della Rossi. She'd been selected for her food expertise. Both the Nashes and Jean-Luc were on a watch list, and recent activity picked up from the Internet suggested something big was being planned. Freddy's death had confirmed it. He was on to them. Tom was able to identify one of his guards from photos taken when the police raided the farm building as the man he saw both in the Piazza Farnese and by the Duomo in Florence.

The Rossis were speechless and Olivia promised that someone would be out to talk with them further, but that they were under no suspicion themselves. They just happened to have an extremely bad neighbor. The plot was many years in the making, giving Jean-Luc, with his Napoleonic desk—Faith chided herself for missing that obvious clue—time to insinuate himself into the local scene. Likewise, the Nashes, also Corsicans, had done so in Britain, easy, as both had gone to school there. Faith learned that what she had overheard them speak in Montepulciano was not their own "pet language" but Corsu, the Corsican language. All those independent side trips had been to rendezvous with the other terrorists, particularly Jean-Luc. What had been a shock, an enormous shock, was that Roderick, the archetypal Wodehouse doddering clubman, was anything but—he had been the brains of the operation and, under his real name, was on Interpol's most wanted list!

No one seemed to be missing the Nashes much. Before the group left for the farewell banquet, Francesca had convincingly explained that the couple sent regrets but had to leave early, as their travel plans had changed. Which was true. Likewise, Jean-Luc sent his regrets. Faith was sure he had many, but doubted they were for anything other than his thwarted plot and the loss of his magnificent villa.

The stall in the bathroom was occupied. Faith was about to leave and wait outside the door when she realized that whoever was using it was probably not engaged in the task for which it was designed; rather the woman inside was crying her heart out.

"Excuse me." No, wait she knew this. "*Scusi*." Now for the "Are you all right" part. Before she could put the phrase together, a trembling voice said, "Is that you, Faith?"

"Yes—Terry?"

The door opened; Terry Russo emerged, clutching a wad of toilet tissue that she had been using to stem the tide of her tears. Her mascara had run. She looked like the band Kiss on a rainy day. Given the frequency of this sort of emotional outpouring—at least on this trip—the woman really should be investing in waterproof makeup, Faith reflected.

"I don't know what to do. You have everything so together. You and Tom. I thought we did, but—oh, Faith, have you ever thought your husband could do something so bad you couldn't stay with him!"

She wasn't crying out loud now, but the tears kept streaming down her cheeks, puddling in her neck, the toilet paper a sodden mess and useless. Faith took a packet of tissues from her purse and handed it to her.

"We've had our ups and downs—some pretty major ones, but I don't know. I guess I'd trust he had a reason, and it had better be a pretty darn good one."

That brought a small smile.

"We're never going to see each other again. That's the way it is on trips, so I can tell you, and besides you're kind of like a priest yourself, being married to one."

Faith had never thought of it this way, and didn't really want to, but she did want to hear what had happened to change the Russos' course from happily ever after to Splitsville.

"A week before we were due to leave, the doorbell rang and it was a young man—early thirties, nice-looking. He asked for Len. It was a Saturday afternoon and he was in the backyard putting the tomatoes in."

Faith nodded. Jersey tomatoes were the best.

"I took the guy back and he announces that Len is his dad. Long story short, when Len was eighteen he got his girlfriend pregnant. They were class couple, wouldn't you know. He wanted to marry her, but she didn't want to, but she *did* want to have the baby. Her family was moving to Florida and her parents must have thought it was fine. Who knows? Anyway, Len kind of forgot about the whole thing. At least that's what he told me. How can I ever trust him again? And how could he forget that he had a kid, for gawd's sakes!"

Her voice was shrill.

First things first. "Why did his son look him up after all that time? What did he want?"

"Nothing. He just found out himself. The man he thought was his father all these years told him after his mother died from cancer. He said he didn't want Len as a father—he had one, as far as he was concerned—but he was curious and wanted to fill in the blanks on his health history. Like he has asthma. Len does, too."

Which, Faith realized, was why the man hadn't looked well at times. All the acacia pollen and everything else floating in the Tuscan air.

Terry was repairing her makeup. A good sign.

"You've been married thirty years. Do you want to be married to him for thirty more? Do you love him, Terry?"

The woman smiled. "As Cher said in *Moonstruck,* 'Aw, Ma, I love him awful.' Yeah, Faith, I love him awful."

"Okay, so let's go have the next course. And, Terry, he's a guy. I have no doubt he was totally able to put the whole thing out of his mind once a couple of years had gone by—maybe sooner."

"Like the moment she crossed the Jersey line with her family on her way to Florida."

When Faith and Terry returned to the table, the waiter was pouring a different wine for the next course and there was a lull in the conversation. Len pulled the chair out for his wife, but remained standing himself. Once he'd seen that all the glasses had been replenished, he said, "I want to propose a toast. Please lift your glasses." He turned toward the Rossis, who were sitting together at the head of the table.

"To Francesca and Gianni for one of the best weeks of my life. I wish you much success and, *paisan,* we'll be back."

"Hear hear," Jack said, and everyone drank. Olivia wasn't on duty anymore and Faith was amused to see her cheeks lose their white pallor as the meal wore on.

Len didn't sit down. He put one hand on his wife's shoulder. "Now some of you know this is our thirtieth wedding anniversary. This toast is for my wife, Theresa, for putting up with me all these years. I hope she'll stick around for the rest of them." He put his hand in his pocket and took out a small box, which he put in front of her. "Because I'd marry you all over again," he said—and Faith could hear the catch in his throat before he was able to say the rest—"and because I hope it's true for you, too."

Jewelry, definitely jewelry. Terry opened the box, stood up, and threw her arms around her husband.

"Oh, honey, an eternity ring! You shouldn't have, but I'm awfully glad you did!"

And awfully in love.

✳   ✳   ✳

"And was this completely your own idea, Reverend Fairchild?"

Tom and Faith were sitting on the terrace of the Sky Lounge Bar on top of the Hotel Continentale's medieval Consorti tower. The Duomo and Palazzo Vecchio were so close, it almost seemed as if they could reach out and touch the bricks. This morning, instead of whisking them off to their train, the Rossis had dropped them off at the luxury hotel.

"Yes it was, Mrs. Fairchild. I wrote to Francesca as soon as I knew for sure we were coming and I even found this place online. The flight home is tomorrow, not today."

"And this, too?" Faith held out her wrist, admiring the Italian Fope rose gold mesh bracelet Tom had given her a few minutes ago after the bartender had brought them two flutes of cold Prosecco. She might never go back to champagne after this Prosecco-drenched trip.

"I have to admit Hope helped on that one."

It was good to have a sister—in more ways than one. Faith couldn't see the consulate from where they were, but it was just down the street. She raised her glass.

"To Hope."

"*Cin-cin,*" Tom said as they clinked.

From an open window nearby they could hear the familiar strains of the Stones singing, "This could be the last time."

Tom took his wife's hand. "It almost was." He kissed her hard.

"To us," she said a moment later. "Always, to us, my love."

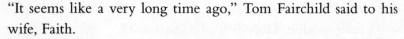

"It seems like a very long time ago," Tom Fairchild said to his wife, Faith.

"It was."

She closed the small travel journal she'd been reading parts aloud from and stood up. They'd been sitting on the deck of their cottage in Maine, watching their family kayak in the cove. Everyone had come for the Fourth of July. Faith had found the notebook in one of the boxes she had brought up to sort through this summer. There had never seemed to be time before, but now they had it in abundance.

"You were a little in love with Freddy," Tom said.

Faith did not disagree but countered with, "And you with Sky, that woman from California."

He smiled. "Very lovely—and very troubled. I can tell you now. They were married, but to other people. She was trying to decide whether to leave her husband. Jack, that was his name, right?"

Faith nodded. This was the sort of thing she remembered. She sat back down.

"Anyway, Jack wanted to leave his wife. He'd run into a neighbor in Florence that day we all went to the big market and he'd realized he couldn't live like that. I guess he'd had to duck into an alley or something."

Or something, Faith said to herself. She remembered this, too.

"She wrote to me that winter care of the church to thank me for listening. She was leaving her husband, and Jack was leaving his wife, but they weren't rushing into anything. They wanted to be sure they loved each other and it wasn't just the excitement of an affair."

"Could never understand that notion," Faith said. "It seems to me you'd be so nervous covering things up that any excitement wouldn't be worth it. All those lies to keep straight, schedules to mesh. Which also reminds me. That's where you bought me the first Fope bracelet—at the jewelers on the Ponte Vecchio." Tom had added two more since then.

"I have very good taste," Tom said.

Faith was still back in the past. "No one was who they seemed at first—except us and the Rossis. All kinds of masks. The terrorists of course. The Nashes weren't even British. I totally missed that one. Even that young man the Rossis hired to be Francesca's assistant turned out not to be who he seemed in the beginning. The Russos, Sky, Jack—everybody was hiding something. And Olivia, big-time. What do you think ever happened to her? No way to find out."

Faith had hoped to stay in touch with the young woman for many reasons, but Olivia—if that was her name—had immediately vanished into the black hole that was Whitehall and the MI6.

"And don't forget those two Southern ladies." Tom started to laugh, and Faith joined him.

Two years after their return from the trip, a cookbook, lavishly illustrated with color photos, had arrived in the mail at the parsonage with Hattie Culver listed as the author. The title was *Buon*

Giorno, Y'All: A Southern Chef Cooks Italian. Sally Culver was listed as her assistant in the acknowledgments. There was no note. Faith had immediately called Francesca, who had received one, too. "I would have helped them! They didn't have to be so sneaky. They must have gone all over Italy doing the same thing from what I can tell from the recipes," she'd said. Cucina della Rossi was not in the acknowledgments, and yes it had been sneaky, maybe worse. But the Rossis had let it go. The *cucina* had been a huge success, and now Gianni and Francesca's children were running it. The Rossis had bought Jean-Luc's villa, expanding their vineyards, olive groves, and the school. It was year-round now, functioning in the winter months also as a language program.

Yes, it had all been a long time ago.

"Happy, darling?" Tom asked.

"Very," Faith said.

Far from the Tuscan hills, they sat hand in hand quietly watching the tide go out—and they'd watch it come back in the morning when they woke up.

Author's Note

Traveling is the ruin of all happiness! There's no looking at a building here after seeing Italy.

—Fanny Burney, *Cecilia* (1782)

I have been a traveler all my life, both metaphorically and physically. The first journey of magnitude that I remember is driving in our station wagon from West Orange, New Jersey, to Readfield, Maine, just outside of Augusta the summer I turned four. We had rented Alberta Jackson's house, found for us by family friends, for a week. It was near a pond encircled by birch groves. Mrs. Jackson had white hair and said, "Ayuh." My younger sister was just learning to walk; my older brother learning to canoe with my father. My mother cooked on a woodstove and I saw my first movie, Disney's *Alice in Wonderland*. Travel had opened up all sorts of vistas, and I was hooked.

Three years later we went to Norway to visit my mother's family, crossing the ocean on the Norwegian American Line's *Oslofjord* in the early fall (always one to march to a different drummer, not unlike the women I have celebrated in all my books, Mom thought we'd learn more on the trip than in school, so we started late that year). It was hurricane season, and although in third class, my brother, sister, and I had the run of the ship from first class on down. All the adults were seasick. We, of course, were just fine—swam in the saltwater pool, had what still seem like Lucullan feasts at the smörgåsbords, and made friends with the crew. The trip took ten days. At the end of this kind of voyage you knew you had truly traveled somewhere.

In 1967 my sister and I worked outside London as au pairs for several months. Sergeant Pepper Summer we call it still. This time we crossed the ocean in a propjet, a charter. It was the first of a number of cheap flights I took in the days when air travel was a novelty, and no one would have dreamed of wearing jeans on a flight. For this one, I wore my little navy blue Jackie Kennedy suit with the Mandarin collar, but left my pillbox hat at home. I seem to recall that the flight took twelve hours. Could that be? It was a college charter, and besides Wellesley, the rest of the passengers were all guys from Cornell, so we didn't mind.

And then there was my honeymoon, or as my friend Julie called it, the "Moonyhon," since it was in July and we had been married in December. Oh that Moonyhon flight! Heaven! Air France, not a no-name charter—and we were going to the country itself! The dinner served tasted exquisite, as did the complimentary champagne.

I did not grow up in a gourmet environment. My mother was an artist, and feeding a family of five was somewhat of a chore, especially as she herself had grown up on a diet mostly of fish and boiled veggies, especially potatoes. She stuck to the tried and true with an occasional mad fling at a recipe from the book *Casserole Cookery,* a source of that northern New Jersey classic dinner-party staple—Green Bean and Mushroom Soup Casserole with Durkee fried onions sprinkled on top. One day someone told her about adding La Choy water chestnuts, and that was about as far as she ventured. When my parents went out, we thought the Swanson TV dinners Mom left for us were an exotic treat. Those and Mrs. Paul's fish sticks. But I stray.

I came to my love of cooking because of my husband, who still teases me about the first time he opened the fridge in my apartment and found only a container of OJ and a jar of herring (we got a full lunch at the place where I was then teaching, and you could tell all the single faculty, since we were the ones chowing down, making it the main meal of the day). Anyway, changing to the train for Lyon in Paris on our honeymoon that July we stopped to eat and I had my Julia Child moment, only it was an even simpler dish—*omelette aux fines herbes* with *pommes frites* and a *salade verte.* I had never tasted anything so perfect—the omelette with herbs, those crispy *frites,* so very unhealthy twice-fried in beef tallow, and the vinaigrette on that fresh frisée. There was much, much more to come. After several weeks with our friends in Lyon and then on to Provence, I realized if you wanted to eat that way you had to cook. I've never looked back. Living in France in the 1980s only made things worse—or rather much, much better.

Now back to this book. *The Body in the Vestibule* was a love letter to France, *The Body in the Fjord* to Norway, *The Body in the Big Apple* and *The Body in the Boudoir* to Manhattan, all the Sanpere books to Penobscot Bay in Maine, the Aleford books to the place where I've spent my life as a wife and mother in New England. Now *The Body in the Piazza* is a *lettera d'amore* to Italy and specifically the trip I took with my friend and fellow writer Valerie Wolzien. We left husbands and hearths, heading first to Rome, where neither of us, despite many travels, had ever been. We felt much like Faith—deliriously besotted. And then it was on to Tuscany. We had both spent time there, but not with the kind of freedom having no schedule provides. As E. M. Forster—and Freddy Ives—advised, "The point of travel is to get lost," so we wandered. Especially in markets. Before we left the United States, we were extremely fortunate to happen upon and book "The Food Lovers Walking Tour" in Florence with Claire Hennessy, assistant extraordinaire to the food writer and chef Faith Willinger. It was a day, and food, to remember always. Claire introduced us to the Baronis among other people and places, many appearing in these pages. I cannot recommend this tour, and this young woman, highly enough—http://www.faithwillinger.com. Claire also serves as a travel consultant (http://www.boutiqueflorence.com).

And so it goes. My husband and I are marking a milestone traveling to Ireland this year, and I'll be returning with Valerie to Italy. We need to sit on more rooftop terraces drinking Prosecco and I'm down to the last drop of the amazing balsamic vinegar I bought at the Mercato Centrale.

The Elizabeth Hardwick quote from *Sleepless Nights* at the opening of this book is one I think about a great deal. For me, even going on a trip to New York City, especially alone, for a day or two grants a kind of liberating anonymity. I don't exist. And then there is its corollary—I could be anyone. Oddly enough it is at times like this when we let go that we are most ourselves.

Finally, besides being a love letter to Italy and the Italians, this is an epistle addressed to two groups of people. The first is my characters, led by Faith Fairchild, who while not Katherine Hall Page, is very close to her, and I'm glad Faith's anniversary trip ended so happily. Jewelry is important. The wonderful mystery writer William Tapply, sadly gone from us, once wrote the following moving words about his character, lawyer Brady Coyne:

> He has neither the cynical world view of some private eyes nor the excessive honor of others. He is, in other words, like you, gentle reader, and he's very much like me. I'd rather have you identify with him than admire him. He's not bigger than life. He's just about life-sized.

I hope the same is true for Faith Sibley Fairchild.

The other group that has become similarly dear over these twenty-five years are you, my readers, many of whom have become friends outright and all of whom have become friends in my heart. I cannot thank you enough.

HAVE FAITH
IN YOUR
KITCHEN

By Faith Sibley Fairchild
with Katherine Hall Page

Spaghetti alla Foriana

1/2 cup toasted pignoli (pine nuts)

1 pound spaghetti

2/3 cup extra-virgin olive oil

4 large cloves of garlic, minced

4 anchovy fillets, rinsed and patted dry

1/2 cup chopped walnuts

1/2 cup golden raisins

Pinch of red pepper flakes

Pinch of freshly ground black pepper

2–3 tablespoons finely chopped fresh
  parsley

To toast pignoli, place them in a frying pan without oil or butter and sauté over low heat, watching very carefully, as they burn easily. As soon as they begin to take on color, remove them from the heat and set aside.

Start the water for the spaghetti and when it boils, add the spaghetti so it will be al dente by the time you have made the sauce. Most brands (Faith likes Barilla and DeCecco) take roughly 8 minutes.

Heat the oil in a large skillet over low heat. Add the garlic and the anchovies. Stir to prevent the garlic from burning and to dissolve the anchovies. As soon as the anchovies have dissolved, add the nuts, raisins, pepper flakes, and ground pepper.

Simmer the sauce for 4 to 5 minutes.

Drain the pasta and add to the sauce along with 1 tablespoon of parsley. Mix well to coat the pasta and serve. Alternatively, you may place a portion of pasta on each heated plate and spoon the sauce on top.

Sprinkle the remaining parsley on each serving.

As always, add more garlic and/or anchovies to taste. The interesting thing about this dish is that the anchovy taste is very subtle and most people will not even identify it until you tell them! It's wonderfully fast—something to serve unexpected guests with a salad of fresh sliced tomatoes or just mixed greens.

Serves four generously.

This is the first dish Katherine's husband, Alan, cooked for her when they were courting!

Pici with Tuscan Ragu

For the pasta:

2 cups all-purpose flour

2 cups semolina flour

1–1 1/4 cups tepid water

Combine the flours in a large mixing bowl. Pour the mixture out onto a clean flat surface. Using your hands, mound the flour and make a well in the center. It will look like a somewhat flat volcano. Add the water in the center of the well, a little at a time, incorporating the flour into it until you have a soft, smooth dough. You are bringing the flour from the perimeter into the center, and using your hands works best, although some cooks prefer to use a fork. You may need more or less water, depending on the humidity in your kitchen. Knead the dough for about 8 minutes until it is elastic and even smoother. Cover and let it rest for 30 minutes.

When the dough has rested, break off a piece about the size of a walnut and think back to when you were a kid in art class and made "snakes" by rolling clay on a desktop. Pici are very long strands. Try to make them as thin and uniform as possible. Place each finished strand on a sheet tray that has been dusted with semolina flour. Each strand should be roughly as long as the tray. Cover the pasta with a clean dish towel until you are ready to cook, after making the sauce.

Making pici is a fun group activity.

For the sauce:

2 tablespoons extra-virgin olive oil

1 medium onion, diced

1 carrot, diced

1 celery stalk, diced

2 cups fresh tomatoes, diced, or canned chopped plum tomatoes

1/2 cup dry red wine

Pinch of salt

For the combination of onion, carrot, and celery or *soffritto*—mirepoix in French—sautéed in oil, the proportion is twice as much diced onion as celery and carrot. Sauté the vegetables in the olive oil until they are softened and the onion has taken on a bit of color. Add the tomatoes, wine, and pinch of salt. Stir, cover, and simmer for 45 to 60 minutes.

For a meat ragu, add approximately 6 ounces of one of the following: ground pork, beef, veal, chopped Italian sausage, or diced *pancetta before* adding the tomatoes, wine, and salt, but *after* sautéing the vegetables. When the meat has browned, add the rest of the ingredients.

You may also add chopped parsley, basil, or oregano to the sauce with the salt. Katherine's sister Anne, who lived in Italy, always adds a teaspoon of sugar to her ragus, or *sughi*—sauces—as they are known in Florence, where she stayed.

Serves four to six.

Fresh Spinach Sautéed with Garlic

2 1/2 pounds fresh young spinach leaves

2–3 tablespoons extra-virgin olive oil

3 cloves garlic, minced

Pinch of salt

Pinch of freshly ground pepper

Lemon (optional)

Wash the spinach leaves well and cut off any stems remaining. Loosely shake them dry in a colander or use a salad spinner. Leave some water on the leaves, which acts to steam them.

Heat the oil in a large skillet or saucepan over medium heat and sauté the garlic for about a minute until golden. Be careful not to brown it. Overcooking gives garlic a bitter taste.

Add the spinach, salt, and pepper. Toss it with the garlic, turn the heat down to simmer, and cover. It will cook *very* quickly, roughly 2 minutes. Uncover, turn the heat to high, and toss once. Continue to sauté for about 1 minute. The spinach will look wilted.

Transfer to a heated bowl, or plates, and serve immediately, adding a squeeze of lemon if you wish.

Serves four to six.

This is a deceptively simple dish that showcases the freshness of the ingredient. Adjust the garlic—more or less—to your taste. On some occasions Faith adds toasted pignoli just before serving. Even spinach haters love this dish, and it is a heart-wise change from the traditional creamed spinach served with steak in the USA (tasty as that is!).

Panna Cotta

3 cups heavy cream or 1 cup whole milk   1/3 cup sugar
    plus 2 cups heavy cream, divided   1 teaspoon vanilla extract
1 envelope unflavored gelatin (approx.   1/4 teaspoon almond extract
    1 tablespoon)

Put 1 cup of the cream in a saucepan and sprinkle the gelatin on top. Let sit 3 minutes to soften the gelatin. Whisk and heat the mixture over low heat until the gelatin dissolves. Add the rest of the ingredients, stir, and heat over medium heat until the sugar dissolves, about 8 to 10 minutes. Do not boil.

Pour through a sieve into a pitcher (easier to fill the ramekins this way) and then fill 6 ramekins that you have placed on a tray. Cover with a sheet of plastic wrap and refrigerate for 5 hours or overnight. You can keep the panna cotta refrigerated for up to two days. To unmold, run a sharp knife around the edge of the ramekin and dip it in a flat pan of boiling water very briefly. If you overestimate and the panna cotta looks runny, just put the ramekin back in the fridge to firm up again. Invert the ramekin over a small plate and serve. You may also pour all the panna cotta into a bowl, cover, and refrigerate before scooping portions out into dessert bowls or martinilike cocktail glasses—very chic.

Serves six.

Garnish panna cotta with fruit, especially summer fruits, which can also be made into a coulis to drizzle over and around it. Fresh strawberries with a few drops of balsamic vinegar, honey, lemon zest, ground pistachios, and ginger flakes are all delicious toppings as well. Using this basic recipe, you may try coffee, hazelnut extract, chocolate, even green and other teas as flavoring. For the cardamom version mentioned in the text, use 1/4 teaspoon vanilla extract and 1 teaspoon ground cardamom.

Yogurt Panna Cotta

1 1/2 cups heavy cream

1 envelope unflavored gelatin (approx.
  1 tablespoon)

2 cups Greek-style yogurt such as Fage
  Total

1/3 cup sugar

1/2 teaspoon vanilla extract

Follow the directions above. The yogurt gives the panna cotta a nice slightly sharp taste, and also a slightly less creamy consistency, which makes it quite special—lovely with fruit and/or honey.

This makes a large amount. You will need 8 ramekins.

Serves eight.

Biscotti

1/2 cup unsalted butter at room
  temperature

1 1/2 cups sugar

3 large eggs

1/4 cup heavy cream

1/4 teaspoon anise oil

1 teaspoon ground anise seed (use a
  mortar and pestle)

3 cups flour

1 tablespoon baking powder

Preheat the oven to 350 degrees Fahrenheit.

In a standing mixer, or using a hand mixer, cream the butter and sugar together. Add the eggs one at a time and mix. Add the cream, anise oil, and anise seed, mixing again. Sift the flour and baking powder together and add to the batter. Mix until you have a firm dough.

Divide the dough in half and form two logs approximately 1 inch by 2 1/2 inches on a floured surface. You may need to add more flour if the dough seems too sticky. Place each log on an ungreased baking sheet, or use a Silpat.

Bake for approximately 40 minutes, checking after 30 minutes. The logs will puff up and should be golden brown.

Remove from the oven and while still warm, slice each log diagonally in 1/4-inch slices. Place the slices back on the sheets and bake for an additional 5 minutes on each side so they brown evenly. Since each oven bakes slightly differently, check to make sure they don't get too brown. Remove and cool on wire racks. Store in airtight containers for up to a week.

Makes three dozen.

Like the *pici*, biscotti are something people think must be very hard to make. They are not. Instead of anise, add 1/2 teaspoon vanilla and 1/2 cup ground nuts. Lemon zest and nuts are also a nice combination. And of course biscotti and chocolate are a natural pairing. Dip one end in melted white, dark, or milk chocolate and refrigerate on a baking sheet until the chocolate is set. Before that, you may also sprinkle the warm chocolate with ground pistachio nuts or colored sugars for the holidays (you can make the cookies ahead before dipping). Faith makes four logs at the holidays to cut for smaller cookies to serve as part of a holiday buffet or to give with other varieties as gifts.